Brother's Blood

A Mediaeval Mystery

D1439746

Brother's Blood

A Mediaeval Mystery

C.B. HANLEY

For my sisters

First published by The Mystery Press, 2016

The Mystery Press, an imprint of The History Press
The Mill, Brimscombe Port
Stroud, Gloucestershire, GL5 2QG
www.thehistorypress.co.uk

Reprinted 2017

British Library Cataloguing in Publication Data.
A catalogue record for this book is available from the British Library.

ISBN 978 0 7509 6614 6

Typesetting and origination by The History Press
Printed in Great Britain

The voice of thy brother's blood
crieth unto me from the ground.

Genesis, ch. 4, v. 10

Praise for C.B. Hanley's Mediaeval Mystery Series

'*The Bloody City* is a great read, full of intrigue and murder. Great for readers of Ellis Peters and Lindsey Davis. Hanley weaves a convincing, rich tapestry of life and death in the early 13th century, in all its grandeur and filth. I enjoyed this book immensely!'

Ben Kane, bestselling novelist of the *Forgotten Legion* trilogy

'Blatantly heroic and wonderfully readable.'

The Bloody City received a STARRED review in *Library Journal*

'The characters are real, the interactions and conversations natural, the tension inbuilt, and it all builds to a genuinely satisfying conclusion both fictionally and historically.'

Review for *The Bloody City* in www.crimereview.co.uk

'*Whited Sepulchres* ... struck me as a wonderfully vivid recreation of the early thirteenth century ... The solid historical basis lends authenticity to a lively, well-structured story. I enjoyed the plight of amiable and peace-loving Edwin, trapped by his creator in such a warlike time and place.'

Andrew Taylor, winner of the 2009 CWA Diamond Dagger and three-times winner of the CWA Historical Dagger

'It's clever. It's well written. It's believable. It's historically accurate. It's a first class medieval mystery.'

Review for *Whited Sepulchres* in www.crimereview.co.uk

Roche Abbey, 1217

To Gatehouse

Bridge

Inner Court

Outer Court

1. Undercroft (below); Lay Brothers' Parlour (above)
2. Lay Brothers' Range
3. Kitchen
4. Refectory
5. Warming House
6. Monks' Day Room (below); Monks' Dormitory (above)
7. Monks' Parlour
8. Chapterhouse
9. Armarium (library)
10. Latrines
11. Infirmary
12. Abbot's House
13. Abbot's Garden

N

West Door

Church

Altar

Side Chapels

Side Chapels

Entrance

Cloister

Monks'
Graveyard

1

2

3

4

5

6

7

8

9

10

11

12

13

Bridge

Prologue

Dover, June 1186

The ship had docked after its long journey, and those on board gave thanks for their safe arrival after many days at sea. At the command of their captain, men began to unload the cargo and soon the sharp, salt-flavoured air was full of shouts and calls as barrels and bales were loaded on to wagons, while gulls circled and shrieked in the cloudless blue sky above.

Three passengers made their way down the gangplank; three men each encumbered by a large pack. Their faces were tanned, and although it was a warm day they shivered and pulled their cloaks closer around them. They reached the shore and moved away from the ship, their legs a little unsteady on the cobbled surface of the harbour as they sought to accustom themselves to the solid ground. They found a corner which was away from the main bustle and lowered their burdens as they stopped to say their farewells.

The eldest of them was a man just approaching middle age, thickset, a few grey hairs standing out from an otherwise dark head. He reached out and placed a hand on the shoulders of the other two. 'So, here we part.' He turned to the youngest, who was not much more than a fresh-faced youth. 'Still determined to take the cowl?'

The young man nodded. 'Yes. In the short time I've been with you I've realised how much I need to read, to reflect, to study. It's the only way.'

The older man squeezed his shoulder and smiled. 'Well then, "Brother", may God go with you.'

The third man, tall, blond, and somewhere between the others in age, made the sign of the cross in the air. 'Yes, Brother, the Lord be with you. And if He wills, may our paths cross again in the future.'

The young man looked a little uncertain for the first time as he squinted up into his companion's face. 'And you?'

'I'm not sure. To start with it's back to St Albans, to see if they'll let me teach at the school there. After all, I have to earn my keep from now on. After that – who knows? It's in the Lord's hands, though I hope His plans involve me being able to read and write after learning so much.'

The youngest nodded in silence, a hint of sadness on his face, while the eldest picked up his baggage. 'And have you got it stowed away safely?'

The third man tapped the canvas of his pack, his fingers making a drumming noise on the wooden box inside. 'Oh yes. It will never leave my side, and I'll guard it with my life if I have to.'

After a final handshake, the three men went their separate ways.

Chapter One

Edwin hadn't thought that he'd ever be comfortable enough in the earl's presence to be bored, but apparently he'd been wrong. Currently his lord was droning – there was simply no other word for it – about fishing rights to his rivers, or something, and Edwin was trying not to doze off as he leaned back against the cool stone wall of the council chamber. He didn't care about fishing rights. Since he'd heard the devastating news that Alys was already married, he'd had no interest in anything. All his previous worries and fears had been about survival, about summoning up the courage to ask the earl for permission to get married, about Alys having endured and lived through the rebuilding of the city after its sacking … the one thing he'd never considered was that she would have married someone else before he could contact her. It had only been what, two months since he'd walked out of the remains of Lincoln. Clearly she hadn't felt the same way about him. In his kinder moments he tried to persuade himself that she'd probably had no choice: a young woman – a girl – orphaned, with three younger siblings to look after, would have needed to find a protector as soon as she could. It was only sensible. Of course it was.

But in his black moments, those times when he awoke sweating in the night, when he looked into his own soul, he knew the truth: that it was because he wasn't good enough. Why would the most beautiful, most courageous girl in all the land want to marry *him*? He'd been foolish even to think he could have something that he wanted so desperately. He should just accept that his life was meant to be miserable. Maybe the earl would send him on another dangerous mission – and there seemed to be plenty of those about with the war against the French invaders still going on – and he wouldn't have to come back. In the meantime he just waited for each day to be over so he could lie down in the dark. Even then he rarely slept but lay awake watching the dawn unfold to herald another pointless day.

He opened his eyes to look across the chamber. There was one window cut into the keep's thick walls, and the sunlight streamed in, illuminating the dancing dust and the fleas jumping up from the floor rushes, to fall upon the desk at which sat Brother William, the earl's clerk. He held a quill in one huge, un-monk-like fist, and he was writing on a piece of parchment as quickly as he could while the earl dictated. In the shadows behind him stood Martin and Adam, the squires: Adam trying his hardest to remain interested in the subject at hand, and Martin looking as woeful as Edwin felt. The earl himself was pacing up and down as he spoke, his movements impatient as ever, the gold on his rings flashing whenever the sunlight caught them. He'd never had a proper clerk before, and he was evidently trying to catch up on several years' worth of correspondence at once. All of them had been cooped up in this room for the last couple of weeks, and if Edwin thought that his lord was trying to keep busy in order to take his mind off the traumatic events of midsummer then he kept that thought to himself.

The voice stopped and Edwin snapped back to attention in case he was about to be asked a question. Since he had gained the earl's confidence he now found that his opinion was asked on some matters, and he had no intention of being caught out. Uninterested he might be, but he wasn't stupid enough to risk the earl's wrath. But his lord was merely taking a sip of wine before continuing.

'That pile of letters there. Pick one and tell me what it contains.' He sat down and drummed his fingers on the arm of the chair.

Brother William pulled out one of the heaped parchments and examined the seal. 'From the Earl of Arundel, my lord.'

The earl grunted and raised the goblet to his lips again as the clerk broke the seal and scanned the contents of the letter. 'In essence, my lord, his younger son is nearly seven, old enough to be sent away, and he asks that you take him into your household as page.'

Edwin glanced across to see that Martin had perked up at this. Someone else in the close household. And there was an opening since …

The earl considered. 'Hmm. I could do with a new boy who isn't a curse. But is there anyone better? Geoffrey?'

Edwin had almost forgotten that Sir Geoffrey, the castellan, was also in the room. He had been standing like stone away to one side so Edwin couldn't look at him without turning round, which the earl might notice.

'My lord of Arundel is now back in the regent's full confidence, my lord.'

The earl's fingers tapped again. 'What about Marshal's youngest?'

Edwin couldn't see, but from the tone he imagined Sir Geoffrey shaking his head. 'Ten, my lord, and already with the Earl of Chester.'

Edwin had once met William Marshal, the legendary regent, and he was surprised to think that a man so elderly should have a son so young. He must be an even older father than Edwin's own had been. But then, he had rather a lot of children, didn't he? He tried to remember his recent conversations with Sir Geoffrey. He was supposed to be learning all these things, but the maze of relationships among the realm's nobility was still bewildering.

The earl was continuing. 'And Chester himself has no sons. What about Marshal's grandsons? By his eldest daughter and Norfolk?'

Sir Geoffrey sounded negative again. 'The eldest is with his uncle, my lord, and the younger ones are, what, five and three?'

'That's no good, then. Maybe in a couple of years – I can always take another one. Very well. Arundel's boy it is then.' He waved to Brother William. 'See to it, and tell Arundel to send him to me at Lewes before St Bartholomew's Day.'

Brother William made some notes, his pen scratching. The earl stood and stretched, one shoulder making a cracking noise. 'I need some air.'

Edwin was mildly amused to see Martin and Adam tensing like hounds who had caught a scent.

The earl laughed. 'Yes, you too. Saddle my destrier and your own mounts. We should be able to cover a few miles before evening, and he needs a run.'

The squires shot out of the room like arrows. The earl turned to Edwin and looked him up and down. 'You will need some riding practice before we set off for Lewes in a couple of weeks, but not today – you wouldn't keep up. For now you can help Brother William get through the rest of those letters. Report to me after the evening meal with anything you think needs my urgent attention.'

Edwin was shocked out of his apathy. Deal with the earl's own correspondence? What if his ignorance led him to miss something? What if …? Belatedly he bowed and said, 'Yes, my lord,' but the earl was already sweeping out of the room, followed by Sir Geoffrey.

A sigh came from the desk, and Edwin turned to see Brother William gazing a little wistfully after the departed men. He caught the other's eye and the monk shrugged. 'I know what you're thinking. But that part of my life is over.' He looked at the piles of parchment and expelled a long breath. 'Still, at least the light is good. Pull up that stool over there and we'll get started.'

Edwin sat, hoping that the worry of this task would push the other concerns from his mind. As he sifted through the letters he wondered about the little boy who would soon be joining the household. A noble, the son of an earl, but still a pawn of the great men to be moved around at will regardless of his own inclination. Edwin chose a random letter and broke the seal, reflecting that nobody had even bothered to ask the child's name.

———•———

Martin enjoyed galloping almost as much as he enjoyed weapons training. To be out of the council chamber, out of the castle, unconfined and away from all the people was bliss. He felt the wind in his hair as he urged his mount forward to yet greater speed, although he had no hope of catching up with the earl, who had let his destrier, his fierce and very expensive warhorse, have its head. Martin didn't have a horse of his own but he was riding the roan courser which was the tallest mount the castle stable afforded. He revelled in the long strides and the freedom of movement as he strove to reach his lord, although his feet were still too far down for comfort. Maybe one day, when he was a knight and had some money of his own, he'd find a horse that was large enough ... but he was still only seventeen, so that day was a long way in the future; he'd have to make the best of things for now.

The earl had paused and was waiting for them to catch up. Martin slowed to a canter and then a trot before reining in, sweating now that the air around him was hot and still. He turned to look for Adam, who was way behind on the ancient pony he'd been using since his arrival at Conisbrough a few months before. Martin watched as the animal puffed its way up to them, the earl shifting impatiently in his saddle.

'When we get back, tell Geoffrey to allocate that boy a better mount, or he'll never keep up when we head to Lewes. That old thing will serve for the new lad if it survives long enough.'

'Yes, my lord.' Adam would be glad, and Martin was pleased on his behalf. He was a good lad who did as he was told and didn't talk too much, and anyway he was surely due a growth spurt which would make the pony even more unsuitable. Martin wondered what the new page would be like and whether he'd be as much trouble as the last one. He would have responsibility for the boy and he was determined to be stricter this time around. Concentrating on that would help to take his mind off ...

The earl's voice cut across his thoughts. 'We'll race across that pasture, round those two trees, and back to this point. Adam, we'll give you a start. Go!'

Adam put his heels to the pony's flanks and was off. Martin thought to himself that his lord was right, as ever: the beast was already labouring despite Adam's best efforts. Indeed, the earl let him get nearly all the way to the trees before he told Martin to be off. Martin surged forward, moving from a canter to a flat-out gallop across the stubble of the hayfield as he chased Adam, already rounding the trees. He had no idea how much of a start his lord had given him, but he could hear hoofbeats drumming behind him. He approached the turning point and slowed, knowing that his mount wouldn't take the sharp turn at speed, and succeeded in passing close to the trees. From the corner of his eye he spotted with some satisfaction that the earl's destrier, excited by the chase, had overshot and that the earl would have more ground to make up. Then it was on to the flat for the race back to the start. Martin whooped, feeling the smile spread across his face, the movement of his muscles at one with the courser and the wind in his hair as he increased his pace and overtook Adam before he was halfway back. But the earl was gaining on him and the great warhorse flew past, clods of earth spurting up from under its hooves just as he reached the end point.

The earl reined in, laughing, looking younger than he had done for some while. 'Good, good! I think we'll call that a draw for now.' He nosed his mount nearer so he could clap Martin on the shoulder. 'Excellent horsemanship. Good man.'

They returned to the castle at a trot and then a walk to cool the horses, Martin hearing his lord's words ringing in his ears all the while. As they neared the gate Martin looked around hopefully, as he always did out of habit, before the realisation thumped into him that it was no good. She wasn't there, and she never would be again. Joanna had gone away with the earl's sister to their new home, following the Lady Isabelle's fateful wedding, and now the whole length of the realm separated them. Despite the sun reflecting off the bright white keep and into his eyes, the castle appeared grey and joyless.

His elated mood gone, Martin dismounted and took the reins of the earl's destrier as well as his own courser. He sniffed the air and realised it was nearly time for the evening meal, so he took Adam's reins as well and sent him to the hall to check everything was ready. Then he led all three horses into the stable and concentrated on brushing, currying and feeding, growling at the groom who offered to help. He needed the time to himself, and the earl wouldn't mind if he was late to the meal. Adam was perfectly capable, and the high table was an empty place these days anyway.

When he emerged from the stable he was surprised to see Brother William's back, as he stood uncertainly in the outer ward. What was he doing here? He tapped him on the shoulder. The monk turned, and Martin apologised, for it wasn't Brother William at all, but another Cistercian in a similar white robe.

'I beg your pardon, Brother. I thought you were someone else.'

The monk made the sign of the cross in the air. '*Benedicte*, my son. Yes, Brother William is here at the castle, is he not? But I have come with a message for the lord earl. Could you take me to him?'

Martin considered briefly the consequences of interrupting the earl's meal. 'He's eating at the moment, Brother, but I can bring you to him afterwards. Can I offer you something while you wait? Would you like to come to the hall?'

The monk shook his head. 'Thank you, but I have no desire to eat.' He seemed agitated. 'However,' he looked towards the western horizon, 'I believe it's nearly the hour of vespers. Is there a chapel where I may say the office?'

Martin nodded and led him into the inner ward, up the stairs to the keep and then up to the chapel. The monk immediately knelt before the altar and Martin hovered uncertainly. He was hungry, and the meal would soon be over. 'Er, I'll just leave you here ...'

The monk was already deep in prayer, eyes closed and hands clasped, oblivious to his presence, so Martin loped down the stairs and over to the hall.

Edwin's eyes were bleary after looking at all the earl's correspondence, so he was glad of the opportunity to sit quietly at the bottom end of the hall and eat his meal of vegetable pottage and maslin bread. He closed his eyes for a moment, not sure if they were watering due to tiredness, the acrid reek of the smoking tallow light on the table, or something else. Thank the Lord the letters had been fairly straightforward, no urgent summons to re-join the war – a couple of weeks ago he'd heard the earl say there had been rumours that Prince Louis was assembling another invasion fleet – or bad news about losses of life or lands. They had mainly been updates from the castellans of the earl's other castles, or requests from his vassals for permission to marry. *Marry*. He pushed the bread too hard into the pottage and slopped it over the table.

Once he had finished his meal he nudged Brother William, who was sitting next to him on the bench and still shovelling in huge spoonfuls of pottage and the Friday eel stew which Edwin hadn't liked the look of. 'We'd better get back so we're ready before my lord gets there.' He looked up to the almost-empty top table, where the earl sat with only Sir Geoffrey for company. Normally the meal up there took much longer, but that was when the Lady Isabelle was there, and Mistress Joanna, and often other guests as well. Neither the earl nor Sir Geoffrey were great or fussy eaters, so although it looked as though they had some fine dishes there, they were nearly finished.

Brother William nodded and took a few last mouthfuls of the stew as he stood; he reached back for another piece of bread and rammed it in his mouth as he walked. Then they made their way over to the keep and up the stairs, deep in conversation until they reached the council chamber and re-checked the correspondence which they had already sorted for the earl's attention. A small fire was burning in the great fireplace, for the stone keep was chilly in the evenings, even in the summer. Edwin took a spill and lit the candles around the room – fine wax ones in here which didn't smoke nearly so much as the rushes at home or in the hall.

He had just thrown the remains of the spill back into the fire when the door opened and the earl entered with Sir Geoffrey – no Martin or Adam, of course, as they would be eating after spending the official mealtime waiting at the high table.

The earl saw Brother William and frowned. 'How did you get here so quickly?'

Brother William looked confused, as well he might. 'I beg your pardon, my lord – I just walked over from the hall with Edwin a short while ago.'

The earl looked between him and the door. 'But weren't you just ...?' He shook his head. 'Never mind. What have you there?' He sat down.

Edwin took a deep breath and listed, as he had been rehearsing in his head all through the meal, the matters which needed the earl's attention. He was relieved when his lord nodded approvingly.

'Very clear. Right – yes to the marriage of Richard of Hooten but no to Simon of Lyndon making a match with the Bolbec girl. He'll have too great a parcel of land all in one place and I don't altogether trust him. Tell him he may marry but he'll have to choose someone whose lands don't adjoin his own.'

As Brother William was nodding and making notes, Edwin wondered about the lives of the people in the letter. He'd never heard of Simon of Lyndon, but was his intended bride someone he cared about? Had the earl just ripped apart two lovers without even thinking about it? Or was the marriage all about the land? These nobles did things differently.

Sir Geoffrey cleared his throat and everyone looked at him. 'This may be as good a time as any to broach the subject, my lord, concerning the question of your own marriage?'

There was a brief silence and Edwin prepared to flinch, but the earl merely waved the remark away as though it were a fly. 'There's nobody suitable available at the moment. I need to ally myself with good blood – my father might have been old King Henry's half-brother, but he was a bastard and there are some who will not let me forget it.' Edwin had only a vague recollection of the old earl, who had died when Edwin was five, as a bright figure on a tall horse who sometimes rode through the village. The earl was now scowling, but he got over it and enumerated on his fingers. 'Blood, Geoffrey, blood. The young king's aunts are all dead. His sisters are but tots, and besides, that might be aiming too high.' And surely they'd be his cousins, thought Edwin, or doesn't that matter? 'So realistically it has to be one of Marshal's daughters, currently all taken, or Chester's sisters, taken also. As soon as one of them comes on the market I'll put in a bid.'

And that was that, thought Edwin. He watched as Sir Geoffrey opened his mouth, but the earl cut him off. 'Yes, yes, an heir, I know. But Gilbert will do for now, and he and Isabelle will no doubt produce a few sons in due course. And besides, I'm good for many years yet. I can wait for the right move.' He clapped his hands together, signalling that the discussion was at an end. 'Back to where we were. Just the question of the fishing rights, was it?'

Edwin nodded. 'Yes, my lord. You were going to give over a tithe of your fish from some of your manors to the abbey at Roche.'

'Yes. Right, Brother William, take this down.' He began to dictate in a toneless voice, speaking slightly too fast for the clerk to keep up. 'William, Earl of Warenne, to his fishermen of Brademer, health. Know that I, moved by charity, have given to God and the church of St Mary of Roche, and to the monks, servants of God in that place, the tithe of the whole of the residue of all my eels from all my fisheries that are in the parish of Hatfield, Fishlake and Thorne …'

Edwin watched Brother William scribbling furiously, glad that it wasn't his job, as his own penmanship was rather scratchy, and then noticed out of the corner of his eye that the chamber door was opening. It was just Adam, so he returned his attention to the earl. '… Wherefore I command you that you ensure they have the aforementioned tithe without any difficulty or delay, and in testimony of this I send you these my letters patent. Farewell.'

There was silence while the sound of Brother William's quill continued for a few moments, along with his heavy breathing. Then Adam spoke. 'Excuse me, my lord, but Martin is outside with a messenger from the abbey at Roche.'

Edwin saw his own surprise reflected in the faces of the others, and the earl crossed himself, muttering that he didn't believe in coincidences.

Martin entered together with a monk wearing a robe of Cistercian white. It wasn't all that warm now, but he was sweating – perhaps being in the earl's presence was making him nervous.

Brother William, on the opposite side of the room, stood and peered in the candlelight. 'Brother Waldef? Is that you?'

The monk acknowledged him with a nod before turning to the earl and bowing. 'Brother Godfrey, my lord, sent to bear you a message from Abbot Reginald.'

The earl, looking a little pale, had recovered himself. 'It must have been you I passed in the chapel earlier. Speak your message.'

The monk folded his hands inside his sleeves, but not before Edwin had noticed that they were shaking. 'Father Abbot has sent me to beg your help, my lord, in his hour of need. One of our brothers has been murdered.'

Chapter Two

Edwin felt hot and a little faint as he heard the words. This was it. This was another mission the earl was going to send him on. What would he do? Would he come out of it alive this time?

The earl looked confused. 'But surely the abbot must know that I have no jurisdiction within the walls of his abbey? Shouldn't he be applying to someone in the Church?'

The monk nodded. 'Under normal circumstances, my lord, that would be the case. But Abbot Reginald is about to travel to the annual conclave in France, which all abbots of our Order must attend each year. He will need to leave two weeks from today, so he fears there will be no time to get a message to our mother house at Newminster which is many days' journey to the north. He has heard that you have a man in your household who is experienced in these matters' – he looked hopefully at Sir Geoffrey – 'and that you might, as an act of charity, send him to Roche for some while to see what he can discover.' He bowed his head and fell silent.

The earl beckoned Sir Geoffrey to one side, so that they were standing nearer to Edwin. 'We don't need to leave for Lewes for another two weeks. The abbey is what, six or seven miles away? We can summon him back any time if we need to.'

Sir Geoffrey nodded and glanced at Edwin, who looked away and pretended he wasn't watching.

The earl continued, though Edwin didn't catch all of it. 'And it's about time … some new responsibilities …' He moved back into the centre of the room to face the monk. 'Very well. I send my man Weaver to your abbey for one week, to render what assistance he may.' He gestured for Edwin to step forward, which Edwin did, trying not to notice the surprise and disappointment on the monk's face.

But the earl hadn't finished. 'I also send Martin with him as guard and escort.' Taken aback, Edwin glanced at Martin, who looked as surprised as Edwin felt, and then back at the earl, realising for the first time that he *liked* catching people off guard in this way. Perhaps he felt he was better served by keeping them all off balance, which Sir Geoffrey certainly was.

'My lord …'

The earl clapped, once. 'Now, Brother … Godfrey, was it? It's almost dark, so you will stay here and set off tomorrow morning. You may make use of my chapel for your offices if you so wish, and Sir Geoffrey will have a man show you the hall where you can sleep.'

The monk looked startled. 'Stay the night? But Abbot Reginald will be expecting me back tonight, and —'

The earl gave him a single look, and he faltered into silence, bowing his head. His shoulders were shaking.

As Sir Geoffrey ushered the monk out of the room, the earl turned to the shocked faces around him and laughed. 'This diversion will do us all some good.' He addressed Edwin first. 'Do what you can. It's Saturday tomorrow – return here once you've sorted it out, or on the following Saturday regardless. If the culprit is a layman we'll turn him over to the sheriff; if he's another monk then the Church will decide what to do with him.'

Edwin had no time to reply before the earl turned to Martin. 'I'm relying on you to keep Edwin safe. A man has been killed, and if there's to be another I don't want it to be him. Take a sword with you and guard him. I place Edwin in your sole care.' His eyes bored into Martin's, and Edwin saw his friend turn pale and clench his jaw, but he didn't drop his gaze. 'I swear it, my lord.'

Adam had been standing silently, as he usually did, and now the earl looked down at him. 'And as for you – temporarily you are my senior squire. See that you do it well.' Well, at least one of us is happy, thought Edwin, as he watched the slow smile spreading across Adam's face.

'Now. Martin, go and look out what you'll need to bring, and then get some sleep. Adam, get the chess set out – Geoffrey and I will have a game. Edwin, go home now, and meet Martin by the stables at dawn.'The matter seemed to be over, and the earl was already moving to sit at the table. Edwin bowed, left the room, and made his way down and out into the evening air.

———•———

The following morning at dawn Edwin stood outside the stable in the outer ward, waiting. He wore his best tunic and hose and his new cloak, even though it was a bit warm for this weather. He carried a scrip containing a spare shirt, a bowl, a spoon, a rosary, a small aleskin and some bread wrapped in a piece of linen. On his belt were his eating knife and a purse containing twelve pennies – he had no idea whether he'd need any money, but he could afford to bring some now, so why not? A second belt, a brand new and very sturdy one which had been a gift from the earl, held the dagger in its ornate scabbard which he now carried everywhere.

He was nervous.

Just as he thought he might need to head round behind the stable for a moment, Martin appeared, accompanied by Sir Geoffrey, the visiting monk, and Brother William. Martin was dressed for travelling, and he carried a heavy-looking sack which made the tell-tale clinking sound of mail. He had both a sword and a dagger belted around him.

Sir Geoffrey didn't look pleased. He greeted Edwin briefly and then took him to one side.

'Brother Godfrey is being difficult. He says his abbot will have been expecting someone … older and may not take you seriously. Therefore Brother William will travel with you, introduce you and vouch for you – Abbot Reginald knows him and will trust his word, though it is an insult to the lord earl that it must be so. Brother William will then return here – he'll be back before nightfall and can inform my lord that you have arrived safely.'

There didn't seem much to say, so Edwin nodded and stared at his feet at the thought of the reception which would no doubt await him. Not old enough. Not rich enough, not noble enough. Not good enough.

Sir Geoffrey broke into a half smile. 'Still, you couldn't be much safer on the road.'

Edwin looked from the warlike Brother William, who had been a knight of some renown before he took the cowl, to the towering figure of Martin, armed and with his long legs now astride a tall horse, and nodded. But before Sir Geoffrey could move away he plucked at his arm and made the knight pause. 'Sir Geoffrey. If anything … happens to me, will you see that my mother is looked after?'

A look which Edwin couldn't quite fathom came over the knight's face and he patted Edwin on the shoulder. 'Yes. Yes, that I will surely do. Have no fear on her account.'

Satisfied, but with a vague uneasiness which he couldn't put his finger on, Edwin turned to the horse which a groom was now holding for him. Fortunately, it looked fairly docile. He managed to mount in a manner which was not elegant but which was at least not embarrassing, and took the reins. There was some alter-cation behind him, and he managed to turn around to see that Brother Godfrey was making a fuss about mounting the mule which had been provided for him. Monks and priests always seemed to ride mules rather than horses, and in his own discom-fort as he tried to face his horse the right way Edwin wondered why. Maybe there was a rule – the clergy seemed to have a lot of rules that made little sense to other people.

'It is not fitting that I should ride, Brother, you know that. I walked here and I can walk back.'

Edwin looked from Martin to Sir Geoffrey and back again, but Brother William, who was already mounted on another mule, was brooking no nonsense. 'It's your duty to get these men back to Father Abbot as quickly as possible. It'll take twice as long if they have to keep pace with you walking, so swallow your humility for now and mount, Brother. You can always confess later if you enjoy it too much.'

Sir Geoffrey, who was talking quietly to Martin – no doubt giving him some last-minute advice – coughed and covered his mouth with the back of his hand to disguise a smirk. Brother

Godfrey looked daggers at Brother William and then heaved himself on to the mule's back, looking uncomfortable as he sat like a sack of beans and muttered a prayer. Brother William slapped him on the back, saying, 'And no doubt you'll be glad to return all the sooner. You look odd out here on your own.' Edwin had no idea what he meant, but when he looked at Brother Godfrey he could see that something was wrong. It wasn't just his discomfort at being on the mule – it was deeper, somehow. He almost looked in physical pain.

There was no time to think further on the subject. A groom finished tying the reins of the packhorse that carried Martin's armour to the saddle of the horse Martin would ride, and they were ready to go.

Despite himself, Edwin couldn't help feeling just a little excited as he went through the village high on a horse's back and on the earl's business. Most of the villagers were already out in the fields, but a few women, children and old folk remained, and they came out to stare as the company rode past. Edwin's mother stood in the doorway of their home and gave a little wave, holding back tears, and Edwin was proud of her. He allowed himself a nod to her as he passed, before the lump in his throat forced him to look straight ahead and concentrate. He had lived in Conisbrough all his life; every stone and blade of grass was familiar to him, but now he found himself staring at it all as though he'd never seen it before. He realised he was seeking to imprint it all on his mind in case he never came back.

———o———

Martin was trying hard not to ride with one hand on his sword. Sir Geoffrey had wished him luck with his first command. Command! Him! Oh dear Lord, what was he going to do if anything happened to Edwin? He needed to think, to plan in advance, that was what leaders did. He should try to remember the lessons Sir Geoffrey had tried to drill into him. *A good commander is always two steps ahead.* Fine, if anyone jumped out at them he knew how to fight, but now he was in charge he would need to think about whether anyone was going to ambush them, and where the likely danger spots might be. He scanned the road ahead.

After they had gone a mile or so without meeting any disasters he began to relax a little. The outlaws who had caused violent havoc in the area a couple of months ago were dead, and there had been no trouble since. Martin had ridden past the execution site on a number of occasions, trying not to look at or smell the remains of the still-hanging, rotting bodies. If he was going to be a knight he needed to cultivate an attitude more like that of Sir Geoffrey, who had calmly surveyed the carnage and noted that local respect for the earl and his laws was demonstrated by the fact that nobody had stolen six dozen or so feet of good rope which was there unattended. Martin remembered the words one of the outlaws had cried out before his death: *The war isn't over yet.*

Some other travellers came into sight along the road, heading towards them, and Martin was immediately on the alert, glancing to make sure Edwin was still to one side of him with the monks behind. He let go of the reins with his right hand and allowed it to hover near his sword hilt, but it looked as if all would be well. First they passed a lone pedlar, tramping along steadily with a large pack; an early arrival heading for the summer market at Conisbrough, no doubt. He stood aside respectfully to let them pass, and Martin rode on, hearing Brother William call out a brief blessing. Next was a covered ox-drawn cart, driven by a solid-looking man and moving very slowly. Really a commoner like that should move out of the way of mounted nobles, but as Martin had neither Sir Geoffrey nor the earl with him, he didn't insist. Besides, those carts were very difficult to turn, and it was so heavily laden that if he made it move aside or stop, it might never get going again. So he led his party into single file to pass the cart by, receiving a touch of the hat and grateful thanks from the driver, which he acknowledged with a nod. Hearing the man speak, a middle-aged woman opened the cover from inside and poked her head out, revealing a glimpse of an interior packed with bales; seeing the mounted group of men she hastily bobbed her head, crossing herself as the monks passed.

At the Crookhill crossroads they met a messenger riding for the nearby manor of Tickhill, who greeted them and said he'd seen no trouble on the roads that day; then a cart carrying barrels of wine to Conisbrough. They passed through the tiny hamlet of Braithwell without incident and followed the road through fields of ripening wheat. If the weather stayed fair for the next few weeks there would be a good harvest, God be praised.

It was when they reached the village of Maltby that a small child, no more than a tot, ran into the road in front of them. Martin's horse shied but he controlled it immediately, ensuring that the packhorse behind was also calmed. Edwin, who hadn't been riding since before he could walk, failed to control his mount and it reared up, throwing him backwards. He immediately panicked, flinging himself forwards and overcompensating just as the horse's front hooves came down again, and falling forwards over the nearside of his horse. Martin shot out a hand and managed to get a handful of his cloak before he toppled off completely, and held him there, straining not to let him drop but unable to lift him with one hand while mounted. He felt the heat rising to his head, but then Brother William appeared on foot and calmly took the weight, heaving Edwin back into his saddle. He was red-faced, but fine.

Martin's head was racing so much that he could barely hear himself bellowing at the child, who shrieked in fear and hid behind the skirts of its mother. He shouted at her as well and she cowered before him.

'Martin. Martin!'

'What?' He turned and realised he was now shouting at Edwin.

'Martin, what are you doing? You're terrifying everyone.'

He looked around to see that a group of villagers had gathered and were looking at him fearfully. He was big, armed and wearing a tunic which bore the earl's badge, and they were frightened. Violence could come their way and they would have no defence against him. But that was not what a true knight would do, and certainly not on his lord's own lands. With a huge effort he tried to calm himself, ordered the woman tersely to take more care, and rode on, forcing the villagers to get out of the way of his horse. They formed in a knot in the road behind the party, and Martin could feel the glares boring into his back as he urged his mount into a trot. The courser was skittish, probably because his hands were shaking.

'Do you want to stop?' Edwin was now beside him.

'No.' And after a few moments, 'Are you all right?'

Edwin shrugged. 'I'm fine. I know I need more practice. Nothing is broken, although I nearly choked when you grabbed my cloak like that.'

Martin noticed for the first time that Edwin had a red welt on his neck where either the edge of the cloak or its clasp had been forced against the skin. 'Sorry.'

'It's all right. My pride would have been hurt a lot more if you hadn't caught me. But are *you* all right? It's not like you to frighten a woman and child like that.'

Martin didn't want to answer that, didn't want to admit even to himself that he'd been scared of the situation he'd created. Sir Geoffrey wouldn't have done that. He hunched forward in his saddle. 'Come on. We're nearly there now and then you can get off that horse. Make the most of such a short journey,' he added, 'when we go to Lewes you'll be riding all day every day for at least two weeks.'

Edwin winced at the thought and allowed himself to fall a few paces behind. Martin increased his speed and forced them all to keep up as they rode on.

———◦———

Edwin had been concentrating on riding, which had helped take his mind off other things, but as they drew nearer to the abbey his nerves returned. He hadn't had much of a chance to question Brother Godfrey on the way as Martin had insisted on riding next to him while the brothers were behind. In fact, he had no idea of what he was walking into, other than that a monk at Roche had been murdered. He didn't even know the monk's name. Who was he? How had he been killed? Why might anyone want to kill him? And he knew absolutely nothing about monasteries. Why couldn't he ever be asked to solve something he knew something about?

He was about to ask Martin if he might ride behind with Brother Godfrey when the squire announced, 'We're here.'

Edwin had thought they were still in the middle of nowhere, but as they came round a slight bend in the road he saw the abbey. It was something of a shock – a huge, soaring church, great stone buildings all round it, and an encircling wall with a tall gatehouse which wouldn't have looked out of place on a castle, all standing there in the peaceful countryside. The stone was very white, and as the sun shone on it he was almost blinded. He shaded his eyes. 'That's odd – it looks a bit like the keep.'

Martin gave him a look. 'Where do you think they got the stone from for the castle? There's a great limestone quarry round behind there.'

How foolish not to have thought of that. And *Roche* Abbey – roche meaning rock. Edwin thought he'd better sharpen his wits a bit before he asked any more questions. But Martin was slapping him on the shoulder, looking a little more like himself than he had since that strange incident earlier. 'Come on. It must be nearly dinner time. And I've got you here in one piece – at least that's something.'

As they approached the gatehouse, Edwin could see that one of the two great wooden gates had a smaller door cut into it. It opened and an aged monk tottered out. He squinted at them until they came right up to him and dismounted. '*Benedicte*, my sons, and welcome. Have you come to pray, or to seek lodging?'

Before either of them could answer, Brother Godfrey stepped round from behind them and spoke very loudly and slowly. 'Greetings, Brother Thurstan. I have returned from visiting the earl and I have brought his men with me.'

The ancient monk peered at him. 'You've been out? Which one are you?'

Edwin heard his companion give a long-suffering sigh. 'It's Brother GODFREY, Brother. Please admit us so I can take these men to Father Abbot.'

'Oh, it's you, is it? Well, you'd better come in. You'll want to take these men to Father Abbot.'

Brother Godfrey made another exasperated noise, and both he and Brother William, who had remained silent all the while, stepped through the little door. Edwin heard the sound of a bar being lifted, and then the large gates opened wide enough to admit them. He took the reins of the two mules as well as his own horse, leaving the others to Martin, and entered the abbey. Then with a heave the great gates were shut again, the bar thudding back into place with a disturbing finality.

Edwin looked around him. He was in a place which looked like a cross between the castle and a working farm. The area in front of him was full of buildings like the ones in the outer ward at Conisbrough: a stable block, workshops, offices, a stone building which looked like it might be a kitchen. Beyond that he could see the abbey itself, the huge white tower of the church soaring into the sky. To his right was a stream crossed by a footbridge, which led out to an open space where he could see gardens, orchards, fish-ponds and a mill. To his left the whole area was bordered by a tall limestone cliff. Apart from the cliff, it wasn't so different to home.

Except that it was. Edwin stood for a moment before he worked out what it was, and then he realised it was the sound. Or rather, the lack of it: back at Conisbrough both the village and the castle wards were full of bustling, jostling, shouting noise, but here there was an eerie quiet. White-robed monks and some other men in brown were walking around and carrying out business, but they were doing it in utter silence.

A bearded man in a brown tunic came to take their mounts, and Edwin handed him the reins. 'A lay brother,' whispered a voice in his ear. Edwin had no idea what that was, but he was glad he'd have Brother William by his side for a few hours at least. As they walked through the precinct the monk kept up a low-voiced commentary in his ear about what he could see, and Edwin picked up a rough idea of what was going on. It really was a bit like the castle, with the area they were passing through being like the more open and public outer ward, an area for work, while the abbey building itself, completely walled but for a few entrances, presented a closed face to the world like the inner ward, a place where only the privileged were granted admittance. The silence was already becoming oppressive, even for Edwin; he cast a glance at Martin and guessed that he would soon be itching to escape from it.

Brother Godfrey did not lead them into the abbey but instead around the outside of it, over another footbridge and towards a separate two-storey building standing in its own small garden. Edwin gathered from Brother William that this was the abbot's house; they entered and ascended the stairs before knocking on the door of the upper room.

Inside were two monks in white robes: a stocky one with very wiry dark hair sticking out in all directions from around his tonsure, and another who was tall and gaunt and wearing a simple pectoral cross. The room was plain: whitewashed walls, a wooden cross, a table and chair and a few stools, a bench over to one side and an open kist in the corner which held rolled-up parchments.

Brother Godfrey and, after a slight pause, Brother William, knelt before the tall monk and kissed the ring on the spindly fingers he held out. He didn't smile but somehow managed to look pleased with them nonetheless.

His voice was sonorous. 'Brother Godfrey. Your return is welcome. How did you fare out on your own?'

To Edwin's surprise, Brother Godfrey began to weep, tears coursing down his cheeks. 'I tried, Father, but it was so difficult! And I didn't know I was to be away overnight, for which I ask your forgiveness – the lord earl said …'

The abbot held up one hand. 'Peace, Brother. You're back safe now, and perhaps it's God's will that you shouldn't be apart. Go now, and know that I'm pleased that you tried. Any fault lies with me.' He watched without any expression that Edwin could discern as Brother Godfrey fled, then turned to Brother William, still kneeling. 'And so the wanderer returns. How do you find your life with the lord earl, Brother?'

'I like it well, Father.'

'And you have as yet no desire to come back to us? I am in need of a travelling companion for my journey to Citeaux, for Brother Alexander was to have come with me.' He sighed and crossed himself.

Alexander, thought Edwin, that must the name of the murdered monk. I wonder why he was going to be the one to travel? He glanced at Brother William, who had an expression of agonised indecision on his face. As well he might – Edwin could imagine him travelling across the sea to protect the abbot and visiting marvellous places on the way. How tempted he must be.

His voice sounded a little strangled. 'Father … I thank you, but as you have sent me to the lord earl, my duty must lie with him. And indeed, he has need of me.' He bowed his head. Edwin, who had come to know Brother William quite well since he had been part of the earl's household, admired his strength of will. Nobody else seemed to notice.

The abbot simply nodded. 'So be it. But why have you come back with Brother Godfrey? Who are these boys? Could the earl's man not be spared?'

Here goes, thought Edwin. He watched as Brother William stood, and then he and Martin moved forward to stand next to the monk. Edwin felt small, in all senses.

Brother William propelled him forward, and spoke a little more heartily than was required. 'He's here, Father. This is Edwin, the earl's man, in whom he has full confidence. He has completed a number of missions for the lord earl with great success. And the other is his senior squire Martin. Have no fear – they will serve you well.'

Edwin flushed as the abbot looked him up and down without speaking, but he didn't lower his gaze. The second monk, who had remained silent all this time, stepped forward to the abbot and stood on tiptoe to whisper in his ear before moving back while smiling encouragingly at Edwin.

The abbot nodded and composed himself before speaking. 'As Prior Henry points out, the Lord's ways are often mysterious to men on earth. It may be that He has sent you to us in our hour of need for some greater purpose. And precept eight tells us that we should respect all men. Therefore, welcome.'

He held out his hand and Edwin, not entirely sure of what he should do, genuflected briefly while putting the ring to his lips. The abbot's fingers were cold, despite the warmth of the day.

The abbot turned to Martin. 'We have little use for arms or soldiers here, but you are most welcome also.' Martin bowed, but didn't move forward, kneel or speak.

There was silence for a moment before the abbot broke it. 'Now, we must speak of the business in hand. Brother William, you may return to the earl with my blessing, and report that his men are safe. I will find another to accompany me to France.' He held up his hand and blessed the monk before dismissing him; Brother William gave Edwin an encouraging pat on the shoulder as he went past.

Edwin hadn't realised that he was going to lose his companion so soon and was assailed by panic. Who else was going to tell him how to behave? 'What's precept eight?' he hissed under his breath.

Brother William leaned in. 'From the Rule of St Benedict, the laws by which we live. Father Abbot quotes it frequently; you'll get used to it.' He straightened. 'Farewell Edwin, Martin. I'll see you in a week at Conisbrough.' He left and shut the door behind him.

The abbot gestured to two stools; Edwin lowered himself on to one but Martin remained standing behind him while the abbot settled himself in the chair and the prior sat on the bench.

Edwin thought he'd better start taking charge of the situation. 'You've called me here, my lord, because one of your monks has been murdered?'

The abbot nodded.

'I'd like to know more. Who was he?'

'He was Brother Alexander, who was master of the lay brothers. He was a good man, a clever man. He joined us some seven or eight years ago.'

'How old was he?'

The abbot spread his hands and turned to the prior, who shrugged. 'In middle age – late middle age, perhaps? More than fifty, certainly, but not yet sixty.'

'But he only took the cowl seven or eight years ago? What did he do before that?'

'He was out in the world. He had travelled widely, which was why he was going to be my companion on the way to Cîteaux.'

'When did he die?'

'On Wednesday morning.'

Three days ago, thought Edwin. Hopefully the trail won't have gone too cold. 'How did it happen?'

'He was stabbed, God rest his soul. In the back.' The abbot crossed himself again.

Well, that ruled out any lingering doubts Edwin might have had about this all being a misunderstanding. 'And may I see the body?'

The abbot looked repulsed. 'No, you may not, as he is already in his grave. And what a very strange and ghoulish request.'

Edwin reflected that he'd had no choice during the last few months but to turn into a ghoulish person. But even so, he should remember that it wasn't the case for others.

After another whisper from the prior, the abbot relented slightly. 'But I can see why you might have asked it. If you are to find out who killed Brother Alexander then you must learn as much as possible. We do not normally allow outsiders within our precinct, but you have my authorisation to go where you will within the abbey and to talk with the brethren, as long as you do not interrupt the canonical hours in the church.'

'Thank you, my lord.' Edwin began to rise, sensing he was dismissed.

'And may God go with you, my son.'

Yes, thought Edwin, as he left the room. If this is all I have to go on, I'll need plenty of His help.

Chapter Three

Martin followed Edwin out of the room and noticed that the prior had accompanied them. He was starving – did these monks not eat dinner?

'Before you go into the abbey proper, perhaps you'd like to go to the guesthouse for something to eat?'

Martin's hand went to his dagger at this evidence of mind-reading, but Edwin was already thanking the prior. He was a cheery-looking fellow for a monk. At least he would be recognisable with all that frizzy hair; Martin had no idea how he was going to tell the others apart when they all wore the same robes. But that was Edwin's problem, mainly – all he had to do was watch Edwin's back. And surely he would have no problem fighting off the monks, who were supposedly peaceful and probably half-starved, anyway. And yet one of them had found the strength to stab his fellow. Maybe it had even been this prior. His hand twitched again.

He walked a couple of paces behind the others while they talked so he could keep an eye on them. The prior seemed keen to chat – he probably didn't get the chance very often, Martin supposed. His face was currently screwed up as if he was trying to remember something as he spoke.

'Daniel, that was it.'

Edwin replied to him. 'Daniel who? Daniel of somewhere? Or did he have another name?'

'Oh, wait now, it will come to me. It was a long time ago he mentioned it – as you'll have understood, we don't speak much in here, and if we do it's only out of necessity. Conversations about our past lives are almost non-existent.' The prior took a few more paces and then stopped. 'Morton, something like that? Ah, no, wait' – he snapped his fingers – 'Morley, that was it. Daniel of Morley.'

'And Brother Alexander spoke of his writings?'

'Yes, and of what an impact they had had on his learning. I'm sorry, that's probably not much use, but it's the only thing I can really remember about him other than his work here.'

'Every little thing is useful to me at the moment, Brother, so thank you.' Edwin looked a bit unsure. 'Can I find out more about Daniel from anyone here?'

The prior shrugged. 'Father Abbot may know more – he is a learned man. Or Brother Octavian, the precentor.'

'The what?'

'The brother who looks after our books – the librarian.'

Martin saw Edwin grimace. 'I'd better start making some kind of list.'

They arrived at the guesthouse, a long, low building at the edge of the precinct, backing on to the stream, and were introduced to Brother Amandus, the guestmaster. He wore a white robe, had grey hair round the tonsure, and stood with a bit of a stoop. He directed them to two beds at the far end of the room, where they dropped their bags. *A good commander plans ahead.* Martin pointed Edwin to the one furthest away, next to the wall, so he would be between Edwin and the rest of the room. Martin didn't know where his armour had got to, but he'd find out as soon as he was able. He was not pleased to see that Edwin took off his dagger and its belt and stowed it away in his scrip. Martin would talk to him about that later – he shouldn't go round unarmed if he could help it, even if they were in a monastery. But more to the immediate point, the monk was pointing them towards a table in the middle of the chamber where bowls were laid out. He grabbed Edwin and propelled him over. The prior, with whom Edwin had been continuing to talk, laughed heartily before attempting, not very successfully, to turn it into a throat-clearing sound.

Brother Amandus waited until he had finished. 'Precept fifty-five, Brother Prior, as Father Abbot would no doubt say if he were here.'

The prior nodded. 'Yes, Brother, I'm sure he would. Now, my sons, I must leave you for the refectory meal and then the noon office of sext. Brother Amandus will guide you to the abbey when you are ready.'

He left, but Martin was already concentrating on the fact that the guestmaster was bringing over a pot of something steaming. He took out his spoon and whispered to Edwin. 'I wonder what precept fifty-five means?'

Edwin leaned in. 'It's from the Rule of St Benedict, which the monks live by. Apparently the abbot quotes it a lot.'

Martin was impressed. How did Edwin know these things? He really was clever. Admittedly he was three years older, but Martin couldn't see that he'd be able to think like Edwin even when he reached that age. But right now he didn't need to – his task was to keep Edwin alive and in one piece.

Brother Amandus ladled something into his bowl and Martin looked with a sinking heart at the mess of beans and vegetables before him. He glanced around surreptitiously to see if a meat dish might be forthcoming, but Edwin was already tucking in, as were two other men at the table. Martin sighed and shovelled up a spoonful.

Once he'd cleared his bowl he could think more clearly. Edwin was already engaged in conversation with one of the other guests, whose status Martin couldn't place. Not a lord, not a peasant – maybe a townsman of some description. He thought he'd better help out by trying to talk to the other one, who was sitting at a slight distance and looking away from the others. Decent clothes, nice belt, scabbard holding a dagger with what was probably an eight-inch blade. The wheel pommel of the dagger was embossed, and the chapes on the end of the scabbard and the belt had the same inlaid design. Nice. Certainly more expensive than the weapon he carried, which was the best he could get for the money his father had sent him.

'Good day to you, sir.'

The other man grunted something and then looked away again, shifting slightly to turn his shoulder to Martin.

Martin didn't like talking at the best of times and had no idea what to say now. Brother Amandus slopped another portion of the meal, which to be fair didn't taste all that bad, into his bowl and he turned his attention back to that.

The monk sat down next to him. 'That's Sir Philip. He often stops here when he travels between his manors, but he's not one for talking.'

'Oh.'

'He normally stays for just a night, maybe two if the weather is bad, but his horse is lame so he'll be here a few days, I expect, while it recovers.'

'Where —'

'I know why you're here. Good Lord, I said to myself when I heard the news about poor Brother Alexander, how could one of the brethren do this? If indeed it was one of the brethren, which must be in doubt. Most of us have been here for many years and we serve God together in peace. I prayed that Father Abbot would be able to find out who did it, but I didn't know he was going to send out for someone.'

'I —'

'And yet here you are. Once you've finished your meal I'll take you over to the main abbey buildings. Once sext is finished you'll probably want to talk to some of the brethren, won't you? Who will you speak to first?'

'I don't —'

'Probably Brother Helias — he's the cellarer, you know — and goes out and about and knows a great many people. Or maybe Brother Octavian: after all Brother Alexander was reading when he ...'

'Thank you, Brother. Really it would be better if you spoke to Edwin. He's the one in charge.'

'Oh, really? I would have thought ... ah, Sir Philip, you've finished? Would you like some more? No? Well then, let me clear your bowl ...' He bustled off, and Martin took a deep breath.

He waited for Edwin to finish. Why did he eat so slowly? He bid farewell to Sir Philip and then they followed Brother Amandus across the precinct, as he talked all the while.

Martin bent his head to speak close to Edwin's ear. 'He's like an old woman.'

'Maybe. But if he is, he's the only woman here.'

Martin looked around. The place looked deserted, but they were probably all in the church, weren't they? But yes, they would all be men, of course. He was used to that. The castle was an all-male environment, except for the Lady Isabelle and …

He kicked a stone. 'Well, maybe we're better off without any women in our lives.' His voice sounded more vicious than he'd intended. Edwin's face fell, and he put on the sad expression he'd had ever since he'd heard back from Lincoln. 'Ah. Sorry.'

Edwin shook his head, though he still looked like he might cry. 'It's no matter. We've business to attend to here, and maybe you're right – we're better off without any women in our lives.'

———◆———

The rhythmic movement of the ox-cart had sent Alys into a doze. She was tired: she hadn't slept very well during the nights while they were on their journey, partly as she wasn't used to sleeping on the ground, and partly as she was wary of the wide open spaces of the countryside. In the whole course of her sixteen years she had left Lincoln's encircling and protecting walls only a handful of times, and she had never been as far away from the city as this. During the day she was safe, though: Master Theobald was a long-time associate of her father, carrying bales of fabric up and down the land, and as his wife Mistress Christiana travelled with him she had some female company, so she could rest easy and catch up with some sleep.

The cart travelled very slowly, the oxen plodding their way through some ten miles each day; they had also stopped off at a couple of fairs to trade, so it had taken many days to travel this far. Still, at least she'd brought her distaff and spindle with her; during the horrible months in the spring that year she'd had no time to devote to it, but spinning was something she'd been doing since before she could even remember, and she'd been glad to take it up again, finding the familiar movements soothing. On their travels she hadn't had much else to do, so she now had several spools of reasonably fine wool in her luggage, which would come in useful at some point.

The ox-cart rumbled on. She opened her eyes and stared drowsily out at the road, which looked very similar to all the others on which they had travelled. She was glad Master Theobald made this journey every year, for surely it would be easy to miss the way if he wasn't familiar with it. And the weather had been kind, for which she thanked the Lord – she had been told tales of winter travels during which the cart could become mired in deep mud, but during these summer months the roads were dry, if sometimes rutted and uneven. Their final destination was the village of Conisbrough: this was the northern edge of Master Theobald's annual circular route, where he would trade the last of his bales from Lincoln at the fair there and stock up on goods from the north. And it was her destination too.

She closed her eyes again. During the long, endless days of the journey she had had plenty of time – too much time, really – to consider and to reflect on what had happened and what she was doing now. It seemed almost unreal. After the letter had arrived there had been a huge argument, which would previously have meant Alys backing down, but she had gained in confidence and determination during the preceding hard months, and had won her case. The end result was that she had now left everyone she had ever known, and was travelling to a place she'd never been to, to find a man she'd known only for a few days. Was she mad? Probably. But anything was better than the alternative.

They had spent last night camped on farmland which belonged to an abbey, which meant they had been safe, but her sleeplessness continued as she realised how close they were to Conisbrough; they would reach it on the morrow. In the morning she had stayed inside the covered cart, comfortable among the bales of fabric, spinning and keeping her thoughts to herself. She'd heard Master Theobald greet a few fellow travellers, and then she'd dozed off to the accompaniment of the creaks from the axles. She wasn't deeply asleep, but was half-dreaming that she was being rocked by her mother. It was lovely, but a sense of unease pervaded the dream, as the part of her mind which was awake was trying to tell her that her mother had been dead for nearly eight years. But she paid that no mind. The sun shone through the canvas of the roof and she lay with her eyes closed, distaff and spindle still in her hands.

'Alys! Wake up, child – we're here.'

The cart had stopped.

Alys came to herself all at once and sat up, heart suddenly hammering in her throat. They had arrived. They were here. In Conisbrough. In a few moments she would see the man on whom her future happiness depended; the man she had helped in his hour of need; the man who had returned to save her life at the risk of his own. The man who wanted to marry her. She smoothed her apron and gown, gathered up her courage, and stepped out of the cart.

Brother Amandus fell silent as they neared the abbey building. They went past the great west door of the church and instead entered via a smaller one further along the outside wall. This led into a short passage; on Edwin's right was another door, and on his left a flight of stairs with an archway underneath.

'That's the lay brothers' range,' said Brother Amandus, pointing to the right. 'They have their own dormitory and refectory separate from ours.' He lowered his voice. 'Father Abbot did say that we were permitted to speak to you, and I thought it might be useful for you to know your way around.'

Edwin nodded encouragingly. 'Thank you. And what's on this side?'

Brother Amandus indicated the arched opening. 'That goes through to an undercroft storage room, and above is the lay brothers' parlour. It's one of only two places in the abbey where speaking is generally permitted – the other is our parlour – as it's used to conduct business with the outside world. Meetings with merchants who buy our wool, that sort of thing. Or the occasional visit to one of the brethren from a relative.'

Edwin let him rattle on as he looked about him.

'That means that we can carry out trade while still keeping the inner part of our abbey pure and dedicated to the Lord. This way.'

He led the way straight on to the end of the passage and then fell silent once more as they all emerged into what Edwin assumed must be the cloister. It was a square open space with grass in the middle and a covered walkway around all four edges. They were in the middle of one side of the square.

Edwin turned to Brother Amandus and opened his mouth to ask a question, but he received a shake of the head so he held his peace while they were led around to the left, along what must be the outside wall of the church, and then to the third side of the square where they entered a room which was more or less opposite the passage where they had come in. Edwin hoped Martin was remembering his way around, as he found himself in a comfortable room, currently empty, with a fireplace and a number of benches and stools.

'The parlour,' explained Brother Amandus. 'The only other place in which the brethren are permitted to speak to each other within the abbey itself, and of course normally only for the brothers, the choir monks. When you need to talk to anyone, if would be best if you could bring him in here. Some of the older brothers who are excused outdoor manual work will be in here shortly, and I will ask them where we might find Brother Helias.'

Edwin nodded, hoping that the cellarer would be less garrulous and more useful than the guestmaster, and moved to sit on one of the benches. Before he got there the door opened again and a number of elderly monks shuffled in; Brother Amandus spoke to one of them in a low voice and then moved to Edwin. 'It appears that Brother Helias is not here. He was called away on business.'

'Oh.' How was he meant to interpret that? Was this something which happened in the normal course of events, or was it suspicious that the monk he ought to be talking to had disappeared? And what was he going to do now? He felt as though he'd been cast into a river, and the flow was taking him far away, and he had no control.

'You mentioned another brother?'

'Did I?'

'Yes, something to do with reading? And the prior told me too, but I can't remember his name, sorry.' Edwin was starting to wish he'd brought some parchment and a quill and ink with him, scratchy penmanship or no.

'Ah yes, of course, Brother Octavian. He's the precentor, the one who looks after the books. Brother Alexander was reading when he died, so he might be a useful man for you to talk to. I'll fetch him here.'

He left. Edwin looked round at Martin, who was fidgeting, and at the row of elderly monks, who were gazing at him in silence. He looked away. He looked back, but their attention hadn't wavered. He sighed and sat down. Reading? How in the Lord's name did a man get murdered while he was reading?

It wasn't long before Brother Amandus re-entered, followed by a small monk who edged into the room behind him.

'Edwin, this is Brother Octavian, the precentor; Brother, this is Edwin, the man sent here to find out what happened to Brother Alexander.'

The small monk crossed himself. '*Requiescat in pace.*'

Edwin did the same and murmured the words, although surely a monk would go straight to heaven, so he needed to worry more about what had put him there than about the state of his immortal soul.

The guestmaster nodded to them both and left. Edwin moved to a seat further into the corner of the room and gestured to Brother Octavian to join him.

'Thank you for speaking to me. I understand you can tell me more about what Brother Alexander was doing when he died?'

The monk looked down at his hands, and clasped and unclasped them before speaking. 'It was distressing.'

Edwin nodded. 'I understand that, Brother, but anything you can tell me might help.'

'Yes. Yes, of course. We were all at *lectio divina* – that is, reading holy texts, which we do every morning after terce. Each of the brethren comes to me to be issued the book he is engaged in, and then they go and sit in the cloister: outside if it is fine, and under the roof if not. Then when they all have theirs, I take mine and do the same. We sit and study until the meal which happens just before sext, and then I return to the armarium —'

'The what?'

'The armarium – the book room, if you will – and everyone comes to return his book to me. On that day I noticed that one was missing, so I went out into the cloister to see who was tardy. And … and I found Brother Alexander, dead. He was sitting peacefully over his book, except that he had a knife in his back.' He twisted his hands together, fiddling with a key which hung from his rope belt.

'Whose knife?'

He shrugged. 'I don't know. One of the ones used to sharpen quills in the scriptorium – there are a lot of them around and they don't belong to anyone in particular.'

Edwin was starting to feel desperate. Were there no distinguish-ing details at all which he could grasp? How was he even to start his investigation? 'So, how many others would he have been sharing this book with? Surely he can't have been stabbed in the middle of a group of other monks?'

Brother Octavian looked confused. 'Share? He wasn't sharing with anyone. The point of *lectio divina* is that we each study sepa-rately, in silent contemplation. At the beginning of Lent each of the brothers is assigned a book, and he reads it throughout the year, meditates on it, prays to understand it better – all on his own. Of course, some of the novices and younger brethren need to —'

'Hold on, hold on.' Edwin held up his hand. 'Each monk has a book of his own? How many monks do you have here?'

'Sixty, including the novices.'

Edwin stared at him in disbelief. 'You have *sixty* books?'

Brother Octavian smiled. 'We have seventy-three.'

Edwin could feel his jaw sagging. Seventy-three books? He hadn't known there were that many in the kingdom. In his life he had seen three books, or at least three proper books, not including the manor and court rolls: the parish Bible, the psalter with which Father Ignatius had taught him to read, and a book with poems in which had belonged to the Lady Isabelle, the earl's sister.

The monk was looking at him more keenly now. 'You can read? You are interested in books? Would you like to see them?'

Would he! Seventy-three books? Dear Lord. But Edwin bit back his immediate yes, surprised by the first surge of real feeling he had experienced in weeks. Think. Would it do any good in his quest? Or was it just something he wanted to do? He looked around the room. Two of the elderly monks now had their heads down over some sewing work, but the others were still regarding him owlishly. Martin's fidgeting had turned to pacing. He wasn't doing any good here, so what harm would it do to go and look? He might be able to find out more. But wait. 'If we leave this room, will we still be able to talk?'

'Yes. Father Abbot has said that we may speak with you if you ask it, as long as we are mindful of the peace of the abbey and the sanctity of the holy offices. And the books are in the armarium, a separate room, so we can talk quietly without disturbing others at their labours.'

Edwin rose. 'Then yes, thank you Brother, I would very much like to see the books.'

They left the parlour, Martin trailing behind, and made their way up part of the same edge of the cloister to a locked door. Brother Octavian took his key and let them into a long, narrow room. It had a window at the far end with real glass in it, which made strange patterns of light across the floor.

Brother Octavian followed Edwin's gaze. 'A necessary expense, for no flame is permitted in here.' He waved his arm, and Edwin looked in wonder at the shelves, floor to ceiling and running the length of the room, all holding books. Dozens of books. Laid flat, individually, on every surface. He was surrounded. Large books, small books, books in new binding, books which looked ancient. He couldn't speak.

The monk nodded. 'You feel it too. Be careful there!' This was aimed at Martin, who, in turning round in the confined space, had knocked the end of his sword against one of the shelves. He mumbled something, and the monk spoke more gently. 'I beg your pardon. I am a man of peace, but it is my duty to look after these volumes and I must do that to the best of my ability.'

Martin moved carefully towards Edwin. 'Is this really serving any purpose?'

Edwin surveyed the room. What knowledge was contained in these tomes? What learning? 'I won't be long, and you never know, it might be useful.' He was fooling nobody, least of all himself. But he couldn't leave until he'd seen at least some of them. 'Look, I hardly need a guard in here, and I can see that you're bored. Why don't you go outside and find someone else to talk to, and I'll come and find you in a while?'

He saw Martin glance at the monk, who was now straightening a volume on a shelf, a volume that was, to Edwin's eye, already straight. 'My lord said I was to take care of you.'

'Yes, but he also said I needed to find out what was going on. And,' Edwin lowered his voice, 'he's not going to talk to me while you're looming there like that and he's worried you're going to damage something.'

Martin looked back and forth between them. 'All right. I'll go outside, find the stables and see that our horses have been properly cared for. And find where my armour has got to. Next time they go into the church for a service, you come outside and find me.'

'Fine. They'll have another service in the middle of the afternoon, so it can't be that long. I'll meet you by the stables. If you meet anyone, try and talk to them.'

Martin nodded, and was gone. Edwin turned to the store of wonders before him and listened to Brother Octavian as he reverently took down the first volume. 'Now, this is the *Carta Caritatis* ...'

Martin tried to get his bearings. Where had they come in, and how would he get back to the stables? He pushed a door and found himself in the church.

Cautiously, he looked around before taking another step. He didn't want to make a fool of himself by interrupting anything. But the place was empty – of course, the monks were about their tasks at the moment, and they'd be back here for the next office, as Edwin had said. What a pain it must be to have to come to church five or six times a day. How did they ever get anything else done? But he supposed that was what they were here for – most of them would be the younger sons of noble and gentle families who would have no inheritance, and who had inexplicably chosen the cloister over the idea of fighting as someone's household knight. They weren't cut out for the real world.

He tried to orient himself. The high altar was to his right, so he must have come into the south transept. The main door would be to the west … yes, there it was.

As he stepped out into the open space of the church he became aware that he was not alone; over in one of the side chapels he could hear someone praying. He peered in and saw a monk kneeling before a statue of the Blessed Virgin, his hands clasped in supplication. Martin couldn't make out the words, but he sounded like he was either desperate or in pain. Martin stepped away as quietly as he could and made his way to the main west door.

He found himself outside the main monastery building but still within the precinct. Right, yes, the guesthouse where they were staying was one of those buildings over there, and the stables were further up back towards the gatehouse. He set off through the precinct, wondering how anyone got used to it being so quiet. It was like watching a load of ghosts, all those figures in brown or white robes gliding round without talking to each other. Back at the castle the outer ward was a hive of activity with men shouting and bawling, or at least greeting each other. This was just wrong. He didn't like it. But he stayed silent all the same.

He reached the stables and entered. After his eyes had adjusted to the gloom he walked down the stalls to find the horses they had left; Brother William had taken both mules back with him, so that meant less to worry about. Edwin's palfrey and the packhorse were together, and Martin was pleased to see they had been well cared for; they had been recently groomed, their hooves were clean and they had racks of sweet new hay. Now, where was his armour? His own mount was in a stall towards the end, but as he stepped in it he jumped, for a man in a brown robe was already there, stroking the roan's neck.

Immediately his hand flew to his sword hilt and he felt the panic rising as it had done on the road. 'What are you doing here? Get away from him.'

The monk – Martin assumed he was a monk or he wouldn't be here, although he did have a beard as well which was odd – stepped back. He inclined his head without speaking.

Martin, realising that the horses must have been cared for by someone, knew he had over-reacted, but still he went to check the courser over. It appeared to be fine. He turned back to the monk, who was still standing there. 'Are you a groom?'

The monk shook his head.

'Well then, stay away from my horse. He's from my lord earl's own stable, and he's a knight's mount, not one of the mules or hobbledehoys which you probably keep here. Understand?'

The monk bowed and left, still without speaking.

The horse was becoming agitated and Martin realised it was probably reacting to him. Why couldn't he calm down? *A good commander is in control of himself.* What would Sir Geoffrey say if he could see him now? Think. What had he come in for? He looked around for his pack – yes, there it was, in the corner of the stall. He picked it up and slung it over his shoulder.

There was one other fairly decent horse in the stable, which he stopped to look at as he went by. It had a poultice strapped to one leg, and Martin recalled that the visiting knight's mount was lame. He considered taking a closer look, but the knight had seemed fairly short-tempered and you didn't want to antagonise men like that, not until you knew their proper rank and position, anyway, so he hefted the armour bag on his shoulder and made his way out.

Once he'd taken it back to the guesthouse and dropped it by his bed, he thought it might be nearly time for nones, the mid-afternoon service. On his way back to the stables to meet Edwin he shook his head again at the utter, overwhelming quiet. How did they bear it? He felt it pressing in on him like a weight.

At that moment the silence was shattered by a scream, a long-drawn-out howl of agony. Everyone in the precinct stopped dead, except Martin, who drew his sword and ran towards the sound.

Chapter Four

Edwin couldn't believe how soon the bell sounded to call the monks to the service of nones. Brother Octavian shut, with regret, the volume of Gregory the Great's *Dialogues* they had been looking at, ushered Edwin out of the room and locked it.

'I must join my brothers at the day stairs.'

'Yes. Thank you for showing me the books. Perhaps if I have time ...'

The monk smiled. 'It's rare to have a visitor who shows such an interest. If we can arrange it then I would be happy to show you more of the books.'

Edwin thanked him and headed back out to the cloister walkway. He stood politely to one side as the aged brothers shuffled out of the parlour, and then passed another who looked nearly as old. This one was harassed-looking and calling behind him.

'Roger! Gerald! Matthew! Stop writing now and hurry, or you'll be late!'

Three very young-looking men, no more than boys, wearing the white robes of monks but without the tonsures, rushed past Edwin, and then there was quiet. The sound of the bell was replaced by chanting coming from the direction of the church. Edwin wandered into the cloister, realising that he'd forgotten, in his excitement about the books, to ask Brother Octavian either anything about the writings of Daniel of Morley or where Brother Alexander had been sitting when he'd been found. He would certainly need to check on the latter point, so he could work out who might have seen anything.

He sat down. The *books*. Never had his mind been opened to such wonder as it had been in the last hour. He was filled with it, bursting with it. The possibilities for learning were endless. He could happily spend the rest of his days reading and contemplating and thinking and reading again.

The chanting continued, a pleasant background to the peace of the cloister. He could almost forget why he was here …

But he couldn't forget why he was here. He needed to do his duty to his lord. And he was supposed to be meeting Martin by the stables.

Reluctantly he stood and made his way across the grass and back towards the door by which he'd originally entered the building. He found himself in the passageway. Was this it? Yes, he was sure it was, for there was the staircase and the walkway, and the second door ahead of him which led back out into the precinct.

As he moved forward something on the stairs caught his eye and he stopped. He bent to pick it up – a small piece of metal in a V-shape, about an inch long, with an inlaid design of some kind. One of the monks had presumably dropped it on his way up or down to the office, though Edwin couldn't immediately work out what it was. He'd ask Brother Amandus about it when he got the chance. He slipped it into his purse and continued on his way.

The precinct was deserted, as he might have expected while there was a service going on. He wasn't quite sure where the stables were, but he recalled they had been near the gatehouse, which he could see over the top of the other buildings, so he headed that way. Eventually the smell told him he was in the right place, and he looked around for Martin. Odd – he wasn't there.

He looked inside the stables but there was nobody there. Puzzled, he walked back to the main gate and roused the elderly monk who had admitted them that morning, who was now dozing on a bench in the sun outside his little porter's lodge.

'Excuse me, Brother.'

His voice sounded shockingly loud in the silence of the precinct, but it had no effect on the slumbering old man.

'*Excuse* me, Brother.' Edwin tried a little louder, and also patted the monk on his shoulder.

This time he woke up. 'Eh? What? Who's there?'

'*Benedicte*, Brother. I'm one of the guests who arrived this morning. I'm looking for my companion.'

Brother – Thurstan, was it? – blinked in the sunlight. 'You're one of the boys who came this morning with Brother William.'

'Yes, that's right. I'm looking for my friend – the OTHER ONE WHO CAME WITH ME. Have you seen him?' Edwin glanced round the precinct again, but there was still no sign of him.

'What's that you say? Stop mumbling. All the young men nowadays, they mumble. Anyway, where's the other one who came with you?'

Edwin sighed. 'Never mind.'

'What's that?'

'I said NEVER – oh, it doesn't matter. Thank you, Brother. I said THANK YOU Brother.'

Brother Thurstan nodded amiably and settled back to his nap.

The guesthouse, thought Edwin, I haven't tried there yet. Maybe he's gone to find something there.

But Martin wasn't in the guesthouse either. Edwin stood in puzzlement. Where in the Lord's name could he be?

Martin ran with his sword in his hand in the direction of where the scream had come from. He paused, faced with several stone buildings which all looked similar. One of them was the abbot's house, wasn't it? Where they'd been earlier? But it hadn't come from there, surely. He wished Sir Geoffrey was here.

The cry came again, nearer this time, allowing him to locate it. He burst through the nearest open door.

He was in a large, long room with beds on either side and a table in the middle. It looked a little like the guest quarters. The noise was coming from the far end so he strode towards it. Was someone else being murdered? Dear God, what if it was Edwin?

'STOP!'

Martin skidded to a halt at the authority of the voice. A monk had stepped round from behind a screen which hid something at the end of the room. Martin didn't think he was a monk he'd seen before – this one was tall and completely bald. In his hands he held a bowl.

The bowl was full to the brim with blood.

The monk moved towards him, and Martin raised his sword. From behind the screen came groans and cries.

'Put that down. You are in a house of God!'

Martin didn't move. 'You put that down first.'

The monk looked at him in surprise, and then at the blood he carried. Enlightenment dawned. 'Ah, I see.' He put the bowl down on the table and folded his arms. He looked steadily at Martin until he sheathed his sword. Only then did the monk speak again.

'I am Brother Durand, the infirmarer. And you are?'

The infirmarer? Ah ... Martin made the best of it and bowed. 'Martin Dubois, squire to my lord the Earl Warenne, and here at his orders.'

'Here to invade my infirmary?'

Martin felt his cheeks grow red. 'No. Well, what I mean is – I heard a scream. And someone here has already been murdered ...'

Brother Durand looked at him steadily until he faltered into silence. Martin felt the eyes boring into him. 'Murdered, yes, but not here and not by me. And even then that would give you no excuse, no authority, to come running in here under arms.'

Martin said nothing and looked at his feet.

'Not that I need to explain myself to you, but the cries you heard were from Brother Richard, who has an abscess of the tooth. He needed bleeding, and I needed to examine his face and jaw. He screamed as I probed.'

'I, er ...'

'So, if that is all, I have matters to attend to. While you are here at the abbey, you will not set foot in this infirmary again unless I give my permission, is that clear?'

'Yes, Brother.'

'Good. Now go.'

It was only after Martin had left the building that he started to think of all the things he should have said, the actions he should have taken. He, senior squire to one of the most powerful men in the kingdom, thrown out of the room like a child! Why, he had a good mind to —

'There you are! I've been looking for you everywhere. Where have you been?' Edwin appeared beside him.

'Where have *you* been, you mean. You're supposed to be here to sort this out so we can leave again, not spend your time looking at books and talking to men too feeble to hold a sword or so weak they cry with the toothache.'

He shoved past Edwin and stalked off.

Edwin stood at something of a loss. The monks were emerging from the church – nones must be quite a short service – and heading in different directions, presumably to work on other duties. Should he follow any of them? But before he could decide, he felt a touch on his arm. It was a monk, a choir monk in a white robe whom he hadn't seen before. This one had reddish hair around his tonsure and was about forty-ish, Edwin would guess.

'You are Edwin? The man the lord abbot sent for?'

'Yes, yes I am – Brother …?'

'I'm Brother Helias, my son, the cellarer. I had word that you wished to see me?'

'Ah, yes, thank you. I was wondering if you could tell me a bit more about Brother Alexander and what he did here? Who did he deal with, did he ever go out of the abbey, that kind of thing?'

The monk nodded. 'I can tell you all you require about Brother Alexander's duties. I have time now while the brethren are undertaking their afternoon's physical labour. But perhaps we would be more comfortable in my office than out here in the precinct?' He gestured and Edwin followed him across the open space, past a warren of smaller buildings and into a room which reminded him very much of the steward's office at Conisbrough. He sat on a stool indicated to him by Brother Helias and looked around at the storage kists and the neat rolls of parchment stacked up on shelves on the wall. He sniffed – a hint of herbs and spices. He felt at home.

'So, being cellarer is a bit like being the steward?'

Brother Helias eased himself down on to a bench and nodded. 'Yes. I'm in charge of all the provisions in the abbey – not just food and drink but also things like leather for our sandals and the lay brothers' boots, and cloth to make our habits. It's one of the more worldly positions here, as I need to talk to men outside the abbey quite often, but it is of some small importance to the brethren, for if I get my orders wrong we might end up with nothing to eat. Which reminds me – Brother?'

Edwin looked around, surprised to see that a younger monk had been sitting quietly in the corner all this time. He was near a small window which cast light on the parchments he was reading, spread out on a table, but he himself was in shadow. These monks really knew how to be silent. Frighteningly so.

The monk stood as Brother Helias beckoned him. 'Have you finished reading the delivery list for the wine?'

The younger man nodded without speaking.

'Good. Take it with you down to the cellar and check it against the barrels which arrived this morning. Take a piece of charcoal with you and mark off each item on the list as you see it in the cellar. Make a note of any barrels without entries on the list, or items on the list for which there are no barrels.'

The monk bowed his head, picked up a parchment and a stick of charcoal from the table, and walked out of the room. Edwin would swear that even his sandals made no sound on the floor.

Brother Helias turned back to him. 'He will be the next cellarer after me, so he needs to learn. If the lists of what we are supposed to have don't match what's actually in the cellar or the stores, it can cause problems.'

Edwin nodded. 'Yes, I know. My uncle William is the steward at my lord's castle in Conisbrough, and he checks everything very carefully. I often help him with his additions and calculations.'

'Ah, you do, do you? An apprentice cellarer yourself? Well then …' Brother Helias allowed a smile to crease his face as he rocked back on the bench, an expression of concentration on his face. 'Tell me, if I ordered three ten-gallon barrels of wine at fourpence a gallon, four ten-gallon barrels of ale at a penny a gallon, and eight pounds of pepper at four shillings a pound, how much would —'

'Two pounds, five shillings and fourpence, Brother, though William would balk at paying four shillings a pound for pepper.'

Brother Helias gaped at him. Edwin shrugged. 'Sorry, Brother, I didn't mean to be impertinent. Adding up like that is something I've always been able to do – I don't know why.'

'It's a gift from the Lord, that's what it is. If you ever decide to become a monk, my son, ask them to let you work with the cellarer.' He continued staring and then shook his head as if to clear it. 'I am sorry I allowed myself to change the subject. Levity is not a desired trait among the brethren – precept fifty-four, as Father Abbot would no doubt say. I shall confess my transgression later.'

He looked serious, but Edwin thought he could discern the ghost of a smile at the corner of his mouth. It was nice to think that at least some of the monks might still be real people underneath. Which brought him back to the fact that he still knew nothing about the man whose death he was supposed to be looking into. 'But anyway, back to Brother Alexander, if I may. Did he also have dealings with people outside these walls?'

Brother Helias sighed and crossed himself. 'Yes, he did. As the master of the lay brothers he was always out and about. Only half of our lay brothers actually work here in the abbey – the others are scattered round and about in different granges, like separate farms – and so he would visit each in turn to check up on their work.'

'And was he popular? I mean, might there have been any of the lay brothers who didn't like him?'

Brother Helias looked shocked. 'My son, none of the brethren could possibly have wanted to kill Brother Alexander. The whole notion is impossible.'

Edwin hastened to soothe him. 'I'm sure they wouldn't, Brother, but the fact is that somebody killed him, and the more I can find out about him and what he did, the better. Especially if he had contact with many people outside the abbey?'

The defensive attitude softened a little. 'Well, yes, when you put it like that … of course it is much more likely that the culprit is someone from outside. Perhaps a disgruntled farmer or trader who wanted to sell to us and was annoyed that we grow much of our own produce? Or a wool merchant? Brother Alexander, with his knowledge of the outside world before he came here, was the one of us who struck the bargains with the merchants to whom we sell our fleeces.'

Now there was an idea which started Edwin's mind working. He had seen traders and merchants often at the fairs in Conisbrough, and knew that they took their prices and their deals very seriously. He had often heard trade referred to as a cut-throat business, but would anyone take the phrase literally? He would need to think about that some more.

But in the meantime, what of this 'knowledge of the outside world' which several of the monks had mentioned? 'Do you know anything about what Brother Alexander did before he took the cowl?'

Brother Helias spread his hands. 'Alas not. All I can tell you is what you probably know already – that he was out in the world for many years, that he travelled, and that he came to the monastic life in his middle years.'

'Have you ever heard of the writings of a man called Daniel of Morley?'

Edwin watched as the monk searched his mind. 'No, sorry. I must admit that I am much less adept at the studying part of our duties than many of the brethren, though I do try.' He sighed. 'I try to love all parts of my life here equally, but I confess I am more at home in my domain here than I am with the books.' He gestured at the office.

'Not to worry, Brother – I just asked on the off-chance. Is there anyone else here who might know more? Not just about the writings of Daniel of Morley, I mean, but about Brother Alexander's life before he came here?'

Brother Helias was in the act of shaking his head when he stopped. 'Well, there is Brother Richard, I suppose. We are not supposed to have particular friends among the brethren, but men being what they are, everyone has some whose company they value more than others, and they were often together. If they were outside the abbey and able to talk, I suppose Brother Alexander may have told him something of his previous life.' He shrugged. 'That is the best I can come up with, I'm afraid. And you won't be able to talk to Brother Richard anyway, as he is confined to the infirmary with toothache.'

Toothache? Hadn't Martin said something about that earlier? He would check – if he could track Martin down, that was. What in the Lord's name was the matter with him at the moment?

Feeling that the conversation was at an end, Edwin was about to stand and take his leave when the younger monk returned. This time he opened his mouth, shaking the parchment in front of Brother Helias and whispering urgently in his ear. The older monk stood and smiled down.

'Alas, it appears we do have a discrepancy, so I had best go and deal with the matter. Please come and speak with me again whenever you wish – unless it is time for one of the offices in church I am normally in here or round about.'

He went out, the younger monk pulling on his sleeve, but poked his head back around the doorway. 'I forgot to say, when we were speaking of those outside the abbey. One of Brother Alexander's other duties was dealing with that witch in the woods. Perhaps you should talk to her. Yes, yes, I'm coming!'

He departed once more.

Martin didn't know how long he had been stamping around before he found the woodshed. He wanted to walk off his temper – better still, ride it off – but he wasn't going to leave Edwin alone in the abbey with all these madmen. Honestly, why would anyone choose to live here if they didn't have to? He had walked around the ward, or whatever they called it; he'd glowered at any monk who so much as looked at him; he'd kicked a stone around; he'd sat in the sun with his back against a wall for a while; and he'd walked again. The place was just too quiet, and it was suffocating. The walls weren't like the ones at Conisbrough. There they kept him safe, but here they were imprisoning him, closing in until he could hardly breathe.

At some point he heard a noise he did recognise – the thump and split of logs being chopped. Of course, with this many mouths to feed the abbey kitchens no doubt got through a fair amount each day so it would be a constant task, just like it was at the castle. Although, judging by the sound, whoever was doing it was very erratic and hadn't got into the rhythm which you needed if you were going to keep at it. Martin didn't do so much of it these days, what with his other duties, but chopping wood had been a major part of his strength training when he was younger, and Sir Geoffrey had made him wield the axe hour after exhausting hour until the sweat poured off him and his arms shook. That was before life got so complicated, and Martin now looked back on those times with some fondness.

He followed the sound until he rounded a fence into a yard full of wood. At one end were new and uncut pieces; at the other a roofed area where split logs were stacked neatly. In the middle, busy turning one into the other, was a monk, just one on his own. Martin watched him for a few moments. He wasn't very good at it – a weedy-looking youth with white arms sticking out of the sleeves of his habit, the skirts of which were clearly getting in his way.

The monk stopped and put his axe down, picked up some logs and staggered over to the woodshed to stack them. As he turned again he saw Martin and jumped and took a step back.

Martin, who was beginning to be aware that people could be intimidated by the mere sight of him, held up his hands. 'Sorry, Brother, I didn't mean to startle you.'

The monk said nothing but continued to look wary. Martin nodded at the white habit, which surely indicated that he was a choir monk. 'Are you supposed to be doing that? Don't you have anyone to do it for you?'

The monk opened his mouth but no words came out. Damn these people. Martin spoke slowly. 'It's all right. I've been sent here by my lord earl, and your abbot said that you were allowed to speak to us.' The monk's stance softened a little. 'What's your name, Brother?'

'B– Benedict.' His voice quavered a little but recovered. 'I'm a novice.'

'And, what, you've been told to chop wood as some kind of punishment?'

Benedict moved closer and Martin saw what he hadn't noticed before – he had no tonsure. 'Oh no, it's not a punishment. It's God's work.'

Martin was confused. 'God's work? Chopping wood?'

Benedict nodded, his face lighting up. 'Yes. As part of our duties we all have to undertake manual labour every afternoon. Everyone has something different: the older brothers might do sewing or shoemaking, and others are scribes or copyists or work in the gardens or the stables. I'm the youngest apart from the three boys, so it's fitting that I should do something heavier.' He heaved a piece of tree-trunk on to the chopping block and hefted the axe enthusiastically, the pale skin on his arms catching the sun as he brought it down, not hard enough, and it got stuck in the wood instead of splitting it. He tried to jerk it back out, without success.

Martin stepped forward to help him, and between them they levered the axe free. Martin looked speculatively at the piles of logs still waiting to be dealt with, and at his companion's gaunt frame. 'Is there any rule that says you can't have some help?'

Benedict's face was immediately confused. 'I don't know. I wouldn't want to fail in my duty to the abbey or to the Lord. I have to do this.' He backed away and gestured vaguely; Martin realised he was losing him again. Pretend he's a skittish horse, that might work.

He took half a pace back so he wasn't crowding the monk, and spoke soothingly, placatingly. 'I'm not saying that you have to stop. You'll still be doing your duty. But ...' he cast around for an idea that would sound right. 'But surely it would be my duty as a good Christian to help with some abbey work while I'm here?' He was quite pleased with himself for coming up with that.

Benedict nodded doubtfully. 'Well, if you put it like that … as long as I keep going as well … I'm sure …'

Martin grinned. He took off his belt and tunic, rolled up his shirtsleeves and spat on his hands. 'Pass me another axe.'

Edwin sat in the church. The open space in front of him, where the congregation would stand and kneel during Mass, was empty; the choir, where the monks sang their services, was away to his right on the other side of the altar screen. He had found a bench pushed up against the side wall, presumably put there for the benefit of those parishioners who were too aged and feeble to stand or kneel, as was the case in the church at Conisbrough, and he had been there some time observing the church from this unusual angle and trying to order his thoughts.

Eventually a bell began to toll somewhere, and a few people made their way in from the western end of the church, the end which led out into the precinct. It must be time for vespers, which parishioners were no doubt allowed to attend if they could. Edwin slipped off the bench and mingled with them, gaining a few looks but no suspicion – the people here must be used to strangers and abbey guests being in their midst. He knelt along with them as the monks filed in, chanting, and the service began. The lay brothers were all along one side of the church and the choir monks away near the altar behind the screen, so he couldn't see them very well. Edwin tried to look around him as much as he could without arousing too much notice. The parishioners all looked like respectable people – no working men among them at this time on a Saturday, of course, but some older folk and a few devout-looking goodwives. The lay brothers – well, frankly, they all looked alike. All bearded, all wearing the same scapular over their clothes, which were in themselves very similar tunics of brown wool.

Edwin said 'Amen' without thinking and then realised that the service was at an end and that people were leaving. He watched the parishioners go out of the west door and decided that now was not the time to try to talk to any of them – better to wait until Mass tomorrow morning when there would no doubt be many more. The lay brothers could wait as well; they might not be too keen to talk to him after a full day's labour and besides, he wanted to take Martin with him if he was going to leave the abbey. Instead he slipped on to the end of the line of choir monks and followed them out of the door which led from the church into the cloister. He followed them around the edge of the square and to the entrance of the refectory, where they filed in and sat in silence at two long tables. Edwin did not like to go in, so he hovered by the doorway. One monk saw him and detached himself to come over. Red hair, middle-aged – yes, it was Brother Helias, the cellarer.

'Can I help you, my son?' His voice was a whisper.

Edwin hadn't meant to be noticed. 'Thank you, no, er, what I mean is …'

Brother Helias moved them both to one side so they were out of the doorway. 'We're about to have our evening meal – the days are so much longer in the summer that we are allowed to eat twice. You won't be able to talk to anyone during the meal, I'm afraid.'

From inside the refectory came the sound of sixty or so men all sitting down at once. Then a single voice started to speak, reading sonorously from what Edwin now recognised as the Rule. Thanks to his early studies Edwin's Latin had always been reasonably good, so he picked up most of it. This bit was evidently about the use of the church: … *used for prayer and not for any other purpose … when the work of God has been completed all are to go out noiselessly … if someone wishes to make a private prayer then let him go in without hesitation and pray not aloud but with tears and with the attention of his heart.*

As the reading continued Edwin could hear the sound of cups, plates and spoons, but there was no other noise, no chat, no raucous conversation as there always was at the lower tables in the earl's hall. He risked a glance back through the doorway. It was very strange watching so many men sitting in such complete silence. Some of them were making obscure gestures to each other.

Brother Helias put his head close to Edwin's. 'Speech is forbidden at meals, but we have other ways of asking the brethren to pass the bread or the beans.' He smiled and patted Edwin on the shoulder. 'I must go back in – I am sometimes late anyway so Brother Prior won't chastise me. And you'd better go back to the guesthouse if you want your evening meal.'

Edwin realised how hungry he was. 'Yes, of course. Thank you, Brother.'

As he made his way to the guesthouse he saw another monk hurrying towards him, no doubt realising he was late. It was Brother Godfrey, who had come to Conisbrough to fetch him, so Edwin nodded his head and spoke a greeting as they neared each other. But Brother Godfrey looked straight past him and hurried on. Edwin stopped and turned to look after him. How strange. Obviously Brother Godfrey was in haste, but it wasn't that he had ignored him because of that – the monk had looked right through him as though they had never met. Edwin felt again the sharp stab of reality. He was unimportant, worthless, his face not recalled, his presence not worth a greeting.

Back in the guesthouse Edwin found Martin and the two other guests whom he had seen earlier in the day already at the table. Martin looked hot and sweaty, and he was shovelling in what looked like a meal of vegetables and beans as though he hadn't eaten for a week, interspersed with giant gulps of ale. He looked up as Edwin entered.

'Come and sit down. I looked for you a while ago but I saw you praying in the church during the service so I reckoned you didn't need me. Come and eat.'

Edwin sat down while Brother Amandus fussed around him placing a bowl and cup on the table. He took out his spoon, then remembered where he was and said a quick grace. The hunger he had felt earlier had dissipated after his encounter with Brother Godfrey, but he forced it all down, clearing the dish and wiping it around with a piece of bread before speaking.

'Where were you?'

Martin was still eating, having held out his bowl for a second helping, and he said something indistinct which Edwin interpreted as 'I'll tell you later.'

The other two guests at the table had finished eating and were stretching their legs out in front of them while they sipped the remainder of their drinks. The knight turned his head away but the merchant called Aylwin, with whom Edwin had spoken briefly earlier, gave him a smile.

'So, you and your companion are staying the night? You're on a journey somewhere?'

Edwin was immediately on his guard. Was that a hint of extra curiosity in his voice? Or was he just making polite conversation? After all, anyone might while away the evening in a guesthouse in idle chat.

'I – er, we're the guests of the lord abbot, so we'll probably be here a few days.' He rushed to cut off any further questioning. 'And you? Are you on a journey?'

Aylwin took another sip from his cup. 'No, this was always my destination. I come here every year to talk to Brother Alexander about exporting some of his wool, but it was only after I arrived yesterday that I found out he'd died.' He crossed himself and Edwin did the same. 'But business is business and must be attended to, so I'm waiting to see who they will appoint to talk to me instead. Hopefully someone who will drive less of a hard bargain!'

Edwin tried to keep his voice casual. 'And did you know Brother Alexander well?'

'No, not at all, beyond our annual discussions.' Aylwin frowned as he thought. 'He was not your usual monk, though – a hard man who knew his way around a business deal. And, not that two men of business would ever come to blows of course, but I always got the impression that if we did, he could probably break my neck quite easily.'

There was an awkward silence.

Aylwin rushed to fill it. 'I beg your pardon. I have no idea why I said that – I have no wish to speak ill of the dead.'

Edwin reassured him. 'Surely it's not speaking ill of a man to think that he would be able to defend himself if necessary, monk or not.' He saw Aylwin nod. If Brother Alexander was capable of defending himself, how tough a man would you need to be to kill him?

'Anyway,' said Aylwin, 'let us speak of other matters. Do you have any news on the war which might be of use to a man of business?' He asked the question generally to the room, and at this the knight turned towards them and joined the conversation. Martin, who had finally stopped eating, pushed his bowl aside and leaned on the table to listen.

Edwin understood the first part of it – that Prince Louis, despite the defeat of his forces at Lincoln, was still holding London and most of the South and was not about to give up on his attempt at conquest – but after that the talk became far too military and technical, with Sir Philip finding a keen discussion partner in Martin. Edwin let the talk of sieges, arms and deployments wash over him until he caught the words 'and Edwin was actually there, of course.'

'What?' The knight was looking at him disbelievingly. 'You were at Lincoln? *You* fought in the battle?'

Normally Edwin would never speak disrespectfully to a man of rank, but it had been a long day and he was tired of nobody taking him seriously. 'Yes, sir. When I met the lord regent he sent me personally on a mission inside the city, and I fought in the battle alongside his nephew John Marshal.' That was perhaps stretching the truth a little, but it was worth it to see the man's jaw sag. 'But if you will all excuse me, I would prefer not to talk about it.' He rose, nodded to them all, and headed for his bed at the far end of the room.

Later on, as the snores of the other two guests indicated that they were asleep, he prodded Martin. 'So, where did you go? And did you find anything?'

There was still some faint light in the room, a pale square of window showing the last vestiges of the day and letting in the cool evening air. Edwin saw Martin raise himself on one elbow and look around the room before whispering. 'I'm sorry. I shouldn't have left you. But I spoke to one of the novices and heard a few things which might be useful.'

Edwin sat up. 'Tell me.'

'Well, it turns out they all have to do some physical labour every day, so some of them might be stronger than they look.'

'Interesting. And?'

'And what?'

'What else did you hear?'

Martin thought for a moment. 'Actually that was about it. The rest of the time he talked about how wonderful it was that he was going to be a monk, how he'd been yearning for it for years and begging them to admit him, but they don't take children here – you have to be fifteen to start as a novice and eighteen to take your final vows, which he will do next year. He had this weird kind of look in his eyes while he was talking about it – I think he might be a bit of a fanatic.'

Edwin was disappointed but tried not to show it. 'Thanks – I'm sure that will all come in useful.' He was about to lie down again when Martin continued. 'Oh, and I met the infirmarer. He's …' there was a pause.

'He's what?'

Martin shrugged. 'I may as well tell you. He's intimidating. I ran in because I'd heard a scream – there's someone in there with toothache – and he told me off and threw me out as though I was a child.'

Light dawned on Edwin. 'So that's why you were in such a foul mood when I saw you.' In the half-dark it would have been impossible to see whether Martin was blushing or not.

'Yes. And I let it interfere with my duty – what if someone had attacked you while I was gone? I'll be more careful next time.'

'It's all right. I was safe with the cellarer.' He outlined the information he'd gained and watched as Martin nodded and eventually fell asleep.

Edwin lay back on his bed, wide awake, and stared at the roof. Brother Alexander was a man of the world who had come late to the cloister. Had he made enemies during his previous life who had come back to find him? Or was his killer someone from outside whom he had met and offended while on abbey business? Or, most chillingly of all, had one of the other monks, all sworn to a life of peace and brotherhood, become so enraged about something that he had stabbed one of his fellows in the back?

He shivered, but he still could not sleep. After an indeterminate amount of time, when the window had long faded to black and he could see the stars, Edwin heard chanting. He sat up and strained his ears. Of course, it would be the monks at one of their night-time services. Well, he was awake anyway, so what harm would there be in going to see? He might find out something that he wouldn't have done in daylight, especially if he hid himself and watched in secret. He slid his legs over the side of the bed. Martin was a very heavy sleeper and probably wouldn't even wake if Edwin poured water on him, but still he put on his boots as quietly as he could before tiptoeing past the other sleeping figures, out of the guesthouse.

Although the day had been warm, it was chilly in the night air and Edwin wished he had brought his cloak. He kept to the shadows as he crept through the precinct, and hesitated at the great west door of the church. Would it be too obvious if he opened it? But the monks would be in their choir right at the other end of the church and behind a screen. He risked taking hold of the great ring of the door handle and turning it. It was well used and turned easily and silently. He pushed the door open as little as he thought he could get away with, and squeezed through the gap before pushing the door closed again.

It was dark at this end of the church, but he could see the candlelight at the far end as he slipped up the left-hand aisle. When he neared the rood screen he stopped in the shadow of one of the archways. From here he would be able to see the monks as they left the choir and made their way back to the stairway which led up to their dormitory. He stood as still as he could, trying to calm his beating heart, breathe slowly and not shiver too much. Why had he left the warm guesthouse and the comforting presence of other men? It was eerie being in such a huge church, alone and in the dark. He looked into the shadows. Did the spirits of dead monks walk with their brothers during the night? He thought he felt a touch on the back of his neck and turned in terror, but it was a whisper of the night breeze. He forced himself to concentrate. Why was he here? He didn't know, but he hoped he might notice something. Were any of the monks set apart from others? Might there be some clue in the way they looked at each other as to whether any of them suspected any of his brethren?

Eventually the chanting ceased and there were sounds of movement. Edwin shrank further back into the shadow, confident that nobody could see him. They would be turning away from him, not towards him, as they left the choir.

Candlelight spilled out of the archway as the first of the monks stepped through. It was the abbot, walking at a measured pace a few steps ahead of the prior, whose earlier jolly expression had been replaced by one of gravity. The solemn presence of God was easier to feel in the dark of the night. The rest of the monks, carrying candles, followed two by two. The faces inside their cowls were illuminated and Edwin recognised Brother Helias, the cellarer, and Brother Octavian, the precentor who had showed him the books. Both looked serene as they almost glided through the darkness. Less tranquil were the older monks who shuffled, stooped and coughed their way along, among them the ancient brother he'd seen with the boys, who weren't there themselves, or at least not that Edwin could see. Edwin examined every face as they emerged from the choir and turned their backs on him, but he could discern no feelings of suspicion or guilt among them. Finally a younger monk, the one Edwin had seen in the cellarer's office, came yawning at the rear and turned away with his light.

Edwin was left in darkness. Well, that had been a useless exercise. He could just as well have stayed in bed for all he had learned. He would go back there now. But wait, what was that?

The light from another candle was spilling out of the choir archway and Edwin froze as two more monks emerged. Instead of heading away to follow their brothers, these ones turned to their right and came towards Edwin. He shrank back into the darkness of the archway as much as he could – what would happen if he was discovered? The stone was cold on his back and he shivered.

And then he looked at their faces.

He was seized with such terror that he would not have been able to move even if he had wanted to. He could feel the hair on his head standing up on end, his skin prickling all over as the apparition came nearer. He couldn't tear his eyes away. It … this … just wasn't possible.

Long after the monks had passed on their way, Edwin sat on the floor in the archway, waiting until his knees had stopped trembling enough for him to be able to stand up again. Then, using the cold stone as a support, he hauled himself to his feet. Shivering, he cast a final look at the space where the monks had gone, and then he ran through the church as fast as he could and fled out into the night.

Chapter Five

Martin woke up and stretched, aware of the slight ache in his arms from yesterday's wood-chopping. It felt good.

It was getting light but it was still early judging by the sun shining very low through the window. Yawning and rubbing his eyes, he took himself out of the guesthouse to the latrine building behind it, conveniently situated over the stream, and then returned to pick up his tunic from the end of the bed. Once he'd got it over his head and manoeuvred his arms into the sleeves – too short, as his sleeves always were – he shuffled over to Edwin's bed to wake him up.

Edwin wasn't there.

Martin felt the cold hand of fear around his heart. *A good commander doesn't jump to conclusions. Be disciplined.* He went back to the latrine building, but it was empty. He looked in and indeed under every one of the six beds in the guesthouse, although he could see with one glance that two were occupied by the other guests and the other four were empty. Edwin's cloak was draped over the end of his bed, and his bag was still there; Martin looked in it and saw that wherever he was, Edwin had not taken his dagger with him. Damn the man!

Striding out of the door even as he belted his sword and dagger around him, Martin wondered where in the Lord's name he should start looking. And how had anyone managed to get past him and capture Edwin during the night? He must have struggled, surely, or made some kind of noise? And yet Martin hadn't woken, and neither, apparently, had the other guests; and there were no obvious signs of a fight. Surely Edwin wouldn't have gone anywhere willingly during the hours of darkness.

The church loomed in front of him as he made his way through the precinct – that was as good a place to start as any. He pushed open the west door and marched up through the middle of the open space. He couldn't see Edwin, but there were chapels and nooks and crannies all over the place. He'd better be methodical. He went back to the main door and began to work his way slowly up one side of the church – he'd look all the way around until he got back to where he'd started. He wanted to shout out Edwin's name, but even panicked as he was he couldn't bring himself to shatter the profound silence.

Eventually he reached the chapel with the statue of the Blessed Virgin, where he'd seen a monk kneeling in supplication the day before. His gaze swept round and he was about to duck out again when he spotted Edwin. He was sitting on the floor with his back wedged into a corner, knees drawn up to his chin, arms around them with fists clenched. He was pale, his eyes were closed and he was not moving.

Martin ran over, grabbed him by the shoulders and shook him. Edwin awoke with a start and started to yell, striking out at him with his fists. His eyes were wild. Martin dragged him to his feet. 'Edwin! Edwin, it's me! What's the matter?'

His words had the desired effect and Edwin gradually calmed down. He grabbed a fistful of Martin's tunic. 'Is it really you?'

'Yes. What in God's name is the matter with you?'

Edwin didn't let go of him. 'I saw a ghost. An apparition.'

'What? When?'

'Here, in the church. Last night. I ran out but then I came back to pray here because I thought it would be safer.'

'What were you doing in the church in the middle of the night? Why didn't you wake me? For God's sake, I'm supposed to be looking after you!'

Edwin didn't answer. Martin fought down the urge to give him a good shake, unsure whether he should be angry that Edwin had gone out without him, or relieved that he hadn't come to any harm. Or at least, no physical harm.

The noise they were making had attracted attention, and Martin turned at the sound of a throat being cleared to see the one with all the frizzy hair, the prior, standing in the entrance to the chapel.

'Are you both all right?'

Martin looked at Edwin, but he didn't say anything. 'Yes, Father – Brother – sorry – Edwin has had a fright. I don't know what happened but he says he saw a ghost.'

The prior raised his eyebrows but remained calm, walking over to Edwin and gently disentangling his still-clenched fist from the front of Martin's tunic. Martin smoothed it down as he stepped back, grateful that someone else was taking charge.

The prior kept hold of Edwin's hand. 'Now, my son, tell me what happened. Where were you when you saw this ghost?'

Edwin's voice was shaky but Martin could see that he was trying hard. 'Here. I was here. In the church. Last night. I … couldn't sleep so I came in to pray. I saw you all coming out of your service and going back towards your stairs, but two monks came towards me.' He was shaking. 'Only, it wasn't two monks. It was Brother Godfrey twice.'

Martin had no idea what he was talking about. What did Edwin mean, twice?

But the prior was now smiling. 'Have no fear, Edwin, for you saw no ghost.'

'But I swear, Brother – he was there, and then he was there next to himself. I thought it was him, and he was dead, and his soul was walking next to him. What else could it have been? I wasn't seeing things, I wasn't. There were two of him.'

Prior Henry was remaining remarkably composed. 'I will show you. Come, stand, there is nothing to be afraid of.' He turned to one of the young novices who was hovering curiously in the doorway. 'Roger, have the goodness to find Brother Godfrey and Brother Waldef and bring them both here to me.'

The boy nodded and shot off, probably, Martin thought, using the excuse to run a bit faster than he was normally supposed to. The three men in the chapel remained standing, nobody speaking, until the novice returned with two monks.

As they entered the chapel, Martin felt his mouth opening in surprise. For there in front of him was Brother Godfrey, who had come to Conisbrough to fetch them; and beside him was Brother Godfrey again.

Edwin had fallen back and looked like he was about to faint, so Martin moved to support him as the prior spoke. 'Edwin, Martin: this is Brother Godfrey and his brother, Brother Waldef.'

Edwin opened his mouth but no words came out. Martin tried to get over his shock and realised how much greater it would have been had he first seen them together in the dead of night, in the cold, dark church. 'Brothers? But ...' He looked from one to the other.

The prior nodded. 'Yes. They are twins – have you never heard of twins? It is when a mother gives birth to two children at once.'

At last Edwin managed to frame some words. 'A woman in the village once had two babies, but they both died. And one was a boy, the other one a girl.'

Martin dredged his memory. 'I met two men at my lord's castle at Lewes once who said they were brothers born on the same day. But they didn't look any more alike than any other brothers.' He stared again at the two men in front of him, exact replicas of each other in every detail he could see. They both smiled at him, exactly the same and at the same time, and he took a step back, resisting the urge to make the sign of the cross.

Prior Henry led Edwin forward towards them. 'Brothers, you will permit me?' They nodded. 'They are both real, Edwin. Here, take their hands.' Martin watched as two identical right hands emerged from the sleeves of their habits. Edwin looked as though he was reaching into boiling water, but he stretched out and touched them both. He had regained a little of his colour.

Prior Henry was continuing. 'From what I can gather from Brother Infirmarer, most twins die at birth because they are too small and it is not God's will that they should live. But some of them survive, and among those are a few who resemble each other like Brothers Godfrey and Waldef here.' His voice turned sad. 'The Lord made them this way, but some men consider it witchcraft, and they were driven out of their manor by their brother after their father died. He agreed to pay their donation and they entered the cloister here. And you are content here, Brothers?'

One of the brothers – Martin had no idea which one it was – spoke. 'Yes, Brother Prior. We are grateful to the Lord and give thanks every day, and again in this chapel every night after the service. May I – may I speak to these men, Brother?'

The prior nodded.

The monk turned to Edwin. 'We do not like to be apart. There was some idea, when we were younger, that we should travel as far as we could in opposite directions, live out our lives in different places, and try to forget about each other. Then each could make a new life among people who did not know of the other. But we could not do it. We cannot be separated.' His voice wobbled.

The other one continued. 'Father Abbot has in the past encouraged us to go separately. He has tried setting us different work in different places, but the further apart we go, the more it hurts. He spoke to us yesterday and said he can see the pain that this causes us, so he says he will accept that it is the Lord's will for us to stay together until death.'

Edwin seemed to be recovering himself. 'So that's why you were so uncomfortable when you came to my lord's castle? You didn't like to be away from your brother?'

He was addressing the one who had spoken last, but it was the other who replied. 'Yes. I thought I would be all right as I was only going for the day and would be back by nightfall, but when I had to stay away all night …' he faltered into silence and his brother gripped his arm.

The prior spread his hands. 'So, we are done here? The hour of Mass approaches and we must not be late.' The three monks inclined their heads and left the chapel.

It was Sunday, Martin recalled. He took the still slightly shocked Edwin by the arm. 'Come on. We'll stay for Mass then we'll find something to eat, and then we'll get on with our task.' He pulled Edwin towards the main body of the church, which was starting to fill with people.

Edwin mumbled something. Martin stooped to hear. 'What?'

'Sorry. I didn't mean to worry you. But it was just —'

Martin patted him on the back. 'Don't worry. If I'd seen them floating around in the dark I'd have run away screaming. Come on.' A thought struck him. 'Let's hope it wasn't one of them who killed Brother Alexander – we'd never know which one to blame!'

That probably wasn't the right thing to say, as Edwin was turning pale again. 'I'm sure it wasn't one of them anyway. You'll find who did it. But let's get through Mass and dinner first.'

Edwin felt the cold stone of the floor through his hose as he knelt during Mass. What an idiot he had been – but then again, how was he to have known that two men could be born identical to each other? And did this mean anything for his quest to find the killer of Brother Alexander? One of the things he'd already noted was that all the monks looked very similar in their habits, so it was going to be difficult for him to tell one from another and even perhaps from those who might have witnessed something.

He wasn't really paying attention to the Mass, just letting the familiar words wash over him, but from a distance he heard *Ite, Missa est* and he rose along with everyone else. Once the monks had filed out of their choir and the lay brothers out of their own part of the church, the parishioners mingled and broke into little gossiping groups. All except one: an old woman who stood alone. Edwin watched and something gave him the feeling that she wasn't unattached by chance; the others were deliberately shunning her. Something Brother Helias had said the previous day came back to him, and he approached a knot of men discussing the weather who appeared to be local. He nodded to them in a friendly manner, aware that for once his clothes, new and smart as they were, were making a good impression. He was also conscious of Martin looming behind him. After some general chit-chat which had Martin sighing and shuffling about, Edwin was able to turn the conversation to the subject of the cellarer's comment about 'the witch in the woods', and he was unsurprised when one of the men turned and indicated the old woman, who had now settled herself on one of the benches vacated by the lay brothers and looked in no hurry to leave. Whispers of disapproval were directed at her from self-righteous gaggles of women, which eventually attracted the attention of the single monk still in the choir, who with something of a sad expression was putting out the candles and collecting up the plates and chalices used during the Mass.

The monk put down the items he was carrying and swept towards her. Edwin couldn't hear what he said to her, but from the expression on his face and the gestures he was making, he seemed to be admonishing her for sitting in the lay brothers' seats – presumably these were not meant to be used by the parishioners.

The woman did not seem overawed by his rebuke; rather the opposite, in fact. She replied with spirit and started waving her hands around. Then she asked him a question, which he did not answer. He put his hands up in front of him as though denying knowledge or pushing away responsibility, and then went back to what he had been doing. The woman made a face at his departing back and then stood.

The church was now emptying, the parishioners no doubt heading back to their homes for something to eat and an afternoon spent with their families: there would be no buying and selling or labour in the fields on a Sunday. Not officially, anyway. Edwin turned away as the old woman passed them, hoping she hadn't noticed that he was watching her. Once she had left through the west door he nudged Martin in the ribs. 'Come on.'

'Where? Back to the guesthouse?'

'No. We have to follow that woman.'

'What? Why?'

'Because she might know something important. Come!' He pulled at Martin's sleeve.

'But what about dinner?'

'You think too much about your stomach. Hurry up or we'll lose her!'

'Can't we go after we've had something to eat?'

'Fine. You go back to the guesthouse and I'll go to the woods on my own.'

Martin rolled his eyes. 'You always know just what to say, don't you? All right. Lead the way.'

The woman made her way through the precinct and out of the gatehouse. She moved surprisingly fast for one who looked to be an old crone. She joined the road outside, but when she reached the fork which led either to the nearby hamlet or to the villages on the way back to Conisbrough she took neither path but veered off into the woods. When Edwin and Martin reached the same spot they noticed a small track which led through the undergrowth.

They looked at each other. Martin shrugged. 'She's one old woman. What harm can she do?' He stepped on to the track, shoving some bushes out of the way as he did so. He peered ahead and then turned back. 'It continues up here – not very well used but you can still follow it. Come on.'

Edwin followed him. 'Quietly then. We don't want to scare her.'

It was quite dark as they made their way along the track, the bushy undergrowth turning to thick trees within a few yards. They stepped as silently as they could, hearing only the sound of birds. Martin had his hand on the hilt of his sword, although he did not draw it.

After a short while the path, such as it was, petered out completely and they stood at something of a loss in a small clearing.

'What do you want?' The voice made Edwin jump, coming out of nowhere.

He held his arms away from his sides and gestured for Martin to do the same. 'Just to talk to you. We mean you no harm.'

The voice sounded again, this time seemingly from a different direction. 'And why should I believe you? What's a well-dressed man with an armed guard got to do with me?'

Edwin turned to face where he thought the voice had come from. 'I'm here to try and find out who killed Brother Alexander. I heard that you knew him so I thought you might be able to help me.'

The woman appeared suddenly, out of nowhere, from a totally different direction to the one Edwin expected, making Martin swear and clutch at his sword again. She made no move to approach them but stood still some ten yards away.

'Brother Alexander? Yes, I knew him. He wasn't as bad as some of the others – it's a shame he died in such a way. If that's what you want to talk about, then come.' She turned and disappeared into the undergrowth. Martin bounded after her, calling back to Edwin, 'It's all right. There's a trail here – not much more than a deer path, really, but it's here.'

Edwin followed, brushing branches out of his face and not entirely sure of which way he was going until he was met by the sight of a cottage – no, he wouldn't even dignify it with the name, it was more of a bothy – squatting among the trees. It was tiny, made of wattle and covered in daub which looked like it needed replacing. There were no windows but smoke drifted out through a hole in the turf roof; a wooden stool stood against the outside wall, positioned to catch the sunlight which made its way into the clearing; a garden of sorts had been hacked out of the forest floor and fenced off, and a goat was tethered to a nearby tree.

The woman settled herself on the stool. 'Come, sit. There's more space out here.'

Edwin glanced inside the building as he passed the doorway. It was cramped: a little hearth, partly covered as she must have left it when she went to church, a pile of bracken or something covered with a blanket in the far corner, a table with a dish and cup on it, and a large wooden cross on the wall. The floor was of beaten earth, worn into a dip in front of the cross. The roof was low – Edwin wasn't sure he'd be able to stand up straight in there, and Martin certainly wouldn't.

He looked down at the ground near where the woman was sitting. Despite the warm weather it was muddy and damp-looking. 'Thank you, but I'll stand.'

She laughed, revealing that she still had some of her teeth. 'Suit yourselves. What did you want to know?'

Edwin hardly knew where to start. 'What's your name? Why do you live here in the woods? And why did Brother Alexander come out to see you?'

'My name is Anabilia. I live here on my own so I can be closer to God; I spend my days praising Him and praying for the world. Brother Alexander came out to see me once every week to bring me my corrody from the abbey.'

'Your what?'

'Corrody. When I left my previous home I gave them every-thing I owned in return for five loaves of bread and three gallons of ale every week, for as long as I shall live.' She emitted what Edwin could only describe as a snigger. 'I think they were expect-ing to get the better of the deal, hoping I would die soon after, but I've been here twelve years now, and God willing I'll be here many more yet.'

Edwin shook his head in disbelief. 'You've been living here twelve years? All on your own? And aren't hermits normally men?'

He'd said the wrong thing. In an instant her expression changed and she hissed at him. 'You're as bad as the rest of them. You have to be a man to be holy, is that it? Those pious monks, so full of themselves and above talking to mere women. Women aren't allowed to set a single foot inside their abbey, did you know that? In case they defile the place with their presence or tempt those oh-so-holy men into sin. No, they're only permitted by such kind generosity into the main church, and even then only if they're not suckling their children. It's an outrage!'

She had half risen from her stool and was waggling a finger in Edwin's face. He leaned back and opened his mouth, but she wasn't finished.

'And even out here, they still don't believe a woman can be holy. A man living here would be a holy man, but me, I'm a witch – that's what they call me, isn't it? I know they do.'

Edwin didn't quite know how to answer that, unsure which answer might make her even more enraged. But Martin's voice came from behind him. 'Couldn't you join a nunnery?'

She turned on him and virtually spat on the floor. 'Pah! A pack of chattering women, living in comfort and vying for position? What good would that do? I am better here where I can talk to the Lord and His saints directly.'

Fairly certain that Martin wouldn't like being spoken to like that and that he might end up in the middle of a fight, Edwin hastened to intervene. 'And Brother Alexander has been coming out to see you – what, once a week?'

Anabilia nodded and sat back on the stool with some dignity. 'Yes. He brings the bread and the ale every Tuesday and takes back the empty barrel.'

'By himself?'

'Yes.' She thought for a moment. 'That is odd, now you come to mention it. You'd think a high-and-mighty choir monk like him might bring a lay brother to do the lifting for him. But he just brought the full one strapped to his back and carried the empty one away the same way.'

'And when was the last time you saw him?'

'Well, it would have been last Tuesday, wouldn't it?'

The day before his death. 'And did anything seem ... different, at all?'

Her forehead wrinkled. 'Not really. Although after he'd gone he didn't do his usual disappearing trick.'

'Sorry, what? He didn't do what?'

She looked smug. 'They might call me a witch but he had some strange powers, too. Maybe he got them from the Devil. I often asked the Lord about it, but I received no answer so I knew He didn't want me to know.'

'But what disappearing trick?' Edwin could feel himself getting further and further mired as the conversation continued. Was the woman addled in her wits after living out here so long?

'He could vanish. I found out some years ago when I realised after he'd left that I wanted to ask him something, so I followed him. He was far ahead of me and I couldn't see too clearly, but he walked towards the stone cliff and just ... disappeared.'

'How? Where?'

Anabilia shrugged. 'I don't know. I was afraid so I hurried home to pray. I followed him a few other times, without telling him, and he did it again and again.'

'And was this always in the same spot?'

'Yes. Near the white stone cliff.'

'Can you show us?'

She rose. 'No, but I can show you where I was standing when I saw it. Come.'

Edwin and Martin looked at each other as she headed behind the cottage and dived into the undergrowth between the trees. Edwin was uneasy. Who knew what strange phenomenon he might be about to see? Was it witchcraft? Was the Devil himself stalking these woods?

Martin put his hand on his sword. 'I'll make sure nothing happens to you. And we'd better hurry or we'll lose her. I've never known an old woman move so fast.'

After an indeterminate time during which Edwin tripped and slipped his way along what could barely be called a path, and tried to keep his face out of the way of branches springing back after Martin had pushed his way through them, the trees thinned and Edwin found himself at the edge of the woods. Some fifty yards or so ahead of them, across some open scrubland, was a tall white cliff. Presumably it was a continuation of the one which ran along next to the abbey, but Edwin couldn't work out which direction that was from here.

Anabilia stopped level with the last trees. 'Here.'

Edwin looked from her to the cliff. 'Here? This was where you were standing when you saw him disappear?'

She nodded. 'He walked towards the cliff and vanished. And you can make of that what you will.' Then she turned on her heel and was gone.

Edwin and Martin stood in silence for a few moments. Edwin shielded his eyes, for the sunlight reflecting off the whiteness of the stone was bright. It was a sheer cliff. There was no break in it, and no way it could be climbed, or certainly not without it being obvious to any watcher. Had he fallen in a hole? But no, surely he would have cried out and Anabilia would have seen and heard. And he wouldn't have done the same thing over and over again.

'Well, perhaps we should …' Edwin took a step forward, but was yanked back by a hand on the neck of his tunic.

'Oh no. No way am I letting you walk across there by yourself. What if you disappear too? How would I ever explain that to my lord?'

'Well, even if Brother Alexander did vanish, he obviously came back, so nothing too evil could have happened to him.'

'Maybe. But still, you're not going. We can go together – or better still, you stay here and I'll go.'

Edwin nodded. 'All right. If I stand here I can be in the same spot that Anabilia was, so maybe I can see what happened. Just …' he gestured helplessly, 'just walk straight towards it and see what happens. And then touch the cliff, and if you can't see anything in particular, walk back again. I'll see if I can see anything from here.'

Martin turned to face the cliff and set off at a steady pace. He didn't actually draw his sword, but Edwin noticed that his hand was clenched around the hilt.

It didn't take Martin long to cover the open ground, even though he was walking carefully and looking where he put each foot, presumably in case he was about to fall into some kind of crevasse, although Edwin couldn't see one.

Edwin continued to watch as Martin neared the cliff. He slowed and then stopped. Edwin saw him reach his hand out, and then turn sideways.

And then he disappeared.

Chapter Six

'He's not here?'

Alys experienced a sinking, sick feeling in her stomach, followed by the first flutterings of panic. She had given up everything to come to Edwin, because he had asked her to, and he wasn't here waiting for her? She turned to Master Theobald, who shrugged without altering his stolid expression, and Mistress Christiana, who looked as bemused as Alys felt.

A small crowd was gathering as they stood next to the cart. The oxen strained forward to reach what little grass they could at the edge of the village green, and a couple of small children skipped back out of the way of the huge beasts. Without thinking Alys turned to make sure that Randal wasn't getting himself into any mischief, and then remembered that it was unlikely she'd ever see her youngest brother again. Or would she? Was she about to be sent back to Lincoln in shame like unsold goods?

She fought back tears as she faced the man who had spoken. 'Where has he gone? When will he be back?'

The man shrugged. 'Don't know. Went out on some business for the lord earl, riding out on a fine horse like the great man he thinks he is now.'

Alys looked around at the people. She saw both curiosity and indifference in their faces, but no sympathy, no hint of help. But then, why would they pity her? She was a stranger.

Everyone was looking at her. What was she to do?

She was saved from having to speak again by the arrival of a woman for whom the crowd parted. She didn't seem to be noble or rich, wasn't dressed in fine fabrics – although her gown was of a superior weave and better cut than some of the others around – but she had a dignity which made Alys feel she ought to curtsey. She bobbed uncertainly.

The woman addressed the man who had spoken. 'Robin? Your youngest came to fetch me. Do you need me?'

The man nodded his head and indicated Alys and her companions. 'They're looking for Edwin, so I said he wasn't here.'

The woman greeted Master Theobald and Mistress Christiana, then looked at Alys properly for the first time. Alys wished she didn't look quite so rumpled after the long journey in the cart. After a few moments the woman's eyes opened wide. 'You're not … are you by any chance Alys?'

Alys licked her dry lips. 'Yes, mistress.'

She was rewarded with a wide and welcoming smile, and was then taken aback to be folded in an embrace. The woman smelled of fresh herbs and flowers, and Alys couldn't help lifting her own arms to half-return the gesture, even though she was confused.

The woman stepped back and held Alys at arm's length. 'There now. Somewhere, somehow, there has been a misunderstanding, but you're here now, so that's all that matters. My name is Anne, and I'm Edwin's mother.' Alys was embraced again and this time felt a kiss on her cheek. 'Welcome to Conisbrough. Now, come home, bring your companions with you – master, mistress, you are very welcome – rest and tell me all about it.'

The sinking, sick feeling receded and Alys let out the breath she hadn't realised she'd been holding. Everything was going to be all right.

Edwin stood dumbfounded as he looked at the place where Martin had been a moment ago. He wanted to run towards it, but his feet were somehow stuck to the ground.

And then Martin appeared again. Thank the Lord. He shouted something but his voice echoed off the cliff and by the time the sound reached Edwin he couldn't make out what it was. He raised his arms in an exaggerated shrug and put his hand behind his ear. Martin waved both of his arms above his head and made an unmistakeable beckoning gesture, so Edwin started to pick his way forward across the scrubby ground.

He reached Martin a few yards ahead of the cliff. 'What happened? I was watching you and you just disappeared, just like Anabilia said Brother Alexander did. How did you do it?'

Martin was grinning. 'I couldn't see it until I was right on top of it, but look.' He pointed.

Edwin couldn't see anything except a sheer cliff face. Martin grabbed him by both shoulders and propelled him so they were standing exactly one behind the other. He reached around and took Edwin's right hand in his own, pointing it. 'There. Look.'

And Edwin saw what he hadn't noticed before; something which would be impossible to see from more than a few yards either side of where he was standing right now: there was a fissure in the rock. He took a few steps back and it disappeared. He moved forward again and it came into view. He did the same a few steps to either side. It was very difficult to see because of the whiteness of the stone, but it was definitely there, and it was big enough for a man to enter.

'Shall we go in?'

Martin nodded and stepped forward. This time he drew his sword out of the scabbard and held it in front of him as he walked into the crack in the cliff.

Edwin followed. The fissure was quite narrow but inside it opened out a little so there was room for both of them to stand and still have space between them; it was high, as the crack reached up into the cliff, so even Martin could stand upright. Edwin looked round at the white rock which surrounded them, with a few shrivelled-looking weeds growing out of it in places. 'Now what?'

Martin looked helplessly at him. 'I don't know. Why would he want to come in here?'

'To meet someone? But who?'

Martin reached out to touch the wall. 'Or to hide something? But where?'

'Have a look round as carefully as you can. Maybe there's a crack in the wall somewhere. The Lord knows what we might be looking for, but it could be something really tiny.'

They scoured the walls, and Edwin moved further back into the cave where the fissure in the cliff became narrower and narrower. When he could move no further he knelt down on the sandy floor and reached forward with his hand into the darkness.

'Ow!'

Martin spun round, knocking his scabbard against the rock. 'What?'

Edwin sat back on his heels. 'I just pricked my finger. There's something here.'

There wasn't room for Martin to crouch down next to him, so Edwin reached forward again, carefully this time, and hauled towards him the stuff he could feel on the ground. Once he was satisfied he'd got all of it they moved it into the centre of the cave so they could examine it properly. It proved to be the rotting remains of a canvas sack and the broken pieces of a wooden box, a packing crate of some sort. It was a splinter of this which Edwin's hand had first encountered, and he sucked at the bleeding end of his finger.

Martin moved away from where he had been blocking the light, and Edwin put his hand up to shield his eyes as the sun streamed in. He went through every inch of the wood and the bag, but there was nothing to be found.

'So Brother Alexander was here, and we can assume that he knew this was here.'

Martin knelt next to him. 'Yes. And something was packed in this. But what?'

'I have no idea. And another question is – did Brother Alexander hide something here? Or did he find something hidden by someone else?'

Martin shrugged. 'There's no way of telling. And until we know what it was, we can't know where it might be now.'

Edwin bundled the fabric and wood up together and shoved it back in the furthest corner. 'Or whether this is what got him killed.' He stood back up and rubbed his hands together to get rid of the fine sand which now covered them.

There was a sudden noise which made Edwin jump before he realised it was Martin's stomach rumbling. Martin made a face. 'I told you I was hungry.'

'Well, you may have missed your dinner but we *have* found something interesting, so it's a good exchange.'

'Huh. I'd still like a plate of good meat.'

'Maybe Brother Amandus can find us something to eat even though the dinner hour is past. I don't think you'll get any meat though.'

Martin grumbled good-naturedly as they squeezed themselves out of the mouth of the cave. Once he'd moved away from it Edwin looked back and was amazed again at how it seemed to disappear from sight. It was definitely a good hiding place, but for what?

Martin looked at the sun. 'I don't fancy trying to find my way back through the woods and getting all turned around, but if we just follow this cliff then it should take us back in the direction of the abbey.' He set off.

Edwin followed, but as he glanced back at the edge of the forest he had a strange feeling they were being watched.

They did manage to get something to eat, as the guestmaster had left them out a bowl of some kind of mush each on the communal table. By the time they got to it the food was cold, but Martin was so hungry he ate it all anyway, having made sure he got the bowl which looked as though it contained a slightly larger portion. Edwin didn't speak during the meal, which suited Martin, but once he'd finished eating he looked at Edwin and realised he wasn't just concentrating on the food – he was miles away.

'So, what are we going to do next?'

Edwin didn't answer so Martin nudged him. 'What?'

'I said, what are we going to do next?'

'I thought I might go and talk to Brother Octavian again.'

'Who? I mean, which one was he?'

Edwin still had that faraway look in his eyes. 'The precentor. The librarian.'

'Oh, *him*. Why? Will he help? Or do you just want to go and look at a roomful of books again?'

Edwin looked ever so slightly guilty, and Martin sighed. How was he to have known that it would be so difficult to keep Edwin on the right path here? Normally he would just concentrate on what he was supposed to be doing for the lord earl until it was done.

'I suppose I'd better come with you.'

Edwin smiled. 'That sounded very enthusiastic. No, you don't need to come. As you say, I'll be in a room full of books, and besides, if you're there Brother Octavian will fuss about you knocking things over or damaging something, and he won't talk to me properly.'

Martin grunted. But still, he really oughtn't to leave Edwin alone …

'Perhaps you could go out and talk to some of the lay brothers? You could exercise the horses while you're at it – it's not good for them to just be in the stable all the time, is it?'

Martin thought this through. Edwin was right – the horses did need a run. And it was certainly tempting to think of a ride out in the air and the space outside, rather than being stuck in here behind these walls.

'Well, if you're sure …'

'I'm sure. Now, if you've finished eating then let's get to it.'

Martin pushed the bowl away and stood. After they left the guesthouse he made sure that Edwin got safely inside the main abbey building before he turned and headed off to the stables.

Now he came to look at it properly he could see that the stable building and its occupants were well cared for. He looked approvingly at the brushed coats, the clean straw on the floor and the filled hayracks as he made his way to the stalls where his three animal charges looked contented.

The packhorse was an old beast who would probably be quite glad of the rest, so he would ask one of the lay brothers simply to walk it around the courtyard while he took the other two out for some proper exercise. He could ride his courser with Edwin's palfrey on a leading rein on the way out, and then the other way round on the way back. He'd saddle both now so he didn't need to swap over while he was out.

Whistling while he worked, he looked over the top of the stall to see two lay brothers at the other end of the stable. He hadn't noticed them before as they went about their tasks in silence; back at Conisbrough the grooms would have been chatting to each other or making jokes. Martin couldn't get used to this quiet, but he supposed they were accustomed to it.

He hailed them as he led his courser towards the door. 'Brothers, I'm taking both my riding animals out for some exercise – could you check on my packhorse and walk it round a bit?'

One of the brothers agreed that he would, the other bowed without speaking. Martin recognised the silent man as the one he'd spoken to the previous day. He tied the courser to a post outside and went back in for the palfrey. Oh well, being mute didn't stop you from caring for animals, he supposed, even if you were some kind of halfwit. The young swineherd in the village of Conisbrough was a bit simple, but he did his job.

Martin stopped to speak to the lay brother on his way back out. 'You have granges near here where some of the lay brothers work? Places where Brother Alexander would have visited?'

The lay brother paused in the act of shovelling dung. 'Yes, my son. We have a number of granges round and about, but the nearest is at Newhall, about four miles away.'

Martin nodded. 'How do I reach it?'

'Out the gatehouse, take the road through the settlement and out the other side, ride on about two and a half miles and then look for a track to your right, which heads off the road next to a split oak tree. Follow the track another mile and that will bring you to the grange buildings. As it's Sunday the brethren there will probably be round and about the buildings rather than out in the fields. You don't have a dog, do you?'

'No. Why?'

'Good. It's just that the track runs through fields of our sheep, and dogs disturb them. If you had had one I would have asked you respectfully to put it on a leash while you went through the field.'

Martin wasn't sure whether such a fellow was entitled to tell him what to do in such a manner, but he could see the logic. 'Well, it doesn't matter anyway as I don't have one. Thank you for the directions, Brother.'

The man inclined his head as Martin continued outside. He made sure the stirrups on the palfrey's saddle were tied up correctly and attached its leading rein with care before he mounted. The Lord knew he didn't want to spend his day chasing after a loose horse. He put his heels to the courser's flank, walking at a collected pace through the precinct and picking up into a trot only once he was outside the main gate. Now this was more like it. A bit of space, a horse under him and no *people* crowding round everywhere. He passed through the settlement, which was much smaller than Conisbrough, at a canter and made his way along the road. What would he say when he got to the grange? What would Edwin want him to ask? He decided he would find out who knew Brother Alexander and ask if anyone had a quarrel with him – that should be straightforward enough.

He would probably have missed the turning for the track had it not been for the oak, which looked like it might at some time in the past have been struck by lightning, although why the Lord might want to punish a tree on lands owned by holy monks, Martin couldn't imagine. He dismounted to move aside the hurdle which blocked the gap in the hedge, led the horses through, and then, conscious of what the lay brother had said, moved it back into place before mounting again. The man was right, there were sheep everywhere, shorn of their fleeces at this time of year, of course, but looking fat and healthy. The thought of roast mutton, so clear he could almost smell it, came to him unbidden and he wondered how they coped with the temptation of keeping all these animals without ever eating them.

As he approached the grange a few men came out of some of the buildings, no doubt alerted by the sound of hooves. They were all dressed like the ones in the abbey, in brown tunics, and they all had beards. Martin had no idea which one of them might be in charge so he gave a general greeting and explained who he was.

One of the lay brothers shouldered his way forward and sketched the sign of the cross in the air. 'Welcome. I'm Brother Sinnulph. We heard you were visiting the abbey and we have permission to speak to you so please, come in.'

Martin dismounted and passed both sets of reins over to another man before following the broad back through the small crowd. Brother Sinnulph led the way into a building and Martin ducked under the lintel to follow him in. He found himself in what must be the main hall of their living quarters: two long tables were arranged down the length of the room with a hearth on the floor between them. There was no fire at this time of year, of course, and although nowhere indoors was ever quite free from the smell, the space was smoke-free; from the light of three unshuttered windows he could clearly see the rafters with their stores hanging down and the sideboard stacked with bowls and cups. There was no high table on a dais as there was in the earl's hall; instead there was a large cross affixed to the end wall.

Brother Sinnulph poured a cup of ale which Martin drank thirstily after his ride in the sun. It was weak but it had a decent flavour, slightly different from the stuff which was provided in large quantities at Conisbrough for the soldiers and the lord earl's servants. He put the empty cup down on the table and stretched his legs out in front of him.

'So, how may we serve you? Can I show you around?' The brother had not helped himself to a drink but had sat in that peculiarly patient way which Martin was coming to recognise as being an attribute of the monks of both types.

'Yes, that would be helpful. I understand that Brother Alexander came here often?'

'He did. Come, and I will show you.' Brother Sinnulph rose and led the way back outside; Martin was pleased to see that his horses had been tied carefully to a post in the shade and provided with water, and he nodded at the brother who was stroking the palfrey's nose.

'He was the master of the lay brothers, is that right?'

'Yes, which means he oversaw our work here, as well as that of the brethren at the other granges and the lay brothers in the abbey itself.'

'How many of you are there?'

'About a hundred all told. Fifty or so at the abbey and the rest of us in the granges. There are six of us here.'

Martin looked back in surprise. 'So why such a large hall?'

Brother Sinnulph reached another building and held open the door for him as he replied. 'Ah, that's because we deal with so many sheep here. There are six of us who live here all the year round to run the place, but at shearing time, which has just finished, we get another half a dozen brothers from the abbey and we also employ a large number of seasonal labourers to help with the shearing – we'd never manage it otherwise – and they stay on for a while to help with the grading and packing of the wool. Part of the arrangement is that we provide their food and ale while they are here.'

He gestured in front of him and Martin saw that he was in a huge barn. The air was chokingly full of wool and dust and he waved his hand in front of his mouth and coughed several times before he could get another word out, his eyes watering. 'I see.'

Brother Sinnulph grinned. 'Sorry. We get so accustomed to it that we forget that others aren't used to the air.' He gestured. 'As you can see, this is our main barn – every one of our animals has been in here to be shorn during the past two weeks. We're now sorting the wool into high, middling and low grades and packing it into bales ready to transport.'

'And who does that? The monks or the labourers?'

'The hired hands help with the packing, but the brothers do the grading. Brother Alexander was very insistent about that, as he once had a bale opened by a merchant who declared that we were trying to pass off inferior wool as high grade.'

Martin tried to sound casual. 'And there was an argument? With this merchant? When was that?'

Brother Sinnulph shrugged. 'Some three or four years ago, I think. I can't remember the name of the merchant, if indeed Brother Alexander ever told me.'

'Oh.'

'Anyway, the bale was swapped and no harm was done, except that the good brother was very insistent about the grading ever after. He was here last week during the shearing to remind us again to be careful about it, and to say that he'd be back to check the bales this week.'

'But he won't be now, will he?'

Brother Sinnulph crossed himself. '*Requiescat in pace*. No, he won't, but the lord abbot will appoint another in his place soon enough. The abbey runs on wool, so the crop can't be left unsold.'

They had been walking through the barn as they spoke, and now the lay brother ushered Martin through a door at the far end into a smaller room. Here there was a table, positioned to catch the light from a window, some shelves and some locked boxes. A monk, one of the ones in a white robe and with a tonsure, was sitting at the table writing something, surrounded by various pens and sharpenings. He looked up and nodded as Martin entered but did not rise or speak. He dipped his quill into a small ink bottle and continued with his work.

'Your office?' Martin hazarded to Brother Sinnulph.

'The grange office, yes. Here we keep our records.'

'And some books.' Martin nodded at some volumes on a shelf. 'This abbey is full of books.'

There was a slight sound – a tutting noise? – from the monk at the table but Brother Sinnulph continued as though he hadn't heard it. 'Not really. They look like books but they're just wool ledgers. See.' He took one down and opened it, and Martin could see that it was full of numbers in columns and other incomprehensible notes and markings. His eyes slid over it without interest as Brother Sinnulph pointed out something or other. 'The main ledgers are at the abbey, in the office in the lay brothers' grange, but we keep our own ones here, separately.'

Martin tried to muster some interest. What did traders talk about? 'I suppose you need to keep track of how much you've sold, what people have paid you, that sort of thing.'

This time there was no mistaking the snort from the table and Martin looked around sharply, only to be greeted by the sight of the monk's tonsured head as he bent serenely over the column of numbers he was writing.

Martin addressed Brother Sinnulph again, a little more loudly than he had intended. 'And did Brother Alexander oversee this as well?'

The scratchy noise of the pen stopped and there was silence for a moment before it continued again.

Brother Sinnulph glanced at the other monk, laid a hand on Martin's back and ushered him firmly back towards the door. 'Yes, yes, he would come and check all the accounts from time to time, but he wasn't here all that often as he had the other granges to visit as well. Now, try to hold your breath while we go through the barn again and then we'll walk around outside and I'll show you the rest of the place.'

Martin stopped halfway through the barn as something caught his eye. He bent and picked up a vicious-looking double-bladed implement from where it had been left on top of a hay bale. It was like a double-ended knife, folded over in the middle and flexible, and the two blades rasped against each other as he pressed the implement in his hand. He held it up questioningly.

Brother Sinnulph took it from his hand, very carefully, and laid it back down. 'A shearing tool. We have many of them, of course.'

'You could do quite some damage to someone with that.'

It was hot in here, but surely the monk was sweating more than he had been a few moments ago? His face looked quite red. 'Yes, I suppose you could. And I have known of careless labourers injuring their fingers or, worse, causing damage to a prize sheep, but thank the Lord we had no such incidents this year.'

They emerged into the sunlight and Martin took a deep breath of the mercifully wool-free breeze which drifted between the grange buildings.

'Can you show me anything else Brother Alexander worked with while he was here? And tell me anything else you know about him?'

'There isn't much else, as this grange really only deals with wool – we don't grow our own crops. But I'm sure you'd find it interesting to look at our garden and some of the other outbuildings ...'

Resigning himself to an hour or so of utter boredom before he could start riding again, Martin followed.

Edwin felt as though he was in a dream. He had spent – he didn't know, about an hour, he supposed, as Brother Octavian hadn't yet been called away to a service in the church – looking at different books and asking questions about them. His mind felt so full that it would hardly fit inside his head.

He picked up another volume and opened it carefully, squinting at the tiny, close-written text.

Brother Octavian peered over his shoulder. 'Ah, now, that one was written by Brother Alexander, may he rest in peace.'

'He wrote it? You mean he copied it out? I didn't think scribing was one of his duties.'

'No, I mean he wrote it. He composed it. This is not his handwriting – the original is in another abbey, but we have a copy made by another scribe. In fact this one is clearer, as I'm told that the original is full of crossings-out and notes.'

Edwin stared at the words, wondering if some knowledge of Brother Alexander might come to him if he read through them all. But it was a hefty volume and the subject matter looked complicated. 'What is it about?'

Brother Octavian sniffed. 'It is not a theological work. It is his *De naturis rerum*, a manual of scientific knowledge and therefore not on our list of recommended works for the novices or the younger monks. He wrote it while he was a schoolmaster somewhere – St Albans, I think – before he took the cowl. Some of the older brothers who have already been through all our religious works have studied it. They have found nothing contrary to our doctrine in it, so it is not a problem, but much of it is just useless information.' He turned a few pages and pointed at a passage. 'See here – he writes that a needle which is magnetised can be of use to sailors in finding their way across the sea. How can that be said to be of interest when compared to his other theological studies? What a pity he spent so much time on this and then never completed his other work.'

Edwin had never really thought about how difficult it might be to find one's way across the sea – he'd never even seen the sea – but now he came to think about it, it would be tricky, wouldn't it? There wouldn't be any landmarks to help you find your way, just water on all sides. He wondered how the needle would help, but there was no time to think about that now. He tore his eyes away from the writing. 'What other work?'

'Ah, well … wait a moment.' Brother Octavian went to the back of the room and reached up to bring a sheaf of parchment down off the top shelf. 'This is what he was working on. It's not finished so it is not bound, but as he will now never complete it I suppose we should bind it anyway in case it gets damaged.'

Edwin shut the science book with care and with regret, and replaced it on its shelf so that Brother Octavian could lay the parchment down in its place.

The monk turned over the first of the loose leaves. 'Now this, this is much more important. This is Brother Alexander's *Speculum Speculationum*.'

Edwin wrinkled his forehead. 'The mirror of mirrors?'

Brother Octavian nodded. 'Yes, you could call it that. It is a theological work of great import.'

'What is it about?'

'Well, the first volume, which he had already completed, was a refutation of the Cathar heresy and its belief in dualism.'

Edwin didn't quite understand that, but he nodded anyway. Heretics were bad, so obviously a learned monk would be able to disprove what they believed, he supposed.

'This is the second volume, and here Brother Alexander was just getting into his stride. See here, where he begins to focus on his key purpose of the application of dialectic logic to the study of theology …'

Clearly the Lord intended Edwin to undergo a lesson in humility. He had always considered himself intelligent – had he even prided himself on being able to understand things which the other villagers didn't seem to grasp? Was he guilty of that sin? – but now he realised that he was hopelessly out of his depth. He listened to the words coming out of Brother Octavian's mouth and he had not a single clue what they were about. He needed to be reminded of his place. Which was evidently not here.

He interrupted. 'So, Brother, do you think any of this might have a bearing on why Brother Alexander was killed? Surely nobody would want to stop him completing this work?'

Brother Octavian looked shocked. 'No. I can't imagine such a thing. Or at least, no good Christian would want to stop this. If there were any heretics or heathens around then they might want to, but there aren't any of those around here.'

Then why, thought Edwin, have you just looked over your shoulder as though you expect one to appear behind you at any moment?

He changed the subject. 'Brother, have you heard of the writings of a man called Daniel of Morley?'

Brother Octavian looked taken aback. 'Of course I have, but how have you?'

Should he reveal the reason for his question or not? 'Oh, it's just that one of the other brothers mentioned his name and I didn't know what he had written – I thought you might.'

'Which brother? It would have to be someone very well read, for Daniel's works are very difficult and we have none here.' He thought for a moment. 'His best-known tract is probably his *Philosophia*. It is divided into two books, on the sublunary and superlunary world, and deals with ...'

Edwin didn't think this was going to help – he needed to concentrate on more immediate practical matters. 'Brother, would it be possible for me to come into the cloister tomorrow while you are all carrying out your reading? Your – I'm sorry, I can't remember the proper name.'

'The *lectio divina*? Well, it wouldn't be normal to have the brethren disturbed at their study, but as Father Abbot has asked us to help you ... I shall ask him directly later today and let you know what he says.'

'Thank you, Brother. I promise not to disturb anyone or even speak – I just want to watch for a while so I can get more of an idea of exactly what Brother Alexander was doing when he died, and how it might have happened.'

They were interrupted by the sound of a bell.

Brother Octavian regretfully started to gather up the loose pieces of parchment. 'That is the call to nones, so I must ask you to leave now so that I can lock the armarium.' He gave Edwin a long look, which Edwin returned for a while before dropping his gaze to the floor. 'I know that you did not understand what I was speaking of just then. But remember: ignorance is not the same as stupidity. If you feel that you have a calling, you can always talk to Father Abbot. Many have joined the brethren and had their minds expanded by a lifetime of study.'

A lifetime of study. Edwin felt his heart beating faster. To leave everything; never again to be sent by the earl on a perilous and terrifying mission; instead to spend his life in peace, reading all morning, working all afternoon and praying to the Lord in between.

The prospect of what such a life could offer, of what might be within his reach if he only asked, of the bliss he could have, was almost as terrifying as the prospect of trying to explain it all to the earl.

Chapter Seven

Edwin was catching the sun's afternoon rays in a corner of the precinct, sitting with his back against a wall and soaking up the heat while trying to make sense of the thoughts – too many thoughts – which were going round in his head.

Did he really want to consider becoming a monk? It was all idle thought at the moment as surely the abbot would object, but still he couldn't help thinking about it. There were arguments both for and against, but he was so confused that it was difficult to line them up and decide which side was stronger. On the one hand, he would live a life of peace, and he would get the opportunity to study. On the other, it would mean giving up his friends and family, and any chance of a life of marriage and children. He leant his head back as he considered. Once, those aspects would have outweighed all else. But his lifelong friend, the companion of his boyhood, was dead these two months, and he still felt the betrayal. His father was dead. Admittedly his mother still needed him, but might she not be pleased that he would be in a position to pray for her? And might she not marry again anyway, possibly giving him a stepfather he didn't want? And as for marriage … the blackness threatened to encroach from the corners of his mind and he pushed it back. If he couldn't have her, he didn't want anyone. And then there was his duty to the earl, to whom he owed his position. Would the earl even let him leave, if he asked? He doubted it, or at least he doubted that he would be released as long as he was still useful. But how useful was he? He had helped the earl out of a few situations so far, he knew that, but could he guarantee that he would keep being able to do it? At the moment, for example, he was no nearer to knowing what happened to Brother Alexander than he had been when he arrived.

He needed to concentrate, to push the distractions away and to think only of the task in hand. What did he know of Brother Alexander already? Think not just of *what* may have happened, but also *why*, for that was the key. His death had not been an accident; someone had killed him on purpose; therefore that person had a reason to do so. Find the reason and it will lead to the killer.

His thoughts were interrupted by the approach of Brother Helias, who smiled as he caught sight of him.

'You look comfortable, my son.'

Edwin squinted up at him. 'I was just thinking, and it's easier to do that when I'm sitting still.'

'Thinking about Brother Alexander?'

'Yes, but also about many other things. And I'm tired because I didn't sleep much last night.'

'Ah, well, that's something we brethren can all sympathise with. One of the most difficult things for new recruits to get used to is the night-time services, although they are a way to get closer to God.'

Edwin stood up, for he was craning his neck and he could hardly ask the monk to sit on the ground beside him. 'I was in the church last night while you were all singing.'

'And did it help you to find peace?'

'Not really. I saw Brother Godfrey and Brother Waldef together and it scared me out of my wits – I hadn't realised there were two of them.' He couldn't work out whether admitting this in the bright light of day made him feel less foolish, or more, but Brother Helias was nodding.

'I remember the day they arrived. It was quite a shock to some of us as well.'

'How do you tell them apart? Does it get easier once you've known them longer?'

'You'd think that, wouldn't you – but I can't tell one from the other and neither can any of the rest of the brethren, as far as I can make out. We just trust that when we say "Brother Godfrey", the right one answers. But the Lord, who can see into the souls of all men, knows each of them.'

'I hope so, for it would be a dreadful thing to come before Him on the day of judgement only to find yourself answering for the sins of your brother.' A cloud crossed the monk's face and Edwin hurried to placate him. 'I'm sorry, Brother, I was just talking idly. I hope that's not blasphemy or anything.'

'As far as I know, my son, it is not, though it is an interesting philosophical point which some of my more learned brethren could no doubt discuss at great length. All I can say is that I trust the Lord to know each man's sins. And He is well aware that not all brothers are as alike as Brothers Godfrey and Waldef.'

Edwin saw Martin ride into the precinct, leading another horse on a rein. He waved, and Martin gestured that he would stable the horses and then come over.

Brother Helias sketched the sign of the cross in the air. 'I must be about my duties, Edwin. I know that we have permission to talk to you, but I have been heading towards idle gossip and I don't think Father Abbot intended that. *Benedicte*, my son.'

He walked off and Edwin sat back down against the wall. It wasn't long before Martin arrived, blocking out the sun and casting him into shadow. Edwin shifted sideways and indicated the ground beside him; Martin obligingly took off his sword and folded himself down into the space so that Edwin didn't have to strain his neck upwards. They sat in comfortable silence for a few moments.

'So, how were the books?'

Edwin laughed. 'They were fine, thank you, but I'm sure you don't want to hear about it. The one useful thing I did find out was that Brother Alexander wrote some of them himself, and that he was halfway through another one when he died. I thought I'd keep it in mind that someone might have wanted to stop him finishing it, but I can't for the life of me think why.'

'What was it about?'

Edwin opened his mouth, but he just couldn't bring himself to confess his stupidity. He waved his hand. 'Something religious. Nothing controversial, though Brother Octavian reckoned that heathens and heretics might not like it.'

Martin made a derisive noise. 'Heathens and heretics don't like anything, do they? That's why we go on crusades to kill them.'

Edwin digested that. 'Anyway, how was your afternoon? Did you find anything out from the lay brothers at the grange?'

Martin picked up a small stone and cast it aimlessly across the courtyard. 'More than I ever wanted to know about wool, that's for sure. Oh, but Brother Alexander did used to go there, and he was apparently really fussy about checking all their accounts and making sure that they graded their wool right.'

Edwin pricked up his ears. 'Their accounts?' Money had been the reason for many a murder before.

'Yes, they shear the sheep and pack all the wool there, and keep lists – ledgers, they call them – of what they sell and for how much. That sort of thing. Some of the ledgers are out at the granges and the rest are in the office in the lay brothers' range here – is that the place up the stairs we saw when we first arrived?'

'Yes, I think so.' That reminded Edwin of something and he reached into the purse at his belt. 'When I came past it again I found this on the stairs, but I don't know what it is – any idea?' He showed Martin the strangely shaped piece of metal.

Martin took it. 'Yes, of course – it's the chape off the bottom end of a scabbard. Look.' He held his sword across his knees and showed the bottom tip of the scabbard to Edwin. There was a piece of metal there helping to strengthen the leather, and Edwin could see the similarity in the shape. Martin looked at him quizzically. 'And your own dagger will have one as well – didn't you notice?'

Edwin shrugged. 'I wasn't paying it all that much attention, to be honest.'

'A fine dagger like that, and you haven't looked it over so many times that you know every detail?' Martin shook his head. 'You're mad.'

'If you say so. Anyway …' Edwin pointed at the chapes in front of him. 'These aren't quite the same. Yours is plain and this one has a decoration on it.'

Martin handed it back. 'Yes. And I know whose it is – it belongs to that knight who's staying in the guesthouse. Sir Philip.'

Edwin paused in the act of stowing the metal back in his purse. 'Sir Philip? But what would he be doing in the lay brothers' office? He's not a merchant, is he?'

'Ha – not likely, and I wouldn't say that to his face, either.'

Edwin pondered that for a while, but came up with nothing. 'Let's leave that for now and go back to the question of the lay brothers. One of them is in charge of these accounts you were talking about?'

'No, it turns out that none of the lay brothers can read or write. I had a talk with one of them, Brother Sinnulph, while he was showing me around, and he explained it all. The white monks – choir monks – come from noble families, so they've got some education. The lay brothers are all from peasant families – some of them ask to join, and some are persuaded to by their families if they have too many sons for their bits of land. You can't move from one to the other – you join one part and you stay there. And the lay brothers just do manual work, not the reading and so on.'

'So how do they do the accounts then?'

'Oh, didn't I say? One of the white monks was there. Sitting at a table and scribbling down loads of numbers – no idea what they meant.'

'Which monk?'

Martin thought about it and then shrugged. 'No idea. They all look the same to me. Youngish, I suppose, but it's difficult to tell when they all shave their heads like that.'

Edwin watched in amusement as Martin ran his hand through his own mop of hair, tousling it, apparently unaware that he was doing so. If there was one man he could guarantee was never going to become a monk, he was looking at him now.

'So, say that Brother Alexander went to look at these accounts and found out that something was wrong with them?'

Martin dropped his hand again, running his fingers idly up and down his scabbard. 'What, like they were stealing money or something?'

'Yes. From what you saw, would it be possible for them to sell the wool at one price, but then write down a different price and keep the difference?'

'I don't know, but I suppose so.'

'Who would that involve?'

'Well, they had lots of men there, but it wouldn't be anything to do with the hired labourers. They just come in at this time of year, shear the sheep and pack the wool, but they aren't involved with the grading or the selling. So that leaves the lay brothers and the monk who comes to do the writing.'

'And we don't know who that is.'

Martin looked down. 'No. Sorry. Now I think about it, I should have asked.'

Edwin was quick to reassure him, conscious of his own current feelings of inadequacy in that area. Perhaps it was time to change the subject.

'I still don't feel like we know much about Brother Alexander himself. Lots of people have been able to tell us about what he did, but nobody has really said what he was like.'

Martin squinted into the sun as he considered this. 'He was a bit tougher than the other monks, I reckon.'

Edwin nodded. 'Aylwin did say that he thought he'd come off worst in a fight if it came to one.'

'Well, yes, though judging by the state of him, Adam could probably best him in a fight so that doesn't say all that much.' He thought for a moment. 'Although, having said that, Brother Alexander must have been quite strong if he's been carrying barrels of ale around by himself – they're quite heavy and I should know.' Unconsciously he flexed his arms, no doubt recalling his years of table service for the earl. 'But no, what I meant was that he's travelled. It takes some guts to get yourself around like that – how many of the other brothers here do you reckon would pack up a bag and rely on themselves to get five miles, never mind over the sea?'

Travelling ... that reminded Edwin of something. 'Brother Octavian told me that before he came here to take the cowl, Brother Alexander was a schoolmaster at St Albans. Do you know where that is?'

'Not exactly, but not far north of London.'

'So nowhere near here then?'

'Oh no. Several days' journey even on horseback. Weeks, I suppose, if you were walking.'

'And there must be some other Cistercian monasteries between there and here.'

Martin made a noncommittal gesture. 'I suppose there must be.'

'So, if you're in St Albans, and you decide you want to become a monk, a Cistercian monk, why would you travel half the length of the kingdom to join the Order here? Why not just find the nearest place?'

'No idea. But then I also have no idea why anyone would want to be a monk in the first place, so I'm probably not the right person to ask.'

Edwin sighed. 'All right. I'll keep that in my head for now. There is someone who might be able to tell us more about Brother Alexander's travels – Brother Helias told me that there was another monk here who he talked to more than the others. But he's apparently in the infirmary with toothache, so I'm not sure if I can just walk in and ask to talk to him.'

Martin gave a mirthless laugh. 'Ha. Good luck getting past that infirmarer. He'll probably throw you out before you have a chance to open your mouth.'

Edwin stood. 'I'll try my best to be polite. And if you've already argued with him then I'd better go on my own. What will you do in the meantime, apart from trying not to upset any more monks so you can't go near them again?' He'd meant it as a joke, but a shadow crossed Martin's face as he also got to his feet. Edwin was used to his height, but every so often he was struck again by Martin's physical presence, and he hoped to the Lord that they would never come to blows. 'I'm sorry, I didn't mean ...'

'It's all right. You're right anyway – I need to learn to act more cautiously around them.' He glanced around. 'But there is one I haven't offended yet. If you'll excuse me, I'm off to chop some more wood.'

'Wood? What ... oh, the novice you spoke to.' Edwin followed Martin's gaze and spotted – Benedict, was it? – making his way across the precinct. 'Good idea. Just get him talking about

anything you can think of, and you never know, he might say
something important.'

'All right. And I wish you well with the infirmarer.' He grinned.
'If he threatens you, come and get me and I'll threaten him back.
I'm turning out to be quite good at that!' He gave Edwin the most
almighty clout on the shoulder and stalked off to follow the novice.

Rubbing his shoulder and muttering under his breath about
knights and squires, Edwin made his way around the outside of
the main abbey buildings, and was directed by an obliging lay
brother to where the infirmary occupied a separate building out
to one side, not far from the abbot's house. He entered quietly
and stood by the door, looking as meek as he could, watching the
tall, bald monk who was attending to an elderly brother in a bed.

Eventually the monk noticed Edwin. Edwin whipped off his
hat and looked at the floor. Judging by what Martin had said,
extreme humility was going to be the way forward here.

The monk approached him. 'This is the infirmary for the
brethren, my son. If you are a guest who needs attention then you
need to go to the guestmaster.'

Edwin risked a look up. 'Pardon me for interrupting, Brother,
but are you the infirmarer?'

'Brother Durand, yes. But as I say —'

'I don't mean to disturb you, Brother, but the lord abbot said
I might speak to any of the brethren if it helped me to find out
what happened to Brother Alexander.'

The monk folded his arms and stared at Edwin for a long
moment. 'So, you're one of them, are you? Well, you've got better
manners than your friend, I'll give you that. To whom did you
wish to speak? Me? Or one of the brethren here?' He gestured
and Edwin saw that several of the beds were occupied by frail-
looking men.

He took a deep breath. 'Actually I was wondering if I could
speak with Brother Richard? I've been told he's here?' He looked
around but he couldn't see that any of the infirmary's residents
looked like they had toothache.

Brother Durand's reply was sharp. 'That won't be possible.'

Edwin tried to remain as mild as he could. 'Why?'

'Because he won't be able to tell you anything.'

'But I have been told that he and Brother Alexander spoke together often.' The infirmarer's face took on a stern look and Edwin rushed to correct himself, not wanting to get anyone into trouble. 'As often as it was permitted, I mean. I'm sure they kept the proper rules of silence, but the brethren here are allowed to talk to each other occasionally, aren't they, as part of their work or in the parlour?'

Brother Durand relented slightly. 'That is true. But when I said that Brother Richard couldn't tell you anything, I didn't mean that he might not know anything – just that he is not in a fit state to speak.'

Edwin held his ground. 'May I see him anyway? Please? It would just be for a few moments.'

Brother Durand shrugged. 'Very well. But don't say I didn't warn you.' He led the way to the very end of the infirmary, where a bed was hidden behind a screen.

Edwin followed him round, but stopped dead in shock when he saw the monk lying in the bed. He crossed himself and asked for the Lord's mercy for the poor man. Dear God.

Brother Richard's head was monstrously swollen, twice the normal size, the skin stretched so tight that Edwin could almost see through it; it looked in danger of bursting at any moment. His nose had sunk into the swelling, his eyes were almost buried, and he didn't look as though he'd be able to open his mouth at all. A hollow reed had been put between his lips, presumably so that he could breathe.

Edwin looked down at him in horror and pity. He was about to back away quietly, all ideas of questioning him gone, when he thought that he saw the eyes watching him. He knelt by the side of the bed and took the monk's hand. 'Can you understand me?'

There was no way that Brother Richard could speak or even nod, but Edwin felt a slight pressure on his hand.

Edwin kept his voice gentle. 'I was going to ask you some questions about Brother Alexander and his travels, and why he took the cowl here, but it can wait until you're better. In the meantime I will pray for you.' He made as if to stand, but the hand holding his did not let go. He looked into the eyes again, and thought he could see a question there.

Brother Durand spoke from behind him, more gently than Edwin would have expected. 'I don't think he knows that Brother Alexander is dead. He's been in here for more than a week, and he only has brief periods in control of his wits.'

The grip became tighter, and the sunken eyes filled with tears. With his other hand Brother Richard made a gesture which Edwin didn't understand, before his arm fell back on to the bed.

Edwin looked questioningly at the infirmarer.

'As you might know, we sometimes use signs to speak to each other. That is the sign meaning brother, another of the brethren. Hearing of the death must have brought him back to himself for a moment.' He leaned over the prone man. 'I'll make up another poultice for your face, Brother, and get you something to drink.'

They both made their way back into the main infirmary room and over to the bench where Brother Durand kept his herbs and medicines.

'May I ask what happened to him?' Now he was away from the suffering man, Edwin realised he was shaking.

'He had been having toothache for some time. When it got too bad I extracted two of the teeth from his left side, the ones which were most rotten. Some hours after this he felt better, and he was able to join the brethren on the refectory for the evening meal. He ate more than he had been accustomed to, and was then struck down for his gluttony: he was assailed by pain and his head began to swell as you have seen. I have tried many poultices, and I have bled him several times, but to be honest there is little we can do except pray for him.' He began to grind some things into a paste, saying the paternoster as he did so.

Edwin's curiosity was aroused. 'Does that make the medicine more powerful?'

Brother Durand smiled without pausing in his mixing. '... *adveniat regnum tuum* ... no prayer is ever wasted, my son ...

fiat volontas tua … but in this case it is because … *sicut in caelo et in terra* … the poultice needs to be mixed for the exact time it takes to say the paternoster twice.' He continued under his breath as Edwin watched, until the mixture was ready. 'Now I'll spread some on his face, and then try to get some of that watered wine into him.'

Edwin must have winced, for Brother Durand nodded. 'It is not easy, and it causes him a lot of pain even though I drip it in one drop at a time. But he must have liquid to restore his humours, or he will die anyway.' He took the poultice and moved away.

Edwin made his way back outside. Clearly there was going to be no point expecting any information from Brother Richard. The poor man. Still, he had at least succeeded in not antagonising the infirmarer so he might be able to go back to him with further questions if he had any.

It was late afternoon, and the precinct was full of monks and lay brothers returning from their labours. Edwin decided against heading straight for the guesthouse and instead turned to walk around to the other side of the infirmary building. He soon found himself in a graveyard – yes, he supposed it was natural that the burial place for the monks should be next to the building in which they were most likely to die. There were mounds laid out in neat rows, older ones at the end nearer to him, which had flattened out and were covered in grass – cut grass, though, with no weeds, he noted, so someone must have the task of taking care of the monks' resting places – and newer ones towards the far end. He walked between the graves towards the last one in the last row, a fresh scar of brown earth.

This must be the final resting place of Brother Alexander, for nobody had mentioned another recent death, and the previous grave looked like it had been there some months at least. Edwin stood in the space next to it, where he supposed the next brother to die would be buried before they had to start another row. He wondered what they would do once the graveyard was full, and how long it would take to fill up the – let's see – twenty-five spaces, if the rows continued in the same pattern.

He shook his head. Concentrate. He knelt down by the grave and said a prayer for the soul of a man he had never met and never would – a man he couldn't even visualise – but whose life and death had become of great concern to him. Then he began to pray for enlightenment, for help with his task. He remembered not to let himself speak aloud: he had once done this at the grave of his father when he was in desperate need of help and advice, and it had earned him some strange looks. But the people in Conisbrough knew him, knew his devotion to his father; here they did not, and he had no idea what sort of punishment might come his way if he were to be accused of trying to commune with the dead.

He listened as hard as he could, in the silence of the graveyard in the middle of the greater silence of the abbey. Speak to me, Brother Alexander, tell me something which will help me find out what happened to you. You are a holy man, so you probably don't want revenge and retribution, but you will be able to rest easier once we know who killed you and why.

But there was silence. Brother Alexander had no word for him from the grave. He was busy making his way through Purgatory while his earthly remains mouldered in the ground, and he had no time for Edwin. Edwin laid a hand on the turned earth, muttered a final prayer, and stood. He was on his own.

He wasn't on his own. He was being watched by one of the monks, whom a closer look revealed to be Brother Amandus, the guestmaster.

'I did not mean to disturb you, my son. Were you praying for Brother Alexander?'

'Yes, I —'

'That is highly commendable of you, for you did not know him during his life. What a shame he should be cut down like that.' He shook his head.

'Did you —'

'But of course every man is called to God when He wills it, and not at any other time. It is all part of His divine plan.'

'Well, yes, but —'

'And we will all lie here one day. Indeed, it seems likely that we will be digging a grave for Brother Richard here before too many more days have passed.'

Edwin remembered the dreadful figure in the bed. How much longer could a man possibly survive that?

Brother Amandus shook himself. 'But there I go again, talking too much. It's why Father Abbot made me guestmaster, you know – unlike many of the other brethren I have to speak as part of my duties, and I think he was tired of hearing me confess to the same fault over and over again. I shall do it again, no doubt – precept fifty-three, "not to be fond of much talking". But now I must leave you and go to prepare the evening meal for the guests. I shall see you at the guesthouse later when you are ready to eat.'

'Before you go …'

Brother Amandus turned back.

'Just out of interest, what did Brother Alexander look like? The lord abbot said he was in later middle age, but that's all I know.'

The guestmaster looked down at the earth. 'I'm not sure what you want to know. He was tall, certainly – not as tall as your friend, but probably next in size after Brother Durand. Tonsured, of course, like the rest of us, with blond hair going grey. And …' he paused for a moment, searching for the right words. 'Thoughtful.'

'Thoughtful? You mean, he cared for others?'

'No – I mean, yes, of course he cared for others, but I mean he always looked like he was thinking of something. He was a very clever man, a real scholar, so perhaps he had thoughts which the rest of us couldn't contemplate. Thoughts which were just between him and the Lord.' He waited to see if Edwin was going to say anything else, and then inclined his head and turned away.

Edwin watched him depart, aware that the whole day had passed and he was no nearer to solving the murder of Brother Alexander – master of the lay brothers, driver of hard bargains, traveller, writer, scholar, thinker – who lay under the ground at his feet.

Martin made his way across the precinct as he followed the novice Benedict. The place was so eerily quiet that he didn't like to call out and draw attention to himself, but he waved and Benedict caught the movement as he turned into the woodshed. He waved back and waited until Martin joined him.

'Greetings.' He sketched the sign of the cross in the air.

'Hello, Brother. I was at a bit of a loose end so I wondered if I might help – if I might serve the abbey again by helping you chop some wood.'

Benedict inclined his head. 'That would be most welcome.' He turned to go in and then seemed to stagger, resting his hand on the gatepost for support.

'Are you all right?'

'I'm fine, thank you. I just turned around too fast in the heat of the sun. Please, come in.'

It was late in the afternoon and the sun wasn't that hot. Martin looked at the flushed patches on his cheeks and the over-bright eyes, but he said nothing.

If he were being honest with himself, Martin would have preferred just to get on with the task without speaking. But that was not his purpose in coming here: he had to make sure he didn't let Edwin down again, and so far Benedict was the only person in the abbey he'd managed to strike up a conversation with which hadn't ended badly. So he discarded his tunic and started. As he got into a rhythm – place the log, lift the axe, bring it down, *thump*, repeat – he considered his next move. Once he had an armful of split logs he swung the axe into the chopping block to hold it and started picking them up while he watched Benedict. He was working as he had done the other day, with little strength and no pattern, which was just going to wear him out.

Martin waited until Benedict had succeeded, at the third try, in splitting a log and then stopped for breath.

'Do you mind if I show you a different way to do it?'

Benedict considered. 'I am here to learn in all things, so please do.'

'You've got to get into more of a steady pace. You need to be able to make the same movement over and over and over again, smoothly. That way you'll do it better and you'll be able to carry on for longer. Look.' He demonstrated, and then stood back to let Benedict have a go. 'That's better, but just hold the axe a bit more …' he adjusted the novice's hands. 'Now, bring it up – yes, a bit further – no, that's too far – yes, about there. As it falls, try to let the weight of it do some of the work, so it's not all coming from your arms.'

This time the log split cleanly and Benedict smiled. He needed a lot more practice, but it was a start. Martin got back to work himself and resumed the conversation.

'So, how long have you been here?'

The novice looked confused. 'You just came in with me.'

'No, I mean, here at the abbey. How long have you been a novice?'

Benedict's face cleared. 'Oh. I see. Almost three years. I shall take my final vows next spring, once I turn eighteen. I can't wait.'

He's the same age as me, thought Martin. What an age to be giving up on life and shutting yourself away. Why does he want to do it?

'You must know most of the other brothers quite well by now.'

Benedict placed another log but did not make a move to lift his axe. 'I suppose so. Some better than others, of course – I have been studying with Brother Jordan, the novicemaster, but I also know Brother Octavian, who tells me what to read, and Brother Walter, the sacrist who prepares the church for each service. I hope one day to be allocated such a holy task.'

'But for now it's chopping wood, eh?'

Benedict looked down at the log on the block and made an attempt to lift the axe over his head. The spots on his cheeks looked even redder as his white arms rose, and he seemed struck by exhaustion. The axe came down and missed the wood completely. 'It's God's work, and I must obey.' He sounded miserable. 'I would rather be praying.'

I bet you would, thought Martin. Now he needed to move forward with his plan. As he added his wood to the stack of split logs, he turned and asked casually over his shoulder, 'And Brother Alexander? Did you know him?'

The reaction was as violent as it was unexpected. 'Him! He had no business here!'

Martin turned in surprise to see Benedict looking animated, his arms waving in front of him, his eyes almost wild. 'Why do you say that?' he asked, keeping one eye on the discarded axe at the novice's feet.

'He had studied with *heathens* – had the temerity to say to Father Abbot that he had learned much from them! How can he claim to serve God as a brother of this house when he has consorted with those who deny Our Lord? How can he live with himself without confessing his sin? How —'

He was spluttering, almost spitting in the grip of his emotion. Martin stepped forward and put a hand on his shoulder. He felt the thin bones, barely covered with flesh, through the fabric of the habit. 'Calm yourself, Brother. Here, sit in the shade a moment.'

Benedict started to protest that he needed to get on with his labours, but Martin propelled him firmly towards the fence where there was a patch of shadow, and pushed him down into a sitting position. He had no wine or ale to offer, but he picked up his tunic from the ground and used it to wipe the sweat from the other's brow. He was hot to the touch. Too hot.

'I heard that Brother Alexander had travelled,' he mentioned carefully when he was sure Benedict was breathing more easily, 'but I didn't know where.'

Benedict looked at him, not as wildly as he had done, but still not calm. 'I heard that he went initially to Paris, but that he did not find the masters there to his liking, so he went south over the mountains, through the kingdoms there and then into the Moorish lands, where he studied with Saracens. *Saracens*! How could he …'

Martin was also appalled that anyone could meet Saracens without wanting to kill them in battle, but saying that out loud wasn't going to help. Think of something to keep him talking. 'But he came back. He came back with more knowledge, and then he came here to use that knowledge.'

The bright eyes were staring beyond him. 'He came back with more than knowledge.'

'What do you mean?'

Benedict leaned in towards him, and Martin could feel the heat radiating off his body. '*Treasure!*'

'What?'

Benedict nodded vehemently. 'Yes. He brought back treasure with him. Brother Walter heard him say so.'

Martin thought rapidly. He had to go and put this all before Edwin, but even he could see the implications. He shook his head to try and clear it. 'What kind of treasure?'

'I – I don't know. But, given his heathenish tendencies, I wouldn't put it past him to have taken Moorish gold or something. He didn't belong here, I tell you!'

He was getting agitated again. Martin put out a hand. 'Look, you sit there, and I'll finish the wood for you. Just rest, just – stay there.'

But Benedict was already struggling to his feet, mumbling that he had to do God's work, and staggering over to his chopping block. Martin didn't feel that he could use physical force to stop him, not here, not a monk, even though he was only a novice. He would keep an eye on him.

Benedict had managed to split one log by the time Martin had done four, and he was placing another as Martin picked up all his pieces and carried them over to the stack. Then there was a strange sighing noise, and Martin whipped round just in time to see the novice collapse to the ground, where he lay unmoving.

Chapter Eight

The smell of cooking assailed Edwin's nostrils as he left the grave-yard and made his way back into the main precinct. He would appreciate an evening meal, although he would remember to pray for poor Brother Richard who would eat nothing.

Edwin poked his head around the gate of the woodshed as he passed it, but there was nobody there, so perhaps Martin was already on his way back to the guesthouse. Edwin wondered if he had found out anything else. He hoped so, for he was getting very short on ideas of what to do next. He slowed as he passed the main door of the church, and wandered inside. It was empty, it being not yet time for the next service – which one would that be? Vespers? – so he took the opportunity to kneel in the cool silence and pray. Although his head was swimming so much that he wasn't really praying coherently – more just letting everything spill out of his mind in a confused heap, in the hope that the Lord might help him to make sense of it all.

After some while he realised that he was not alone in the church; he could hear a sound coming from one of the side chapels rather than from outside. At first he couldn't make out what it was, so he stood and crept forward as quietly as he could. He shivered as he remembered his shock of the night before when he thought he had seen a ghost, but this was no spirit – it was a real man, a choir monk, kneeling before the small altar in a side chapel and clearly in great distress. The sound that Edwin had heard was the monk trying to swallow his sobs.

Edwin was in a dilemma. He could not bring himself to inter-rupt a man in such need of speaking with the Lord privately, but what if it had some bearing on the murder of Brother Alexander? For why else would a monk be crying like that unless he had done something wrong? He seemed to be begging for something, and maybe that something was forgiveness. Edwin craned his neck to try and see more, to identify the man at least, but the monk had his back to him and all he could see was a bit of dark hair around the tonsure. He felt frustration rising. Why were they all so difficult to tell apart? All he could work out was that it wasn't one of the novices, who were untonsured, it wasn't the infirmarer, who was completely bald, and he was fairly sure it wasn't one of the very elderly brothers who had greying or white hair. But that still left, what, the other forty or so choir monks? He had to move forward, he had to talk to the man.

He didn't move.

Eventually he gave up and backed away into the main body of the church, and then out the door into the evening sunshine.

On his way to the guesthouse he saw Brother Helias, presumably making his way back from the cellarer's office for his own evening meal. As Edwin greeted him he mentally crossed the cellarer off his list, firstly as he didn't think the weeping monk could have got out so quickly, and certainly not without having some signs of his distress around his eyes, and secondly as he had forgotten that Brother Helias had reddish hair not dissimilar to his own.

Brother Helias nodded to him and was about to pass by. Edwin wondered if he might know anything about the weeping monk in the church. 'Brother, may I speak with you please? Privately?'

Brother Helias inclined his head and indicated the nearby guesthouse. As they reached the building Edwin stood back to let the monk enter first. To his surprise he heard Sir Philip addressing the new arrival in a low hiss. 'I thought we agreed only to talk while we were in the ...' He saw Edwin and bit back his words, turning away.

The merchant Aylwin rose as they entered, and greeted them. 'Brother Helias, do you have any idea of how long it is going to take the lord abbot to appoint a new master of the lay brothers? I need to speak to him really quite urgently about this year's wool, and while I am kicking my heels here I am not out doing business elsewhere, which is ...'

Brother Helias held up a hand. 'Peace, Master Aylwin. I appreciate your business concerns, but the appointment of such a key obedientiary cannot be rushed. Father Abbot needs to consider carefully who will be best for the position, and to pray for guidance.'

'But —'

'As soon as I am aware of the identity of the new master of the lay brothers, I will make sure you are informed. Now,' he turned to Edwin, 'what was it you wanted to ask me, my son?'

Edwin had forgotten that they wouldn't be alone in the guest-house, and he didn't feel comfortable airing before others what was probably a private matter for the monk concerned. 'Oh, er, it can wait, Brother. I don't want to make you late for your meal.' He tried to give Brother Helias a significant look to indicate the reason for his change of heart, but he wasn't sure it worked.

After Brother Helias had left, Edwin sat down at the table where Brother Amandus was setting out the meal. Edwin saw that there was egg and cheese to add to the normal beans and vegetables, maybe because it was Sunday, he guessed, and thought that Martin would be pleased. Come to think of it, where was Martin?

—————

Martin swore out loud as he saw Benedict crumple to the ground; he dropped the wood he was carrying and ran over, throwing himself down next to the still form and turning him on to his back.

'Brother, Brother, can you hear me? Are you all right?' He tapped the side of Benedict's face. 'Wake up.'

Benedict made no reply and Martin wasn't sure he was breathing. That wasn't good, was it? And should his eyelids be fluttering like that? Well, there was only one thing to do. He put his arms under the prone man and lifted him, standing up as he did so. He was immediately thrown off balance by how light Benedict was. Dear Lord, he weighed nothing! Regaining himself, Martin clasped the unconscious novice to him as he hurried out of the woodshed and in the direction of the infirmary.

He should have guessed that the sight of a panicked stranger carrying what looked like the body of a dead novice would cause much alarm, and he was soon surrounded by an anxious crowd of monks and lay brothers.

He brushed them off as he thrust his way through. 'He's not dead – taking him to the infirmary – will be easier if I carry him —'

One of the white monks took charge, shooing the others away and telling a lay brother to fetch Brother Jordan to the infirmary, whoever he was.

Martin tried not to think of the welcome which was going to await him as he kicked the door open and burst into the building. And indeed Brother Durand's face turned purple as he saw who entered.

'I told you not to – *what in God's name have you done?*'

'Nothing! I have done nothing! But you have to help him.' Martin moved to the nearest spare bed and knelt to lay Benedict on it. As Martin watched he took in a breath, and Martin sagged with relief.

He felt himself being pushed aside by the infirmarer, and stood hovering at the end of the bed.

'What did you do to him?' Brother Durand thundered as he knelt to examine Benedict, looking for any signs of a wound.

'I told you, nothing. I was helping him chop wood and he just fell over and I couldn't wake him, so I thought —'

'Don't lie to me! Don't tell me that something just *happened* to assail him while you just *happened* to be nearby —'

Martin felt his own anger rising and he pointed an accusing finger at the infirmarer. 'If you were any man other than a monk I would knock you senseless for calling me a liar!'

Brother Durand stood. Martin had the unusual sensation of being face-to-face with a man almost as tall as he was, as the monk lost his own temper, spitting out his words. 'Knock me senseless? Your answer to everything, no doubt!'

'What have you got against me? Ever since I —'

'Who do you think you are, coming here and —'

'Brother Durand, calm yourself please.'

Martin turned, for the voice had come from behind him, to see that the monk who had taken charge outside was the prior, who had followed him in. He now stood unmoving, his arms folded in the sleeves of his habit. Martin belatedly realised that he was in an abbey building, facing off furiously against one of the senior monks, and that the elderly men in the surrounding beds were cowering. He took a pace backwards.

Brother Durand also came to himself and, in a move that Martin recognised from his own years of obedience to authority, bowed his head immediately. 'Yes, Brother Prior.'

Prior Henry moved forward to stand next to Martin at the foot of the bed. He sighed and shook his head. 'Ah, Benedict, I thought we had moved on from this.'

Dear Lord, in his anger Martin had almost forgotten the stricken novice. 'You know what ails him?'

The prior's voice was sad. 'He is keen to suffer in the name of the Lord – too keen, and Father Abbot and I have both had cause to speak to him about it during the last couple of years.'

Martin didn't understand. 'What do you mean?'

'We have a restricted diet here, as you know, but this is not enough for Benedict. He seeks to earn the Lord's favour by starving himself, which is not the best way to serve as it means he does not have the strength for his labours and for the services. Brother Jordan, the novicemaster, is supposed to have been watching him carefully and instructing him to eat properly.'

Martin wondered how on earth anyone could possibly want to starve themselves, but as he had already worked out that Benedict was a very different man from himself, he tried to feel sympathy.

Prior Henry sighed again as he looked down on the figure in the bed, now moaning and whimpering although he still appeared unconscious, his eyelids moving rapidly. 'Oh no …'

'What?' Martin's voice was sharper than he meant it to be, but the prior took no offence.

'Turn him over, Brother. On to his stomach.'

Brother Durand, who had his hand over Benedict's heart, looked puzzled, but he obeyed. Martin stooped to help him as they manhandled the novice into position. He was still hot, but some of the moaning stopped.

The prior nodded. 'As I thought. Loosen his robe and look at his back.'

Brother Durand did so and expelled a harsh breath. Martin didn't want to appear too curious, but he leaned forward as far he dared. Benedict's back was covered with a criss-cross of ugly red welts, some of which were oozing an unpleasant substance. Martin looked at the two monks, who were exchanging a glance.

The prior explained. 'He has been scourging himself. That is strictly against the rules of the Order and Father Abbot expressly forbade him from doing it.'

Brother Durand was now bustling about his business. 'I have a poultice which can be used for the bleeding and the discharge, and he must be bled to help relieve his fever. If you will excuse me, Brother Prior …'

Martin briefly touched Benedict's hand. 'Will he be all right?'

The prior was muttering a prayer, and he crossed himself before he replied. 'If it is God's will.' He regarded Martin with some sympathy. 'But yes, I hope so.'

A noise from the doorway heralded the arrival of an elderly monk who was puffing and breathing quite heavily. 'I came as fast as I could.' He staggered inside. 'The poor boy. Is he —' He wheezed his way over to the bed and saw Benedict's back. 'Oh.' He dropped to his knees.

The prior's voice assumed a stern edge. 'Brother Jordan. You and I need to have words. Please come with me to see Father Abbot.'

The new arrival looked both horrified and forlorn. 'Yes, Brother Prior.' He struggled to rise, holding on to the bed for support, and Martin grabbed him under one arm and hauled him to his feet, then watched as the two monks left the building.

Brother Durand returned with a bowl of something which smelled evil and knelt by Benedict's side. 'You can go.' His voice was brusque.

Martin shuffled his feet. 'Yes, Brother. I – I hope he recovers soon.'

'Whether he does or he doesn't is in God's hands. Your sword can't help him, and neither can you. Now leave, and don't come back.'

Martin opened his mouth but the infirmarer was already kneeling and dipping his fingers in the paste. Still smouldering at being called a liar, Martin turned on his heel. *A good commander must be in control of himself at all times.* Or so he kept telling himself as he fought the urge to kick things on the way out.

When he reached the guesthouse Edwin rose from the table to greet him. 'I was wondering where you'd got to. Here, sit down and have something to eat.'

Martin folded himself up on to the bench and accepted a bowl of food. He shovelled it in without really noticing what it was, thinking of Benedict being presented with such tiny rations all the time and then refusing some or all of it anyway. What could possess a man to act so?

Edwin was talking to him, but he didn't fancy telling him everything with the other two men sitting at the table, especially about his latest encounter with the infirmarer, so he muttered that they would talk later and then turned the conversation to more general matters, asking Sir Philip about his horse's recovery. As he spoke he looked at Edwin in case he was going to raise the subject of the scabbard chape he had found. But Edwin, somehow reading his mind, gave a very slight shake of the head so Martin kept his mouth shut. The evening passed in strained chat and a few cups of weak ale.

———

Eventually the guests took to their beds. Once the others were asleep Edwin turned his face towards Martin and listened to a whispered summary of all that had happened that afternoon. Edwin considered the implications of Benedict's announcements and his behaviour, even as he told Martin of his lack of success and the unlikelihood of being able to speak further with Brother Richard.

'But treasure, though – that has to be important?'

Martin yawned at him and nodded. 'I thought so.'

'And he didn't say what it was?'

'No. I did ask, mind, but he didn't know himself.'

'That's a shame.' Edwin lowered his voice even further. 'He must have kept it in that cave. In the box we found.'

'Yes. But it was empty, remember?'

'I know.' Edwin considered for a few moments, aware that Martin's eyes were starting to close. 'Perhaps we missed something. We'll go back there tomorrow and have another look.'

'Fine.' Martin's voice was drowsy, and as Edwin watched he saw the exact moment when his friend fell asleep. He wished he could drop off as easily, but it seemed he was in for another night of thoughts jumping up and down in his head. He tried to order them but they would not obey, and after a while he sat up again. He'd had several cups of the small ale, not enough to make him feel drunk, but as he was still awake he now found that he needed to relieve himself. He put his bare feet on the floor – no need to lace himself into his boots just to go to the latrine behind the guesthouse – and tiptoed past the other guests. As he did so, he caught a flash of something from one of the beds – a reflection of the light from the burning rush on the table twinkling from one open eye. Now he looked again, both eyes were closed and the man appeared to be fast asleep, but Edwin had the definite feeling that Sir Philip had been awake, and he wondered how much of their conversation the knight had overheard.

The following morning Edwin felt as though his head was full of sand. He groggily raised himself to a sitting position and then put his fingers to his lips as Martin looked like he was going to say something. Martin gave him a questioning glance but took the hint and said nothing, merely stretching and yawning as he pulled his tunic over his head.

Once they had left the guesthouse Edwin checked all around him to make sure they weren't being overheard. Sound would carry much further here than it would at home because there was so little background noise. He explained that he suspected Sir Philip had heard them last night. 'I'm not sure about him.'

Martin lowered his own voice. 'It does seem a strange story, him staying here because his horse has gone lame. Surely he must own more than one, and he could send a servant to fetch another? And where's his squire?'

'He might be a knight, but I don't think he's very well off. Not all of them are.'

'How can you tell?'

'Well, the lack of a squire, for one thing. Maybe he can't afford one. And his clothes are wearing thin and a bit frayed around the edges – didn't you notice?'

'No.'

Edwin couldn't resist it. 'A fine knight like that, and you haven't looked him over so many times that you know every detail? You're mad.'

But Martin didn't get the joke. 'Well, come to that, I'm not so sure about the wool merchant either. Maybe he's in on this cheating which might be going on in the grange?'

'Maybe,' said Edwin, unwilling to commit to the theory at the moment. 'But he didn't get here until after Brother Alexander was already dead.'

'Oh yes, I forgot that. Anyway, where are we going? I thought we were going to head back to that cave to have another look around?'

'We will, but it will have to wait until this afternoon. This morning we need to watch the *lectio divina*, and before that the monks have their Chapter, their daily meeting, and I want to see if they will let us in.'

'The *lectio* what?'

'It's reading.' Edwin felt guilty, but he wanted to have Martin with him so they could both watch and then compare notes. 'We're going to watch the monks reading.'

'*What?*'

They stopped outside the door to the abbot's house and Edwin turned to squint up at his friend. 'I know you won't like it. But two pairs of eyes are better than one, and you might see something I miss.'

Martin sighed. 'All right. But you're going to owe me a day's hunting in the forest once this is all over, you know that, don't you?'

Edwin managed a tired smile. 'All right. Just because I know I'd hate that as much as you're going to hate this. But first we must speak to the lord abbot.'

It took Edwin some persuading to get the abbot to give them permission to attend the morning Chapter meeting, as this was normally for the monks only, unless there were very honoured guests to be received – to which category he did not consider that Edwin and Martin belonged, evidently – but he eventually admitted that these were exceptional circumstances and that the two of them could attend as long as they stood at the back, remained silent and did nothing to make themselves noticed by the brethren. The abbot added that after the service of sext at noon he would expect Edwin to visit him to apprise him of progress so far, and then with a brief reference to precept twenty-eight – Edwin thought he really must go and look these up somewhere – he swept off through his garden in the direction of the chapterhouse. Well, that will be a short meeting, thought Edwin, as he and Martin took the longer way round into the abbey building through the lay brothers' range.

The monks were already assembled in the chapterhouse when Edwin and Martin arrived and they slipped in as quietly as they could. It was a rectangular room into which light flooded at this time in the morning, thanks to the three windows at the east end; nearer the door it was a little darker and they managed to find themselves a shadowy corner behind a pillar where they could watch proceedings unobtrusively. The abbot and the prior, who were facing them, might be able to see them if they stretched a little, but the other monks were facing their superiors and so not likely to spot them unless they turned around. Edwin scanned the backs of their heads and realised again how difficult it would be to pick out the one he had seen crying in the chapel. It could have been any one of up to about half the monks. He had forgotten to mention that to Martin but he couldn't do it now as they had promised to remain in silence. He made a note to himself to do it later.

Chapter started with a reading from the Rule of St Benedict, the text which governed how the monks should live their lives, which Edwin had also heard being spoken aloud during the meal the other evening. He let it wash over him but then snapped back to attention when the abbot invited any of the brethren who needed to do so to step forward and confess their faults.

An elderly brother hauled himself to his feet and shuffled forward. Edwin felt Martin's breath in his ear as he leaned down to whisper, 'That's Brother Jordan, the novicemaster. I saw him yesterday in the infirmary.' Edwin nodded, recalling that he had seen the monk in the company of the three untonsured boys on the day they had arrived.

Brother Jordan had made his way to the open space in front of the abbot and the prior, and lowered himself creakingly to his knees. His voice quavered as he spoke. 'Father Abbot, Brother Prior, Brothers, I confess to you that I have failed in my duties with regard to the novice Benedict.'

The abbot looked down on him, and Edwin could not detect a trace of sympathy. Dear Lord, he was as inflexible as the earl. 'Continue, Brother Jordan, and explain your fault fully.'

'I have failed in my duty of care. Against your express wishes, Father, he has been starving and scourging himself, and I failed to notice this and to stop him. The fault is not Benedict's, but mine, for he is but a youth and had he been better guided by me he would not have misunderstood the Rule and acted in such a way. I humbly ask for punishment and forgiveness.' He leaned forward and lowered himself with aching slowness to the floor, lying face down with his arms stretched out to the sides. Edwin wondered how he would ever get up again.

The abbot looked around the room. 'Does anyone wish to speak on this matter?'

At a nod from his superior the prior stepped forward. His usual jollity was absent but he looked with compassion on the elderly man on the floor. 'Father Abbot, if I may, I would like to state that I do not believe there was any deliberate neglect on the part of Brother Jordan. Rather, I believe that his duties are becoming too onerous for a man of his age and it was this which led to the lack of oversight of Benedict.'

He stepped back and the abbot nodded thoughtfully. 'Does any other here wish to speak in support of, or against, Prior Henry?'

Brother Helias raised his hand and was invited to stand. 'I would add my voice to that of the prior, Father, to say that Brother Jordan would not purposefully neglect his charges. Many of us here were novices under him in our time, and we know his devotion to his labours.' He became a little less formal. 'And we are all aware that the three younger boys are a bit of a handful, Father.'

He sat and the abbot's eyes swept the room again. When he was met with only silence and a few nods, he addressed the prostrate man. 'Brother Jordan, how long have you been the novicemaster here?'

The monk raised his head far enough from the ground to reply. 'Thirty-four years, Father.' His forehead returned to the floor.

'You have served the abbey well during that time, and it is my will that you now be relieved from the post so that you may spend more time in prayer and that you may be provided with labour more suited to your age.'

This time the reply was aimed at the flagstones. 'Yes, Father Abbot.'

'You will remain as novicemaster for a further week while Brother Prior and I pray and consider who will be best suited to fill the office. While Benedict lies in the hospital you will visit him at any time when you are not otherwise engaged in services or labour, and you will read to him from the Rule, ensuring that he is aware that his behaviour was wrong. When he is sufficiently recovered he too will make confession here, to acknowledge that he has become wild.'

'Yes, Father Abbot.'

'Rise, now, and take your place beside your brethren.'

As Brother Jordan struggled to rise the abbot himself stepped forward and lifted him to his feet, making sure he was steady before directing him back to his seat. Edwin caught a glance between abbot and prior which set him thinking.

The abbot addressed the room. 'Does any other wish to confess a fault?'

Edwin watched as several other brothers came forward to admit to what seemed to him to be very minor transgressions, and each was dealt with. Nobody confessed to anything which could have the remotest bearing on Brother Alexander's death, nobody mentioned wool, and none of the penitents appeared to be the man Edwin had seen in the chapel. He sighed and Martin elbowed him to remind him to be silent; he hoped nobody had noticed. Martin himself was standing so still that he had virtually become invisible, and Edwin remembered that he'd had plenty of practice due to the hours and hours he spent in attendance on the earl.

As the Chapter moved into daily notices Edwin considered the abbot's words. Benedict had been allowed to behave in a way which was not conversant with the Rule. He had become 'wild'. And from what Martin had said, he nursed a hatred for Brother Alexander, or at least a hatred for the way he had travelled and learned. Just how wild had Benedict become?

Chapter Nine

Edwin settled himself into a corner of the cloister as he watched the monks prepare for their morning reading. Each one queued at the armarium and was issued his book, and then found himself a spot on one of the benches around the edge of the cloister or those placed on the open grassed area in the middle. That would be a fine place to read today, thought Edwin, but surely they can't sit there if it looks like rain or the books would be ruined. I wonder what the weather was like on the day Brother Alexander died – I don't think it was wet but I must remember to check. One of them will know.

The monks were by now all seated individually, each with his book and each with his cowl up, covering his head. To give them more privacy and help them to concentrate, Edwin thought, though it made them even more indistinguishable from each other than they were normally. Each of them was reading aloud to himself, but quietly so as not to disturb the others, so the whole cloister was filled with the sound of murmuring as the monks ran their fingers along the text of the page in front of them. Every so often one of them would stop reading and fold his hands – contemplating something he had learned, no doubt.

After what Edwin judged was about half of the allotted time for *lectio divina* he leaned over towards Martin, who had been sitting next to him unmoving all the while and clearly bored out of his mind. He whispered as quietly as he could. 'Notice anything?'

Martin shrugged and replied in an equally low voice. 'Nothing except that they're all reading and I can't tell who is who.'

'Agreed.' But Edwin had also noticed something else, and now he cupped his hand to Martin's ear. 'See that door over there? The one that leads through the lay brothers' building and out into the precinct?'

Martin nodded.

'Can you walk over there, go through the door so I can't see you, and then walk back here as quietly and calmly as you can? I want to try something.'

Martin nodded again and rose. He sauntered around the walkway at the edge of the cloister until he reached the door, and then disappeared through it. Then he reappeared and strolled back, walking this time across the grassed area. As Edwin expected, none of the monks really paused in their reading and studying, but a number of them looked up at Martin curiously before lowering their gaze to their books once more.

Martin took his seat again. 'And?'

Edwin leaned in. 'I'll tell you later, but I think it's important.'

Once the *lectio divina* was over, each of the brothers closed his book with care and then queued in silence to hand it back to Brother Octavian before heading towards the refectory. The librarian took each volume one at a time, placing it precisely back in the armarium before coming back for the next, so the whole exercise was going to take some time. Occasionally he spoke in a low voice. 'Brother Walter. How are you getting on with the *Lives of the Fathers*? Brother Eugenius – I'm glad to see you making sense of ...'

Edwin's attention was caught by the arrival in the cloister of one of the lay brothers. Bearded and wearing a brown tunic like all the others, he made his way over to the prior and bowed before handing him a slip of parchment in silence. That seemed odd – perhaps they weren't allowed to speak in here at all? But Edwin could still hear Brother Octavian in the background, 'Ah, the works of St Jerome – thank you, Brother Waldef,' and the prior was also clearly audible as he thanked the lay brother, who seemed to be called Brother Guy. How strange. The lay brother departed without breaking his silence.

Eventually Edwin and Martin were alone, but Edwin still checked all about him to make sure before he spoke out loud.

'Like you said, they all look the same. And they all look the same because they are choir monks, white-robed monks. The lay brothers don't come in here while the reading is going on – did you see that one waited until it was all over? – and neither do any of the guests. As soon as you started walking around, a lot of them noticed.'

Martin looked perplexed. 'So?'

'So, if Brother Alexander was killed during the *lectio divina*, it can only have been by one of the other choir monks.'

'Sorry, what? Why?'

'Because they are the only ones who wear white robes. That lay brother in brown stood out among them, and so did you in your tunic – they would notice immediately anyone who was wearing a different colour.'

Comprehension started to dawn on Martin's face. 'You mean …'

Edwin nodded. 'Brother Alexander was murdered by one of his brothers.'

Edwin raised his hand to knock on the door but let it fall again. He was not really looking forward to his interview with the abbot. However, it must be done, so he must go in. He squared his shoulders and smoothed down his tunic.

He still didn't knock on the door.

After a short while he realised he was going to look foolish standing outside the room if anyone came along, so he rapped his knuckles on the wood in what he hoped was a respectful manner. He was admitted to the parlour, where he knelt and kissed the ring on the abbot's hand before being invited to seat himself on a stool. The abbot placed himself in the chair on the other side of the table and folded his hands. 'Well?'

Edwin took a deep breath. 'I should start, my lord, by saying that I do not yet know who killed Brother Alexander, but I have made some progress and I know more about him than I did before.' He explained what he had discovered about the dead monk's past. The abbot nodded in recognition at the details of how seriously Brother Alexander took his duties in the abbey and that he drove a hard bargain with outside merchants; he looked thoughtful at the news that Brother Alexander had been in St Albans before arriving at Roche, that he had travelled abroad and that he had apparently brought something back with him.

'But,' Edwin concluded, 'this is all outweighed by the things I don't yet know about him. Most pressingly, why did he come all the way here instead of joining a monastery nearer to London, what did he bring back with him, and why did he keep it? Oh, and what if anything has someone called Daniel of Morley got to do with all this?'

The abbot raised one hand. 'One thing at a time. First, I am surprised to find you are familiar with Daniel of Morley, as his writings are very challenging. How did you hear of him?'

'When I first arrived, your prior said he didn't know much about what Brother Alexander had done before he came here, but that he had mentioned that someone by that name had been a great influence on him. That's all I know.'

'He was a man who travelled widely, both within and outside Christendom, and his work deals with the creation of the world, matter, the elements, the nature of the stars, and so on. Some of it relies on Arabic sources which are not considered proper by the Church, and we do not have any of his texts here.'

'Wait, you said he *was* a man who travelled widely? Is he still alive?'

The abbot shook his head. 'No, he died – about seven or eight years ago now, perhaps? I heard the news from fellow abbots at our annual conclave.'

Edwin honestly couldn't see what any of this had to do with his present task, so perhaps it was just a dead end. The prior had said it probably wasn't important, after all.

'Let's leave that for now, then. What about the "treasure" that Brother Alexander brought back with him?'

'That cannot be. Every man, when he enters the Order, must give up all personal possessions. There are no exceptions. Besides, if he had something then we would have found it after his death. When his place in the dormitory was cleared we found only the permitted items which all belong to the abbey: his belt, his eating knife, his boots, his spare robe. All were returned to the abbey stores ready to give to another. Even the robe he was wearing when he died was put back in the wardrobe after the washer-women had cleaned and mended it.'

Edwin thought that he wouldn't much like to be allocated the robe in which a man had been stabbed, but he supposed that the next wearer, whoever he was, wouldn't know about the garment's history.

'But what if he kept it somewhere else?' Edwin didn't want to go into too many details about the cave, but he could speak generally. 'Brother Alexander was often outside of the abbey due to his business – maybe he could have kept whatever it was in another place?'

The abbot's lips were starting to form a thin line. 'You are verging into speculation, my son, and you are doing the memory of Brother Alexander no credit. Precepts seven and fifty-two: not to bear false witness, and to guard one's lips from uttering evil or wicked words.'

'But —'

'I will not have a decent man slandered after his death. I must ask you to cease on this line of questioning.' His tone was firm and Edwin recognised authority when he heard it.

'Very well, my lord. Perhaps I can ask you something else.'

'Go on.'

'Yesterday, when I was in the church I caught a glimpse of one of the monks – one of the choir monks – kneeling in a side chapel, praying and weeping as if his heart would burst. Martin says he also saw someone doing something similar soon after we arrived, but we're not sure whether it was the same man. The one I saw had dark hair around his tonsure and I don't think he was one of the oldest brothers, but I couldn't identify him further than that. Do you have any idea who it might have been? If he was crying from guilt and praying for forgiveness then that might have a bearing on my quest.'

The abbot nodded. 'From what you say, I would guess that the man you saw was Brother Walter, our sacrist.' He sighed. 'He is not suited to his life here in the cloister, but he tries hard and he prays constantly that he might improve.'

'Why must he stay here, if he is not suited to it?'

'He is not obliged to stay. Indeed, I have offered him the opportunity to leave the Order on several occasions – you may think that we seek to keep men imprisoned here, but like many of my fellow abbots I recognise that we can all serve God in different ways, and in Brother Walter's case it may be that he would achieve that better in another way.'

Edwin was fascinated by this insight. He had always thought that once you were a monk, you were a monk and there would be no escape, no second chances. But something puzzled him. 'But Brother Walter doesn't wish to leave?'

The abbot shook his head. 'No. He is determined that the fault somehow lies with him, that if only he tries harder, prays harder, makes more of an effort, that it will all become clear to him and he will be content here. He wants to stay, but he also wants to *want* to stay, if you see what I mean.'

Edwin could certainly sympathise with that situation, but he wasn't about to think about it just at the moment. He moved on. 'And what is his role in the abbey? You said he was the …?'

'The sacrist. It is a highly responsible post, for Brother Walter is in charge of all our sacred vestments and vessels, meaning that he has to set them all out before each service, collect them in and take care of them.'

Edwin thought about that, and about other things he'd seen and heard. And then it started to fall into place. 'And you appointed him to that post on purpose? So that he is often in the church, so that he has a greater opportunity to pray and perhaps to become closer to the Lord?'

The abbot sat back in his chair, a look of surprise on his face. 'You have great insight, my son. I did indeed, and for exactly the reasons you describe. It hasn't worked, I admit – I am sure that Brother Walter has a vocation, but it has not yet been revealed to me what that vocation might be. But how did you know?'

'I —' How could he put it into words?

'You may speak freely.'

'I … well, when I first met you, my lord, I thought you stern.' He looked at the abbot in case he had already gone too far, but the abbot nodded.

'This is something I recognise about myself,' he said. 'Have no fear – continue.'

'But since I've been here I have already learned how much you know about all the brothers, and how you care for each one of them individually. They aren't all just monks to you – I mean, they are monks, obviously – but what I mean is, to you they are all individual men with individual needs, and you try to help them.'

The abbot closed his eyes in brief prayer. 'Yes, I try, for it is written in our Rule that the abbot should show the stern discipline of a master, but also the loving affection of a father. And what father does not seek to help his sons find their path? But sometimes I fail, as I have done so far with Brother Walter. The brethren might look the same to you, but in my eyes they are each unique among God's creatures, and I must find a way. "The abbot must realise how difficult and arduous the task is that he has undertaken, that of ruling souls and serving men of many different characters." That is also contained in the Rule, and I must seek to understand each individual. The Lord will show me the way if I pray hard enough and am deemed worthy.'

'I hope so, Father,' said Edwin. 'He has already shown you the way with Brothers Godfrey and Waldef – think how much easier it is for them to serve God and the Order when they are allowed to be together, when others might have forced them to separate. And Brother William, whom you let out of the abbey to come and serve my lord earl.' The abbot nodded in acknowledgement. 'And this morning, you were kind to Brother Jordan. You had already arranged with the prior that he would speak up, hadn't you?'

The abbot narrowed his eyes. 'You are extremely perceptive. I can see why the lord earl puts so much faith in you. I too was deceived at our first meeting, for I thought you an inexperienced boy. I can see now that I was in error.' He continued to stare and Edwin started to feel a little uncomfortable under his gaze. 'Have you ever considered taking the cowl?'

'What?'

'You have only been here a few days, but I am already persuaded that you would make a fine brother of the Order. You have a keen mind and a thirst to know the Lord better, or so I hear both from Brother Helias and Brother Octavian.'

Edwin felt sweat break out on his forehead. 'I – er, that is —'

The abbot raised his hand. 'You do not need to decide anything now. But while you are here you might like to give the matter some thought. Once you have found out what happened to Brother Alexander, would it be so difficult to consider staying here instead of going back to the lord earl?'

Edwin opened his mouth but no words came out. He stood abruptly. 'Thank you, my lord. I will think, as you say.' He started backing away towards the door.

The abbot remained seated. 'Peace, my son. I had no wish to alarm you. Have no fear – if you decide to walk away from the abbey then so be it. I have no desire to keep any man here against his will.'

Edwin was almost out the door by now, but the words chimed with something the abbot had said earlier. 'Father?'

'Yes?'

'While we were talking, you said that you were sure that Brother Walter had a vocation, but you weren't sure what it was?'

'I did.'

'It's not my place, but … have you considered making him the new master of the lay brothers?'

The abbot sat up even straighter than he already was. 'Why do you say this?'

Edwin shrugged. 'I don't know, Father, but if constant prayer and reflection are not working for him, perhaps more action, more activity, might be good for him and might reconcile him to the abbey? That way he can see that we can all serve the Lord in many ways.'

As I serve my lord earl in many ways, he thought, as he bowed and left the stunned abbot in the room. But for how long? Might there be another way?

Alys looked around the cottage as she sipped her ale, thinking to herself that it was a better brew than she had ever managed to produce. In some ways it was very different from her home – the place that had been her home – in Lincoln: it was made of wattle and daub rather than wood, and it was all on one storey with no upper floor. She was in the main room, but she could see that there was another off to one side which she assumed was a bedchamber. Another difference was that back home the front room of their house was a shop, opening on to the street, and they lived above and behind it; here all the space was for living.

But although the space looked different, there were also similarities: the cottage was well kept, with fresh rushes on the floor and stores hanging from the rafters; the fire was well tended, a bubbling pot over it, and the furniture was in good repair. She had striven to do the same in Lincoln, to make the house into a welcoming home, or at least she had until – but better not to think of that. She took another sip of her ale.

Mistress Anne, for so Edwin's mother was called, was ladling some kind of savoury pottage into a bowl, and now she placed it on the table in front of Alys, along with a piece of bread. They were alone; Mistress Anne had explained that she was a widow, which Alys knew already as she had first encountered Edwin shortly after his father had died. Alys had started to speak, to try and explain, but she had been gently shushed, for Mistress Anne said she would like her sister and her sister's husband to hear the tale as well. 'And it might distress you less if you only have to tell it once.'

Alys was grateful, and also not a little jealous that Edwin had not only a mother but also an aunt and uncle. What she would have given for such adult family support when she had lived through the siege, trying almost single-handedly to keep her younger brothers and sister safe.

The pottage was warm and delicious, and Alys was just wiping the last piece of bread around the bowl when the doorway darkened and another woman entered, calling out a greeting as she did so. She was a similar age to Mistress Anne, perhaps a few years older, and although they were not terribly alike there was enough of a resemblance for Alys to work out that this must be Edwin's aunt. The sisters embraced and Alys stood, smoothing down the front of her apron. Another shadow blackened the door and a man entered, stooping to lower his head under the lintel and leaning on a stick. He straightened and Alys started backwards in fear, for his face was twisted, distorted, like the very devil.

Mistress Anne hurried to her and patted her shoulder in reassurance. 'Have no fear, child, for William is not as frightening as he looks. He was wounded in battle many years ago.'

Alys looked at the newcomer, taking in the horrific scar which disfigured the whole left side of his face, and the torn and part-missing ear. She curtsied and said nothing.

'None of that, now, none of that. I'm no lord for you to bow to.' His voice was gruff but a little lighter than she had expected; she watched as he heaved himself laboriously over to a stool and sat down, laying the stick on the floor next to him. He nodded to Mistress Anne. 'Although she has her manners about her, I'll give her that.'

Mistress Anne made a tutting noise and placed a cup of ale down in front of him. 'Alys, this is my sister Cecily and her husband William, who is the steward at the lord earl's castle.'

Alys had noticed the castle as she had approached Conisbrough – well, you could hardly miss it, could you, it was a landmark for miles around – and she felt a little overawed at meeting someone who worked in such a fine place. Her dealings with the castle in Lincoln, and the folk who lived there, had been scant. But she had no time to think further on the subject for she was being embraced by Edwin's aunt, who smelled of herbs even more strongly than her sister and who felt comfortable.

They all sat and everyone looked expectantly at Alys.

She took a deep breath. 'Mistresses, Master – from what you've said already, I think there has been some confusion.'

William thumped his cup down on the table. 'You can say that again. First the lad mopes about like a calf because he's left you there, then he decides to ask the lord earl can he marry you, and then he mopes about even more because you're married already.'

Alys tried not to stare at his disfigured face. 'I beg your pardon, but I am not married and I never have been.'

Mistress Cecily spoke soothingly. 'So that is where the confusion has arisen. Why don't you explain it all to us, from the beginning?'

And so Alys told them of the siege, of the attack on and subsequent death of her father, of her two eldest brothers both being missing, and of the discovery of the body of one of them, Nick, on the doorstep. She faltered and felt tears coming to her eyes when she described the scene, remembering the fear, the terror … and the comfort of having with her the man who had come to dominate her thoughts ever since.

Mistress Anne patted her hand and William muttered something about war. Alys steadied herself and wiped her eyes on a corner of her apron before continuing.

'And then it was over. The other army came, there was a great battle. The city was looted but our house was saved by a knight, Edwin's friend. The children and I hid. But within another day they were all gone, and the city had to try and right itself again.'

She looked around at her audience. 'And then a miracle happened – or at least I thought it was at the time. My eldest brother Thomas had been away from the city since before the siege started, away on business for his master – he was an apprentice, you see.' She wasn't sure whether they would know what she meant, but they nodded in understanding so she continued. 'When he didn't come back I was worried, but in fact he'd been staying with one of his master's business partners about a dozen miles away, and once the city fell they said he'd be better off staying with them and not going back, because it would be too dangerous. So he stayed there during the whole siege.'

William interrupted. 'Leaving a girl and a pile of children in a besieged city? Some brother he is.'

In her heart of hearts Alys would have liked to agree with him, but she ought to show some family loyalty. 'Well, my father was still alive at that time and Thomas had no reason to know what would happen to him – or to Nick – after.'

She expelled a breath and looked up at the ceiling and back down at the floor. 'While he was there, he got to talking with the merchant about his apprenticeship, about Father's business and so on, and he obviously thought Thomas would be a good catch, for when he arrived back in the city after the siege he brought a wife with him – the merchant's eldest daughter.'

Understanding was dawning in Mistress Anne's eyes. 'And it was she whom Turold – the lord earl's messenger – spoke to when he entered your shop?'

Alys nodded, a lump coming to her throat. 'Yes. And neither she nor Thomas told me about the visit until it was too late, until he had long gone and I couldn't chase after him.' She remembered the bitterness of the feeling as they had eventually admitted it. She might not have known at all had she not seen her little brother Edric with a halfpenny and asked him where he got it, and heard the story of the messenger on the fine horse.

'They deceived him, for they didn't want me to leave. She was fine with being married to Thomas, and being now mistress of the house because my father was dead, and showing off about it to the customers, but she didn't want the bother of looking after the children or running the house – that was for me to do as I was the unwed sister.'

The tears were coming again but she didn't care. 'So I asked them straight about what the man had said, and they gave me the letter, saying it didn't matter now as the messenger was long gone. I took it to Father Eustace and he read it out to me, and I cried and cried.' She wiped her eyes again. 'You see, I didn't know Edwin for very long but I'd been thinking about him ever since he left, wondering if he was thinking about me, and then to find out that he wanted me to marry him … and I'd missed the chance …' She buried her face in her apron.

Alys felt a touch upon her shoulder and arms about her; Mistress Anne had come to kneel beside her. The older woman made gentle noises and stroked her head until she was steady again. 'But you didn't miss your chance, did you? What did you do?'

Alys sniffed hard. 'I – I had to decide. Was I going to stay there and be their maid for the rest of my life, with them keeping me in service until I was too old to marry anyone else? Was I going to give up on the man I lo— on the man I'd been thinking about? Or was I going to do something?'

Her voice became fierce as she remembered. 'I remembered Master Theobald came up north this way once a year, so I made an excuse to visit his shop and turned the conversation that way. When I heard he came as far as Conisbrough I spoke to him and his wife. They said they wouldn't take me, not without Thomas's permission, so I went back and faced him about it. I told him all that I'd been through while he was keeping himself safe out in the country, I told him that we all owed our lives to Edwin and his friends, and I told him that I was going no matter what he said, even if I had to walk all the way in bare feet and rags.'

'Good for you, girl.' William was impressed.

'Anyway, he caved in like I knew he would eventually, and said to Master Theobald that I could go and that he'd give me some of the bolts of cloth as a dowry.' She allowed a slightly derisive note to creep in. 'Not any of the most expensive stuff, of course, for he said I wouldn't need that out in the country, but I didn't care. And he wouldn't have any cloth at all if it hadn't been for Edwin and his friends.' She folded her arms.

Mistress Anne surmised the rest. 'So you set off. Why didn't you let us know you were coming?'

'I'm sorry for surprising you, mistress, but how could I get a message to you? The only way would have been to send word with Master Theobald as he's the only one who comes this far, and if I did that and then waited to see if Edwin could get a message back to me, it would have been next year before I could come as Master Theobald only makes his way here for the summer fair.'

The others all looked at each other before Mistress Anne spoke. 'Well, you're a brave and resourceful girl. Edwin will only be gone a few days and he'll be overjoyed to see you when he gets back.'

Cecily nodded her agreement and William grunted, lifting his cup. 'And it will be good to see the lad happy for a change.' He raised the cup in salute. 'Here's to a wedding before the month is out.'

Martin had been extremely glad when the monks' reading was over. The thought that they did this *every day* was almost too much. He'd kicked his heels around a bit while Edwin was seeing the abbot – he considered going to see Benedict in the nearby infirmary but he thought better of getting into another argument with Brother Durand.

Eventually Edwin had emerged, and he'd been very quiet ever since. Martin wondered what they could have been talking about – well, he had a fair idea, obviously, but he had no idea why it should have affected Edwin so deeply.

He clouted his friend on the shoulder. 'Come on. Let's go out and find that cave again. A bit of air and a walk will do you good.'

Edwin rubbed his shoulder, muttered something under his breath that might have been agreement and might not, and they set off to the gatehouse. Once they had waited what seemed like an hour for the ancient brother to dodder his way into opening the small wicket-gate, and stepped through it, Martin looked about him. 'I think we might be better off trying to find it by retracing the steps we took to get back last time. If we try to go through the woods without following that woman then we're bound to get lost. What do you think?'

'All right. It was this way, wasn't it?' Edwin gestured off to his right and Martin agreed.

'Yes. All we have to do is follow the cliff around.'

Martin didn't like walking – his boots were always too small and they hurt his feet – but there was no point bringing the horses into such terrain. And there wouldn't be anywhere to tether them outside the cave anyway. So they made their way on foot over to the edge of the white face which soared high above their heads and began to walk next to it. Their path took them through some undergrowth and then through a bit where the forest came right up to the edge of the stone and they had to push their way through. Martin remembered all this from their journey back last time, so he was confident they were heading in the right direction, although of course it all looked a bit different when you were going the other way.

After some time they reached a space where there was more open ground around the cliff, and the edge of the forest was some way off across scrubland. Martin slowed and then stopped. 'It's around here somewhere.'

Edwin gazed around. 'Yes,' he said vaguely. He still looked distracted.

'So, what did you talk about with the abbot?' There was no point in beating around it – he may as well ask straight out.

Edwin looked at him sharply. 'About Brother Alexander, of course. What else would we have been talking about?'

There was something in his face which Martin didn't quite understand. 'I don't know. It's just that you seem ... you look like you're thinking about something else.'

'I've got a lot to think about, that's all. Anyway, are we going to look for this cave or not?' He reached out to touch the rock face and began to feel his way along it. Martin joined him, running his fingers along the white stone.

It was surprisingly difficult to find. They had almost given up when Martin fell into it almost by accident. 'Here.'

Edwin was about to go inside, but Martin had spotted something and pulled him back. 'Wait.'

'Why?'

Martin crouched down and edged his way through the fissure in the rock, banging his elbow as he did so. Inside he moved so that what light there was struck the floor. 'I think someone else has been here.'

Edwin's head appeared. 'How do you know?'

'I don't *know*, exactly, but look – did we scrape the floor this much?' He touched the sandy surface lightly.

'Maybe we did? I mean, we did both walk round a bit and then drag that bag and that broken box out.'

Martin wasn't convinced. 'Well, let's get it out again and see what we can find.' He crawled to the very back of the space and reached his arm forward until he felt wood. 'Here, I'll pass it out to you.'

Piece by piece, he pulled out the broken crate, and then the canvas bag. Then he leant as far forward as he could, patting around and hoping nothing was lurking in there which might bite him, and felt something soft – more fabric? 'There's something else here.'

'There can't be.' Edwin knelt beside him.

'Well …' Martin grabbed a handful and dragged it out. 'What's this then?'

It was a rolled-up ball of some kind of cloth.

'It's too dark to see it properly in here,' said Edwin. 'Let's take everything outside.'

Once they got out into the light, Martin looked first at the pieces of the box and the bag. 'That's what you found the other day.'

'Yes.'

Martin rearranged some of the bits on the ground. 'Well, judging by the size of it, the crate wasn't all that big, and it would have fitted in the bag. So that maybe tallies with the idea of Brother Alexander bringing back "treasure" – it needn't have been of any great size. It could have been bags of gold or jewels or something.'

Edwin didn't look convinced. 'Perhaps.' He pointed at the thing Martin still held in his hand. 'But what's that? That definitely wasn't here the other day.'

'Are you sure? It was right at the back behind the other stuff.'

'I'm sure. I went in as far as I could and felt around on the ground, and it was empty after we'd got the rest of it out.'

Martin put it down on the ground and knelt to unroll it. It was wool, just a length of unbleached woven wool. No, wait, there was stitching there. It wasn't just a length – it was a shape which was sewn together out of several pieces, and another separate bit. He stretched it out and then sat back in shock, for there was no doubt that what they were looking at was a white robe and hood, the clothing of a choir monk.

Chapter Ten

Edwin looked at the robe on the ground before him. 'Do you know what this means?'

'Yes, or at least, I think so.'

'You do?'

'Well, surely the explanation is that one of the monks has run away. He's come here, changed out of his robes into something else, and made off. And if he was here, in this cave, then he must know something about Brother Alexander, so he's likely to be the man who killed him. So all we have to do is track him down and catch him!'

Martin started to stand and Edwin admired his confidence, his enthusiasm; he looked like he would happily chase after his missing man right now, on foot and with no idea where he was going. 'Wait, wait.' He waved his arm and Martin sat back down.

'What?'

'There is another explanation.'

'Is there?'

'Yes.' Edwin sighed. 'And it's not one I like, but I think it's more probable.'

'What?'

'Well, what if someone wasn't trying to get out of the abbey? What if they were trying to get in?'

Martin looked puzzled. 'Why would anyone want to do that?'

'We've both said, over and over again, how difficult it is to tell one monk from another in their robes. And it's especially difficult when they've got their hoods up. So, if you wanted to get in the abbey and walk around unnoticed, all you'd really need to do is to put on a robe and put the hood up, and nobody would give you a second glance.' He looked at Martin who was showing glimmerings of understanding. 'It wouldn't work in the long term, of course, as they'd soon notice an imposter at night, or even at one of the services, but if you wanted to slip in when the place was busy, do something and then slip out again, you could.'

Martin spoke slowly. 'And if the thing you wanted to do was to murder one of the brothers …'

Edwin nodded. 'Especially when they were all sat at their reading – sixty or so of them, all in their robes. They'd notice if somebody dressed differently came in, but who would pay attention to another white monk in the cloister?'

Martin whistled. 'So that's how it was done?'

'It's a possibility. But the main thing,' said Edwin, his heart becoming heavier by the moment, 'is that it could have been anyone. There I was just thinking that we'd narrowed it down to the choir monks, but with this robe our pool of potential killers has just widened to include all the lay brothers, the visitors, and every man in the village.'

'Oh.'

'Yes, quite. Look, I need to think. Let's take all this back to the abbey and then I'll find somewhere to sit for a while, while I try to get a few things straight and work on what we're going to do next.'

'All right.' Martin began to gather the broken pieces of the box together. He put them in the bag, and then rolled up the robe and hood and stowed them on top. The bag was old and full of holes, and Edwin wondered whether it would survive its loaded journey.

It was early evening by the time they reached the abbey again, and the monks and lay brothers were returning from their afternoon's labours. Edwin asked Martin to take the bag and store it in the guesthouse for now. He himself needed to find a quiet space in which to think: he first considered the church but then realised that the brothers would soon be on their way in for vespers. But that in itself gave him an idea, so he wound his way around the precinct until he came to Brother Helias's office.

This was as much an atmosphere of home as he was likely to get, so he placed a stool against the wall and leaned back. He could be fairly confident of having the place to himself almost until dusk, for the monks would go from vespers to their evening meal and then probably straight to compline without returning to their places of work. And if Brother Helias should by any chance come back in between, Edwin would be able to explain why he was there. The cellarer wouldn't mind.

Edwin breathed in the scent of spices and closed his eyes.

He tried to visualise the figure of Brother Alexander, but the nearest he could get was a tall, shadowy figure in a white robe, whose face he could not see. Who would want to kill you? thought Edwin, but the figure did not speak. So, who might have wanted the master of the lay brothers dead? The novice Benedict was critical of his previous involvement with heathen masters and teachers – fanatical, even. And his own behaviour showed him to be unstable. But would this have led him to murder a brother, a professed monk? Surely even he could see that this would be against the Rule of the Order he so desperately wanted to join, against the will of God, and that it would send him to hell. Or was he so far gone in his hatred that he didn't care? Did he see Brother Alexander as a heathen himself, and thus worthy only of death, as Martin had noted so dismissively?

Edwin considered the case against Benedict and put him to one side for a moment. He would not have needed to use a borrowed white robe, for he wore one already. Who else from outside the ranks of the choir monks needed to be considered? There was the question, which was only a question at the moment, of whether some form of swindling had been going on at the lay brothers' grange with regard to the wool. That would bring into question both the choir monk who worked there – and Edwin didn't know who that was at the moment – and also the lay brothers, particularly the one Martin had met, Sinnulph. Edwin would need to go there for himself to see if he could pick up on anything else. Suppose Brother Alexander had found out that the abbey was being defrauded and had threatened to tell the abbot. One of the lay brothers could have dressed himself in the robe and murdered him to stop him talking.

But how would the lay brother know about the cave in the cliffs? He wouldn't likely be wandering around there when he had work to do at the grange, which was several miles away, and it was hard to see how he might have found it by accident for it was so well hidden. The only people who knew about its location were Brother Alexander himself, anyone he might have told about it, and the hermit Anabilia – although she didn't know of its actual existence, only that Brother Alexander had somehow 'disappeared'.

Edwin jumped as a bolt of wakefulness shot through him. Had he been dozing off in the quiet comfort of the office? What was it that had alerted him? Oh yes, there was one other who could have known of the cave: Sir Philip, the knight who had been awake and who Edwin thought had been listening when he and Martin were talking during the night. If he had learned of the cave he could have gone out there while Edwin and Martin were busy with other matters, for it had been many hours in the time between their whispered conversation and their trip out to the woods. Perhaps Sir Philip had murdered Brother Alexander and now sought to hide the means by which he had done it. But then why would he stay around? Surely if he had murdered a monk his safest course of action would be to get away as quickly as possible afterwards. And why would a knight want to murder a monk anyway? And what had that odd remark to Brother Helias meant? None of this made sense. However, he would keep it at the back of his mind in case it started to become clearer later on.

Brother Alexander had brought back treasure when he returned from the Moorish lands. But what was this treasure and who might want it? Monks were sworn to have no possessions, so Brother Alexander must have kept it against the rules, which was why he had hidden it. But what good would gold be if he could not spend it? And therefore what good would it do any of the other monks to have it? The monastery was prosperous, and although Edwin guessed that the abbot might not actually turn down any additional wealth which came his way, he was fairly sure he wouldn't kill for it. He was a good man. And besides, if he had killed one of his monks, he would hardly have sent for Edwin, would he?

So had someone else crept into that cave and stolen the treasure? And had they done so before or after they killed Brother Alexander? He could have been murdered to stop him alerting anyone to the theft – although that would put him in an awkward position as he would have to explain why he had the treasure in the first place. So perhaps he had been killed by someone before the theft. If so then that someone had planned everything carefully: stealing a robe, sneaking into the abbey, murdering a monk in front of his brothers, leaving again, going to the cave, stealing the treasure and leaving the robe. No, wait, not leaving the robe, for that had not been done until later.

Edwin's eyes were heavy and his head nodded towards his chest. Something important was nagging at the back of his mind. He'd just thought of it a moment ago; what was it? He searched … oh yes, that was it. Someone else might know the location of the cave if Brother Alexander had told him about it. And Brother Alexander spoke most often to Brother Richard. But the robe had certainly been hidden there in between Edwin's two visits, for he was as sure as he could be that it had not been there the first time. And that meant that Brother Richard could not have hidden it there, for he was confined to the infirmary with a condition that was certainly not faked. Edwin wished he could speak to him again, but there seemed little hope of that, and he did not wish to cause the ill man any further pain, for he had seemed genuinely upset when he heard of Brother Alexander's death.

But now the figure of Brother Alexander was stepping forward out of the shadows. As Edwin watched, he pulled back his hood. Edwin shrank back in horror, for the face was dead, the skin dark and rotting around the empty eye sockets and the bared teeth. Then the figure reached behind it and pulled out a bloody knife, holding it out, dripping, as it advanced on Edwin, crying out for revenge …

Edwin woke up. His heart was pounding so hard that he could feel it in his mouth, and he looked around the office in horror. But there was no ghost, no corpse, no blood. He was alone. He was haunted. He needed to get more sleep.

He opened his dry mouth and stretched his stiff arms. He sat for a few moments before attempting to stand. And on top of all this, there was the abbot's question to him – *have you ever considered taking the cowl?* He couldn't give that proper thought at this point in time, but now that the question had been asked, now that it was a real possibility, it was going to weigh on him until he made a decision one way or another. For what was there for him in the outside world? A lifetime of being sent by the earl on difficult and dangerous missions, until the inevitable happened and one of them ended up killing him.

He was tired. But he was also hungry, so he stood to make his weary way back to the guesthouse. As he left the cellarer's office he heard a noise behind him and turned, in case he hadn't shut the door properly – just in time to see the edge of a white robe disappearing inside.

He should have ignored it and walked on, but some prickling of his neck, something about the way the man had moved into the building, made him stop. Perhaps it wasn't Brother Helias? But what would anyone else be doing there?

Edwin concealed himself in the shadow between two other buildings and watched the office. No light was lit within, but there was still enough to see by in the dusk, so it would be unlikely that anyone would light a candle or rush if he was only going to be inside for a few moments. As indeed appeared to be the case: after a very short while Edwin saw the monk leave the building again, and he cursed himself for his overactive imagination – it was the young brother who was the cellarer's assistant, and he was carrying a piece of parchment and a small sack. No doubt the kitchen had run out of something and he had been sent to fetch it and account for it on a list. Kitchen. Food. Yes. He made his way to the guesthouse.

———•———

Martin dumped the bag on the floor of the guesthouse in between his bed and Edwin's. Nobody should need to walk past it, for theirs were the last two berths at the end of the room, but it looked a bit out of place and might arouse curiosity. Martin scanned around him for possibilities, and then picked up Edwin's cloak. He draped it over the bag and kicked it all as close to Edwin's bed as possible. It wasn't hidden, but a casual observer might just think it was travelling luggage stacked untidily.

He stretched. The ceiling of the guesthouse wasn't all that high and his fingertips brushed the rafters. Lord, when were they going to get *out* of here? He'd never felt so confined.

It wasn't time for the evening meal yet, and he wasn't about to stay cooped up in here any longer than he had to. He couldn't really leave the precinct again, either, but he could head over to the stables and check on the horses, which hadn't been ridden today. He cheered himself at the thought that he'd have a good excuse to get out somewhere tomorrow as they'd need some exercise.

The sun's rays were slanting in through the open stable door, illuminating the dust in the air and the neat rows of stalls. The mute half-witted lay brother was just coming out of the one which contained Sir Philip's horse, and he stood back with a bow as Martin pushed past him. Martin looked suspiciously at all three of his animals, but had to admit – grudgingly – that they were being well cared for and that the place was clean and tidy. He doubted even that Arnulf, the long-serving stablemaster at Conisbrough, would have been able to find fault with anything. Not that he wouldn't try, of course.

Martin stood for a while with his courser, glancing idly over the barrier at Sir Philip's horse, and was still there when the knight himself came in. He cut off Martin's greeting with a curt nod which clearly indicated that he should mind his own business and Martin turned away. As he unnecessarily brushed the coat of Edwin's palfrey he reflected that Edwin had been right – as usual – when he pointed out that Sir Philip probably wasn't well off. Now he'd had a closer chance to look at it, he could see that the horse, a courser no better than his own, was getting on a bit and wasn't in very good condition. Except —

'You there!' Sir Philip was addressing the lay brother, who looked up enquiringly from the stall on the other side of the knight. 'Get me some hot water so I can replace this poultice.'

The lay brother bowed and left the stable in silence, but not before Martin had seen him give a very sharp glance indeed at the knight.

Martin didn't attempt to engage in any further conversation with Sir Philip. Instead he concentrated on the smooth, even strokes of his brush as he contemplated two things. The first was that perhaps the lay brother wasn't as half-witted as he might seem. And the second was that, from what he had seen, Martin was as certain as he could be that Sir Philip's horse was not lame.

———◆———

Brother Amandus was his usual garrulous self as he ladled out bowls of food for his four guests. Edwin wondered how often he had the same people staying for so long – surely most of the men who stayed here would only be doing so for one night. He ate to try and give himself some strength and even mustered the energy to poke a thoughtful-looking Martin in the ribs. 'Never mind. You'll soon be back at the lord earl's hall and eating as much meat as you can stomach.'

Martin stopped with his spoon halfway to his mouth. 'Why? Have you found something?'

Was it Edwin's imagination or did both the other men at the table stiffen slightly?

'Oh, no – nothing in particular, not since I saw you earlier. I just meant that you'll be back within a few days whatever happens.'

Martin grunted and continued with his meal. Edwin finished his, and then pushed a piece of bread around the bowl for no reason. Nothing was getting any clearer. Just the opposite, in fact: the more he went on, the more confused he was getting. He needed something. He needed a sign.

Brother Amandus had been speaking with someone at the guesthouse door, and now he came over to Edwin. 'Pardon me for interrupting, my son, but I have a message for you.'

Edwin's curiosity was aroused. 'For me?'

'Yes. You were showing a particular interest in Brother Richard, I believe?'

'Yes, that's right. Is he recovering?'

Brother Amandus shook his head and spoke sadly. 'I'm afraid not. A message has just come to say that he is dying, so the brethren are summoned to his bedside to pray. Brother Durand said that as you had spoken with him so recently, you might want to be there as well.'

Edwin put down the piece of bread and rose. 'Of course, Brother.' He looked at Martin, who was also half out of his seat, and put a hand on his shoulder. 'It's all right, you don't need to come. You've never met Brother Richard, and anyway I don't want Brother Durand getting upset with you again. Why don't you stay here and talk?' He hoped that Martin would guess the implication of the slight emphasis on that last word, and draw the other guests into conversation to see if he could find out anything further about them. Martin had been giving him strange looks since he came in, anyway, but hadn't said anything. He must make time to catch up properly. But first, he had to go to a deathbed.

Edwin sighed and wiped his hands on his tunic before belatedly realising there was a cloth on the table exactly for that purpose. Oh, never mind. He didn't have time right now to be worried about what others thought of his manners. He followed Brother Amandus out of the guesthouse and around towards the infirmary, where a line of other monks was entering. The guestmaster talked without ceasing as they crossed the precinct, telling him all about the elaborate-sounding rituals they went through every time a brother lay dying and for once Edwin wished he would just shut up. He rubbed his eyes and felt grateful when Brother Amandus fell silent as they reached the door.

Edwin crept quietly towards the end of the infirmary, conscious that all the other monks were silent. The sick man, head still grotesquely swollen, lay prone, his skin pale and waxy. Candles had been set around the head of the bed and the screen moved out of the way so that there was more room. The abbot, the prior and some fifty or so other monks – all the ones who weren't either too infirm themselves or too far away to be summoned, guessed Edwin – were gathered around the bed, kneeling, heads bowed. They began to chant a prayer. He hesitated.

Brother Durand saw him and beckoned him over. 'We are praying to Our Lady, patron of our abbey, and to St Apollonia, patron of those who suffer from toothache. Please, join us. Brother Richard seemed to know you were there when you visited before, and that is the last time he seemed to be in control of his wits.'

Edwin dredged his memory for those long-ago lessons with the village priest. St Apollonia ... she had been martyred by having all her teeth pulled out with pincers, one by one, before being beheaded. If any of the saints in heaven could sympathise with Brother Richard's plight, she could. He knelt tentatively by the edge of the pushed-back screen, behind the monks, and looked at the abbot; when he received a nod he began to pray. He drove all other thoughts out of his mind and concentrated on the plight of the agonised and dying man. Please, St Apollonia, you must have suffered terribly, could you not intercede with the Lord to ask Him to save Brother Richard from this terrible fate?

Brother Richard opened his eyes and gave a groan, which rose in pitch to a wail. As Edwin watched, the left side of his throat, hugely distended, started to crack. Then, suddenly, as though it had been pricked by an awl, it burst and a mass of foul-smelling discharge poured out. The monks exclaimed and jumped back, all except for the abbot who raised his hands and his face to the heavens. 'A miracle!'

Edwin looked from the ecstatic abbot to the man in the bed. The swelling was subsiding rapidly, his eyes, nose and mouth reappearing. Edwin's legs felt wobbly, and he didn't think he'd be able to rise off his knees if he tried. He had seen the mercy of the Lord.

Abbot Reginald and the monks were raising their voices in a hymn of thanks and praise. Then the abbot looked directly at Edwin. 'A miracle indeed. God shows us His grace and delivers our brother from his suffering. And He does so the instant you begin praying. Today you have been the instrument of the Lord.'

Edwin's legs were still shaking, but he scrabbled backwards in panic and managed to get to his feet. 'I ... er ... I ...'

He turned and fled.

Once he got back to the guesthouse he ran straight past the others, still sitting at the table, ignoring their looks and questions. He tried to stop his fingers shaking long enough to remove his boots, and then got into bed and pulled the blanket over his head. *Today you have been the instrument of the Lord.* That hadn't really happened, had it? He had prayed and Brother Richard had experienced a spectacular recovery.

He heard the sounds of surprise from the others at the table, but thank the Lord nobody came over. Martin would know he wanted to be on his own. It was hot and airless under the blanket, but to put his head out of it again would mean re-joining the world, and he wanted to be apart from the world a little longer. He shifted the blanket to make a space for air to enter, making sure it was on the side which faced away from the table so nobody would notice.

He heard the sound of Brother Amandus returning, his exclamations to the others about the miracle he had witnessed, and how it had come about. He heard Aylwin and Sir Philip saying they would go out for some air before they retired, and then them leaving. He heard Brother Amandus clearing the dishes and cups from the table. He heard Martin getting into his bed, and the creaking noise of the wooden frame as he did so.

What he did not hear was the voice of the Lord, telling him what to do next. He closed his eyes.

———•———

The following morning Edwin staggered bleary-eyed out of the guesthouse. Should he have told Martin where he was going? He couldn't think straight. But Martin was asleep and he was only going out to clear his head for a while – he'd be back before Martin woke up. It was very early. The choir monks were probably up at some service or other, but the rest of the precinct had that first-thing-in-the-morning feel that he had sometimes encountered in the ward at Conisbrough when he'd arrived before everyone else was awake. He could hear birdsong, and the smell of baking bread wafted across from somewhere. The slight chill of the breeze helped him to wake and he wandered over to the footbridge which crossed the beck dividing the precinct from the outer court with its gardens and orchards. He leaned on the rail and listened to the birds and the sound of the water. He stared across at the outer court, the fishponds, the mill, and allowed his eyes to close.

After a while, he realised that the water didn't sound right. He opened his eyes. Yes – instead of a kind of regular flowing and gurgling noise, there was a lot of splashing. Edwin looked over the upstream side of the bridge: the water was streaming down the beck and under the bridge as it should. He moved to the other side: the water was coming out much less fast than he would expect – a little more than a trickle, but nothing like the flow that was going in. There was a splashing noise coming from underneath, so he knelt down and leaned forward, tipping his head as far under the bridge as he could. There was something there – some object was in the water, blocking the stream. The incoming flow was hitting it, which was what the noise was, but very little was getting past it. Soon the water would back up around it and cause an overflow, which would be immediately noticeable, but right now you would really only notice if you were standing on the bridge.

Edwin moved to the bank and considered his options. There wasn't really much point in finding or waking anyone else until he knew what it was under the bridge – if it turned out to be a dead cat then he'd feel rather foolish if he'd caused an alarm. He sat down, took off his boots and hose and rolled up his linen braies.

The water was chilly, much colder than he'd expected it to be during such a warm season. Still, it was bearable. He was downstream of the bridge so the current of water around his legs was minimal, not much more than knee-deep, and he had no problem wading through it. He reached the bridge, crouched, held on to the wooden planking just in case, and stretched one arm underneath. His fingers touched something – which he was fairly certain wasn't a dead cat – but he couldn't shift it. Taking a firmer grip on the planking he strained as far forward as he could and managed to grasp the object more firmly. He braced himself and pulled as hard as he could, and it came towards him.

Of course, what he hadn't considered was that releasing the object would also unblock the beck, and a large wave of freezing water hit him in the face and chest. Gasping and clutching the object to him, he held on to the bridge until the first wave had passed, and then waded towards the bank. As he was shaking the water out of his eyes and hair he felt himself grabbed by the shoulder of his tunic and hauled out on to dry ground.

Martin was standing over him. 'What in the Lord's name are you doing? I can't leave you on your own for one paternoster, can I?'

Edwin spluttered and regained his footing. 'I'm fine. I'm sorry, I didn't mean to worry you – I just came out for some air and I noticed that the water wasn't right, and …'

'What? Anyway, never mind that now. Come back inside and dry off. What's that you have there?'

Edwin's teeth were chattering. 'I have no idea. Something very wet.'

'Well, we can look at it once you're dry. Come.' Martin picked up Edwin's discarded boots and hose and propelled him back towards the guesthouse.

The movement helped Edwin to warm up, and by the time he was back inside he felt a little recovered. The other two guests were still in bed so he stripped off his sodden tunic and shirt as quietly as he could, found the spare in his pack, and put his dry hose back on. Then he sat on the edge of the bed and looked at the dripping object.

It was a book – or, at least, not a whole book but the parchment leaves from inside it. The pages were so sodden and stuck together that it was impossible to see what the contents might have been, and Edwin regarded it helplessly.

Martin leaned over his shoulder. 'Maybe if we can dry it out …?'

'I'm not sure how much that will help – look, the ink has run – but it can't do any harm.' A shaft of sun was coming in through the window so Edwin placed the pages on the floor directly in the light. It was the best he could do.

Aylwin and Sir Philip were now rising, and Brother Amandus bustled in with some bread and ale. He looked at Edwin and shook his head in disbelief. 'Remarkable. I have heard from Brother Durand that Brother Richard is further recovered this morning after a night's sleep, and he seems certain to live and to regain his health. A miracle! *Gaudete*, indeed.'

In the excitement of his find and his dousing Edwin had almost forgotten about the events of last night, but now it all came crashing back in on him. Was this the sign he had been waiting for, the sign that told him that he should stay here and live his life in peace and study, rather than returning to the earl and his dangerous existence there? He sighed and tried to force down a piece of bread.

Once Aylwin and Sir Philip had left the guesthouse – and exactly how long were they going to stay here, anyway? – and Martin had gone to check the horses, Edwin went back to the pages. There was a puddle of water around them on the floor, and most of the leaves were still very wet, but the ones which had been on the top in the direct sunlight were a little drier. The parchment was wavy and the ink smeared, but maybe there was hope of finding out something. Edwin carried it over to the table.

He couldn't make any sense of it. What he could see, despite the condition, was that the pages had not come from a fine illuminated volume – it was just parchment and ink, no traces of paint or colour. And if there had been some, surely he would have seen the remains of it even after it had been in the water. No, it was just writing. But it seemed to be going in a funny direction – he turned the pages round and round, in case he was holding it the wrong way up – and the ink had run so much that he just couldn't read anything; it all just looked like squiggles. He pushed it away from him and sighed.

He was alerted by a noise behind him, and he tried to put his arms around the pages so they couldn't be seen. It was futile, of course – it was perfectly obvious what was on the table in front of him.

It was Aylwin, who walked over to his bed and was rummaging in his bag. 'I forgot my hat.' He retrieved it and placed it on his head, turning to leave. As he did so, his eyes fell on the pages and he walked up to the table. 'I didn't know you were interested in wool.'

'What?'

Aylwin gestured at the pages, currently spreading a damp patch on the table. 'It's a wool ledger. Not in very good condition, clearly – where on earth did you find it?' He didn't seem to expect an answer, but instead leaned forward over it.

'How can you tell?'

'Well, look here – you can't read it very well because the ink is smeared, but this is how you arrange the figures in columns, with the grade of wool, the weight and the price.'

Edwin stared, and as he did so, some of the mess on the page seemed to become clearer. That was why the writing had seemed the wrong way up – because it was in columns and not in long lines across the page. He looked up at the merchant standing over him. If Aylwin had had something to do with dubious wool deals, or with hiding this ledger, surely he would not be standing there so brazenly looking at it; he would not have volunteered to Edwin the information about what it was, he would look a bit … guiltier?

Edwin decided to take a chance. 'If you were to look through this ledger – when it's dried out, I mean – would you be able to tell whether there was anything wrong with it?'

Aylwin frowned. 'Wrong with it? What are you suggesting?'

Edwin should have known that a man didn't become a respected and prosperous merchant without being intelligent. 'Nothing, nothing. I just thought that maybe someone had thrown it away because the numbers were wrong, or maybe it's really old and they don't need it any more.' That sounded feeble, even to him, for nobody would throw parchment away – they would scrape it clean and use it again and again, until it eventually wore right through.

Aylwin was looking doubtful. 'It's very wet and difficult to read, I grant you, but I'm willing to have a try if you like. I'm still waiting for the lord abbot to tell me who I'm supposed to talk to, so I'm only waiting around in the meantime. Please God they'll appoint a new master of the lay brothers soon.' He sat down on the bench next to Edwin.

There was no point in them both looking at it. 'Thank you, Master Aylwin. I'm very grateful to you. I'll leave you to it as I have something else to attend to, but perhaps we may speak later?'

The merchant grunted, already engrossed in trying to make sense of the ink splatters in front of him. Edwin made his way out of the guesthouse to find Martin, because one thing was certain – he needed to go to the lay brothers' range.

Chapter Eleven

Martin was at the stables, waving his arms around at one of the bearded lay brothers, a burly fellow Edwin had seen before … ah yes, he was the one who had delivered that message to Prior Henry while Edwin had been observing the *lectio divina*. The man was standing in silence with his head bowed, making no effort to reply to Martin.

Edwin attracted Martin's attention and he stalked over. 'These lay brothers are from the peasantry, and I'm just not sure they know how to look after fine horses properly.'

'Why? What's wrong with ours?'

'Well, nothing.' Edwin looked at him and raised his eyebrows. Martin was virtually spluttering and he continued, much more voluble than Edwin had ever seen him. 'But they're much better quality than the mules and suchlike that they keep here normally. And that fellow just won't talk to me when I ask him in detail about their feed. Yesterday I was just starting to think that he … but anyway, I've told him that the abbot said they were all allowed to speak with us, but he just stands there. I think he must be simple.'

Edwin had no idea what Martin was talking about. 'If there's nothing wrong with the horses, they must be doing something right. Anyway, I have news.'

'News that can get us out of here all the sooner, I hope.'

Ah. So that was it. Edwin actually felt quite comfortable within the enclosing walls of the abbey, but he had the feeling it was driving Martin mad. He kept his tone mild. 'Maybe not completely out, not today, but we do need to go out to the lay brothers' range which you visited the other day. I want to talk to the lay brother – Sinnulph, was it? – that you spoke to.' He saw Martin making a move towards the stables. 'I suppose it's too far to walk?'

Martin looked at him as though he'd just suggested flying. 'Walk? When we have horses? Don't be ridiculous. I'll saddle them up now.' Looking a bit happier, he hurried off into the stables.

Edwin sighed. He supposed he was going to have to get used to riding on horseback, if he was going to continue in the earl's service. Or maybe he wouldn't need to, if he stayed here. But that would mean facing down the lord earl, looking him in the eye and asking to be released from his service, only weeks after being formally accepted as his man. Edwin winced at the thought. And anyway, didn't he owe duty to the earl above and beyond that? The earl, who trusted him, who had raised him up? Edwin expelled a long breath. It looked impossible whichever way he looked at it.

Martin led the horses out of the gatehouse and Edwin heaved himself up on to the back of the one he'd ridden from Conisbrough. Would he ever be comfortable in the saddle? 'How far is it?'

'About four miles. Won't take long. Come on!' And Martin was off.

Four miles might not seem long to Martin, but Edwin was quite glad to get down off the horse and hand the reins to a waiting lay brother once they arrived at the grange. Martin, as ever, swung down easily and looked no worse for wear, and Edwin was momentarily jealous.

A second bearded lay brother was approaching, and he greeted Martin. '*Benedicte*. And this must be your companion?'

Martin shoved Edwin forward. 'Yes, this is Edwin. I told him about my trip here the other day, and he said he'd like to come out and see for himself, to meet you. Edwin, this is Brother Sinnulph.'

'To meet me?' The brother sounded surprised, but Edwin detected a hint of fear underneath. Had he been expecting someone to come here and question him?

Edwin didn't want to make him hostile before he'd even started. 'Not just you, Brother, although I hear you gave Martin something of a lesson on wool production which I'd like to hear about. No, I'd like to talk to all of you, particularly about anything you might remember about Brother Alexander, anything he might have said or done in the last few weeks which you didn't think was important, but which might help me if I were to hear it.'

Brother Sinnulph relaxed a little, and Edwin tried to keep his voice innocent. 'I'd also like to talk to the choir monk who comes here to do your accounts. Is he here? Brother … I'm sorry, I don't even know his name, but Martin met him here before.'

'That would be Brother Eugenius. He doesn't work here all the time, he just comes out two afternoons a week because it's part of his other duties. He'll be here about mid-afternoon today, if you can stay that long.'

Was he trying to get rid of them? Edwin exchanged a glance with Martin. 'That will be fine. Perhaps I could speak with you and then the other brothers one at a time while we wait for him?' It was heading for noon, so they could surely kill some time.

'Of course. Please, come this way.' Brother Sinnulph led them into a building where there were two long tables with benches down each side, and bade them sit. He fetched them some ale. 'We only eat twice a day, so there is no meal prepared, but I could find you something if …?'

'Thank you, we have already …' Edwin looked at Martin. 'Why yes, anything you might be able to provide would be most welcome. Some bread, perhaps?' Martin looked unenthusiastic, but what did he expect them to come up with?

Brother Sinnulph gestured to another brother and then took a seat on the opposite side of the table. 'Well then, let us begin. You wish to talk of Brother Alexander?'

Edwin started with a few general questions, to try and put him at his ease – how many days a week did the master of the lay brothers visit, what were his duties, and so on. He was aware that Sinnulph had already told all this to Martin, and from what Edwin could gather he gave no answers now that differed from what he had said before. A plate of bread arrived with some hard cheese and a couple of onions. Martin rolled his eyes but nevertheless tucked in while Edwin crumbled some bread and ate a little out of politeness.

He turned the conversation to more personal matters. 'So, are you a local man yourself?'

Brother Sinnulph nodded. 'Born and bred on the Maltby manor here. And you must be local yourself, from your voice?'

'Yes, I'm from Conisbrough. My father was the bailiff there for many years.'

The lay brother's face creased into a smile. 'You're never Godric's son? Godric that they called the Weaver?'

Surprised, Edwin put down the bread he had been toying with. 'Yes, yes I am. Did you know my father?'

'Aye, and a fine man he was too. Sorry, lad, I should have said right off that I was sorry to hear that he was dead. He was a good man, and all knew it.'

'Thank you.' Edwin was surprised to find out that he did not feel overwhelmed at the mention of Father's death. Sad, yes, but he didn't want to run away and cry. He could continue in an even tone of voice. 'Of course, if you're from Maltby you might have seen him when he went out there every quarter.'

'That's right. And a fair man he was too. Courteous to all, even villeins like my father, listened to all, spoke the truth, never took more than he was due. Like I said, a fine man. There aren't many of them around. Well, well, Godric's son, here and all grown up.'

Edwin began to feel more at his ease. 'So, your father was a villein on Lord Richard's estate here at Maltby? How did you come to join the Order?'

'Ah, too many brothers, that was my problem. Or it was back then, anyway.' A shadow crossed his face but it was gone before Edwin could interpret it. 'That was all right when it came to giving service on the lord's land, for we could share it about, but our own holding wasn't enough to support us all. My eldest brother married and had children of his own, but there was no chance for the rest of us, so I thought, if I'm not going to marry and have a family anyway, why not try for a lay brother? The work is pretty much the same and you get a good meal every day – two in the summer – not to mention getting closer to God. Even such as I might go to heaven if I work hard enough.'

Martin pushed away the empty plate and leaned forward. 'So all the lay brothers come from the local peasantry, do they?'

'Most of them, yes. Like I said, the work isn't too different and we get fed regardless of what the harvest is like. In return we take vows, the same as the choir monks, so we're part of the abbey and not allowed to marry or have children.'

Martin nodded, and Edwin wondered what he was driving at.

'So, most of them are local and would know their way around?'

Oh well done, thought Edwin, he's seeing if anyone might know about the cave.

'Yes, I suppose so, from when they were running around as lads. Although even as lads we all had plenty of work to do.'

Martin's next question was forestalled as Brother Sinnulph continued in a thoughtful tone.

'Of course, that's not quite true. Most come from the peasantry, but not all. Take Brother Guy.'

Edwin was confused. 'Brother Guy?'

'A lay brother at the abbey. Great burly fellow, bigger beard than most. Works a lot with the horses.'

'Oh yes. I saw him and you've spoken to him a few times, haven't you, Martin? Was that him you were talking to when I arrived at the stables this morning?' Edwin wondered why Martin had started to look uneasy.

'Yes, yes I have. What about him?'

'Well, before he joined the Order he was a knight, quite a famous one if the tales are true. He travelled to the Holy Land a long time ago with old King Richard's crusade, and then again to Constantinople about fifteen years ago. He was a great warrior.'

Martin looked like he was going to be sick. 'Really?'

Brother Sinnulph was getting into his storytelling. 'Oh yes. He was a lord, a man of renown. Of course, some men do come back from such campaigns and then wish to take the cowl. But they mainly become choir monks – more suited to their rank, you see. Brother Guy, now, I remember the day he arrived. He begged entry, but he had a great many sins on his conscience so he wished to demonstrate his humility before the Lord by becoming a lay brother.'

'He did?'

'Of course my lord abbot – Abbot Osmund it was then – tried to talk him out of it. But he was determined. And from that day to this he has never once spoken of his past, never shirked the heaviest or foulest duties. Most of the lay brothers take advantage of working in the fields or the granges to talk to each other, but not Brother Guy – he took a vow of complete silence and he sticks to it. He has never said what his sins were, but surely he's atoned for them by now.'

Edwin looked at Martin and felt he had to take back charge of the situation. He opened his mouth.

Sinnulph hadn't finished. 'He never speaks of his past life – well, he couldn't, could he – but sometimes, just sometimes, I wonder what stories he must have, what tales of kings and popes, battles and deeds, of the treasures of the East. He could probably tell stories every night for a month if he wanted to.'

Now *that* started Edwin's mind off a new and different path. 'Treasure? What sort of treasure?'

The lay brother shrugged. 'I don't know. Nothing particular. I just heard there was lots of treasure out in the East. I heard tell that the crusaders came back with some wonderful things. Gold and jewels and silk and suchlike.'

Edwin sat in silence. Martin still looked dumbstruck and also said nothing.

Brother Sinnulph looked from one to the other. 'So … if you've finished talking to me, I'll get back to my work, shall I? And send one of the other brothers to talk to you?'

Edwin recovered himself. 'Yes, thank you. That would be kind.'

He spent an hour or so talking to the other brothers but gained little of interest. Martin sat in stony silence throughout and Edwin wondered what in the Lord's name could be wrong with him. Eventually he sent the final lay brother out and leaned over to whisper. 'It must be nearly time for Brother Eugenius to arrive. Can you go out and wait for him? I don't want Brother Sinnulph to get the chance to talk to him first.'

Martin roused himself. 'What? Oh, yes, of course. I'll bring him straight in, and I'll give you a nod or a shake of my head to let you know if he was the one I saw here last time.'

Edwin wasn't waiting long before the doorway darkened and a monk stepped in. Because he had the sunlight behind him Edwin couldn't immediately see his face, but he could see that behind him Martin, a head taller, was nodding vigorously. So this was the man that Martin thought had been acting suspiciously with Brother Sinnulph.

The monk came further into the hall and was illuminated by light from one of the windows. Edwin saw his face, and suddenly several things fell into place. He stood to greet him.

'Brother Eugenius. I didn't realise your duties involved coming out here as well as assisting Brother Helias in the cellarer's office.'

The monk looked slightly bewildered. And maybe a little nervous?

Edwin bade him sit. 'Please, Brother, just a few questions before we leave you to get on with your duties.'

Brother Eugenius perched uncomfortably on the very edge of the bench. 'Yes?'

'Why are you and Brother Sinnulph stealing from the abbey?'

'What?' The monk tried to jump out of his seat but Martin's hand on his shoulder pushed him back down.

'I believe you heard me, Brother.'

The monk's face went red and sweat broke out on his forehead. 'I – er, I …' He twisted the sleeves of his habit in his hand but did not deny the accusation.

'He did it because I asked him to.' The voice was Sinnulph's as he entered the hall from outside. He sighed and sat down on the bench next to Brother Eugenius. 'We may as well tell him all, Brother, for he clearly knows some of it anyway.' He looked directly at Edwin. 'And if he truly is Godric Weaver's son, he'll listen to us.'

Brother Eugenius was almost in tears. 'It was out of charity … I didn't mean … oh, what will Father Abbot say?'

Edwin turned to Sinnulph. 'Perhaps you'd better tell me.'

The lay brother spread his arms. 'You heard me say I once had brothers. Not any more – they all died. And my sister's husband too, leaving her with four children and nobody to look after them. And I've taken my vows so I couldn't go back. What was she to do?'

'That's no exc—' Edwin waved Martin into silence.

'Your sister and her children were hungry.'

'Yes. The oldest boy is about twelve, so he couldn't do a man's full day at work. The holding got taken off them and they had to labour where they could to earn food.'

Edwin nodded. 'You felt responsible.'

'I did. And on top of that we had thieves, outlaws, around here earlier this year and they stole some of the stores.'

Edwin winced as he remembered his own dealings with the band of men who had terrorised the area for some weeks. 'I know. They've all been caught now, and hanged.'

'So I heard. But that didn't get the people back what they stole, and Lord Richard wasn't too sympathetic – said everyone still had to work in his fields and pay his rents regardless.'

Perhaps Sir Geoffrey ought to hear of this, for Lord Richard held his land from the earl, didn't he? Edwin had better check. It made no sense, even for a noble, to allow the villeins and workers to starve, for who would till his fields the following year? The family near Conisbrough who had suffered the most from the outlaws had been sent home with food and supplies when they came to break the news. He felt himself sympathising with Sinnulph, but he had to harden his heart to find out the truth.

'So what did you do?'

Sinnulph looked at Brother Eugenius and patted him on the shoulder. 'My sister's boy came here one day to tell me all. To start with I just gave him my food, off my plate, for I reckoned that was fairly mine to give. But how far was that going to go among five of them? So I took more bread, more vegetables, some grain, and handed them over.' His voice became weighted with guilt. 'I mean, here I was surrounded by good food, and how I could eat my two meals a day while she starved? It's not like she could take orders and join the abbey to do the same – or the children – so I did what I could.'

Brother Eugenius now broke in. 'I started to notice very small discrepancies in the accounts, of what we should have compared with what we actually had. I asked Brother Sinnulph about it and he confessed all. I should have put a stop to it – I should have —'

'You should have what, Brother? Allowed my sister to starve? And her children too?' Sinnulph turned to Edwin and his voice became urgent. 'The fault is mine, and mine alone. Brother Eugenius is young, he didn't know what to do and I persuaded him to keep quiet about it.'

'You threatened him?'

Sinnulph opened his mouth to deny it but then changed his mind. 'Yes. Yes, I threatened him. So no blame can attach to him.'

'He did not threaten me.' Brother Eugenius's voice was resigned. 'He is right that he persuaded me that it was the only way to save them, but he did not threaten me, and I will not have him confess to a sin he has not committed. I should have gone straight to Father Abbot, but I did not, and that I must confess.'

'So, when I saw you coming out of the cellarer's office last night, with a bag and a piece of parchment in your hand ...?'

Brother Eugenius looked shocked. 'You saw me? And I thought I had been so ... well, yes. *Mea culpa*. Obviously the stores at the abbey are in much greater quantity, so I thought I could make up what was missing here from there, and then rewrite my accounts before Brother Helias saw them.' He hung his head.

Edwin waited for the rest, but when it was not forthcoming he prodded further. 'And the wool?'

Brother Eugenius and Sinnulph exchanged a puzzled glance before the lay brother spoke. 'What wool?'

'The wool ledgers. Have you not been falsifying them?'

They both looked so utterly horrified that Edwin couldn't believe they were acting.

Brother Eugenius managed to splutter out a few words. 'Falsify the ledgers? Are you mad? Why, that would be ...' He tailed off into silence at the enormity of the thought.

Edwin was confused now. 'When Martin was here the other day and he mentioned Brother Alexander, he said you both looked worried.'

Sinnulph replied. 'Yes, but we were worried that he'd find out that a few bits of bread had gone missing, and he'd make us stop and my sister would starve. We would never tamper with the wool accounts.' His eyes opened wide as he grasped the severity of the implication. 'You … you thought we were falsifying the wool ledgers, to – what, to keep the money? And, dear Lord, you thought we might have killed Brother Alexander to stop him finding out?' He sagged back on the bench in shock.

Brother Eugenius had turned completely white. 'Dear Lord.' He crossed himself. 'I see now how committing one sin can lead to the suspicion of other sins. But we did not kill – I mean, the idea is impossible – how could we – dear Lord.'

This was not quite going the way Edwin had expected, but he pressed on. 'So, just to be clear. Did you, either of you, tear out some pages from a wool ledger and throw them in the beck at the abbey?'

They both looked totally confused and were shaking their heads. 'I did no such thing,' answered Sinnulph, 'and I'm sure Brother Eugenius didn't either.'

The monk shook his head. 'I also did not.'

There was silence for a moment. Edwin felt that everyone was looking at him. He needed to think fast. 'Right. This is what we are going to do. The two of you must, *must*, confess everything to the lord abbot. I will give you a day to do this, and if you have not told him by noon tomorrow then I will tell him myself. And I'm sure you realise it will sound better coming from you.'

They nodded.

'You must accept whatever punishment he metes out.'

They nodded again.

'You, Brother Eugenius, will also make a confession to Brother Helias. I have no doubt that he will eventually find something wrong with the accounts, and if you tell him before that happens then you will save him both from worry and from the suspicion that something much worse has happened.'

'Yes. I will do this. And I deserve whatever punishment comes my way.'

Sinnulph started to speak but Edwin held up his hand. 'And you will confess all of your part in this, and the influence you brought to bear on Brother Eugenius, but you will not exaggerate or confess to anything you have not done. The Lord will know, even if the abbot doesn't. And,' he drew a deep breath, 'you will ask the abbot to release you from your vows so that you may go back to your family.'

'He won't do that, surely?' Sinnulph asked in astonishment.

'Try him. You may be surprised. If you explain that you wish to go back to the outside world so that you can provide for your sister and her children, he might see that as a different way of serving God. And he may even speak with Lord Richard about your family's holding so that you have something to live off.'

Both of them were staring at him with desperate eyes, holding back tears and hanging on his every word. Another responsibility to add to the unbearable weight on his shoulders.

Edwin sighed. 'But none of this gets me any nearer to finding out what happened to Brother Alexander. If you can, please say a prayer for me.' He stood and beckoned Martin to follow him out, aware that he'd solved one problem only to create another.

Once Edwin felt the sunlight on his face he shook himself as if to get rid of the shadows. 'You've been very quiet.'

Martin shrugged. 'You seemed to be managing quite well without me.'

Edwin didn't push it. 'Anyway, you'll be pleased to know we have another ride ahead of us.'

'Where, back to the abbey?'

'And beyond. We may not have solved the mystery of the wool ledger or of Brother Alexander's death, but something Brother Sinnulph said has given me an idea on another subject. There's someone we need to talk to.'

Martin wondered whether, if he prayed hard enough, a hole in the ground would appear so he could bury himself in it. The man he'd told to stay away from his horse, the man he'd shouted at, called a peasant, treated as simple, was a knight. And not just a knight but a crusader, a great warrior who had travelled to the East with the famous King Richard; he had fought battles against the Saracens and won glorious renown. What had he been thinking as Martin spoke, treating him like dirt? Oh dear Lord.

He wasn't really paying attention to where they were going, so when he eventually looked up he found that they had gone past the abbey and its gatehouse and were now heading for the woods.

'Where are we going?'

'To see Anabilia, the hermit.'

'Why?'

Edwin grinned, unusual for him these days. 'You'll see.'

'All right. But stop here and we'll dismount. If we're going to go through all that undergrowth then we'll be better off on foot and leading the horses.'

Martin watched as Edwin got down – he couldn't really call it a dismount, not when he just pretty much fell off – and made sure the stirrups were shortened on both saddles. 'Can you manage leading your own horse? If not then I'll take both, but it might be easier going single file.'

'I can manage. I'll go slowly.'

They left the road and entered the forest. Martin stood uncertainly. 'Can you remember the way?'

Edwin also looked doubtful. 'Let me think. There was a little path which led off somewhere – is this it?' He pushed aside some branches.

'It could be. Yes, look – there's a footprint in that patch of soft ground there.' Martin placed his foot in the mark and it fitted perfectly. 'It's mine.'

They made their way through the undergrowth, stopping every so often to wonder whether this broken branch or that odd-shaped tree was a reminder that they had previously come this way. And then, quite suddenly, they found themselves in the clearing where the woman lived. The hovel was still there, the garden was still there, even the goat was still there, but the hermit was nowhere to be seen.

Martin took both sets of reins and tied them safely to a sturdy tree branch. He pointed to the roof of the dwelling. 'Smoke. She can't have gone far.'

'I'll try calling her. You stay there and try not to look too threatening.'

Martin stood and watched as Edwin put his head through the doorway and then went all round the hovel, calling Anabilia's name. 'We don't want to hurt you or trouble you – I just need to ask you something. Something important.'

There was silence.

Edwin tried again. 'I know that you didn't kill Brother Alexander. You're safe, but I really do need to talk to you.'

Martin was surprised. Did they know that? He didn't, but who knew what was going on in Edwin's mind?

'About what?' Martin's head shot round as he heard the old woman's voice, but he couldn't for the life of him work out which direction it was coming from.

'Please come out. We will not harm you, you have my word.'

'Your word? What good is that to me?' Martin put his hand on the hilt of his sword, still turning this way and that.

Edwin sighed and his face took on that sad look again. He made the sign of the cross in the air. 'I swear on the soul of my father, in his grave these two months past, that we will not harm you. Please, come out so we can talk.'

Anabilia appeared from the undergrowth, much closer to Martin than he would have thought possible, making him jump. He forced himself to let go of his sword. She was an old woman, in the Lord's name. What harm could she possibly do? But still he calculated the distance between them as she approached Edwin. If she tried to attack him, he could get there and stop her well before she could do any damage.

Edwin opened his arms wide. 'Shall we sit?'

She folded hers. 'No.'

'Very well. I just have one question to ask you, and please, you must tell me the truth before God.'

She inclined her head. 'Very well.'

'Was it you who hid the monk's habit in the cave?'

To say that Martin was thunderstruck would have been an understatement. How on earth had Edwin worked that out? His start of surprise had frightened the horses and he moved to calm them as he listened to the conversation in the clearing.

'Yes.'

Edwin nodded. 'I thought so.'

The woman's curiosity had been aroused. 'How did you know?' Now she indicated the space outside her home and the two of them sat down. Martin circled around the edge of the clearing, but quietly so as not to alarm her. He wanted to hear this.

Edwin settled himself. 'Earlier today someone pointed out that his sister could not join the abbey community. Because she is a woman, of course. Which led me to think of another woman who has dealings with the abbey, another woman who ranks herself in holiness along with the monks there … another woman who might have wanted to get inside the abbey buildings?'

She laughed, a dry, croaking sound. 'You're a sharp one, boy. So, why would I want to do that?'

'I haven't quite worked that part out yet. To see what it was like? To see if you really would want to live there if you were given the chance? Or … no —' he snapped his fingers. 'To save up the experience so you could offend them with it one day by letting them know that a woman had penetrated into their enclave?'

She was nodding. 'Very good. Them with their holier-than-thou attitudes, just because they are men. There's as much sin in there as there is in the outside world – they just hide it better and call it by different names.'

Edwin leaned forward. 'What did you see?'

Anabilia also bent forward, so that her face was very close to Edwin's. Martin tensed. 'Nothing that I'm about to tell you.' She sat back and Martin unclenched his fist.

Edwin appeared calm. 'Very well. But let us speak of when and how you entered. You could not have been in one of the services, or at Chapter, because someone would have noticed you.'

'That is true. I went in one afternoon while they were all at their labours. There are more of them milling around then, so I thought it would be easier.'

'And what did you do?'

She shrugged. 'Nothing, really. Just walked around, had a look at everything – oh, and I went in the choir of the church, where they don't allow women at all, just so I could say I'd been there if I ever needed to. Then I left again.'

'And the porter didn't notice?'

She snorted. 'Him? Blind, deaf and stupid.'

Edwin acknowledged her point. 'And how did you get the habit in the first place?'

'Oh, they might hate women and not allow them to soil their fine religion, but they don't mind giving them their dirty laundry to wash, do they? Oh no, that would be too menial for a monk to do, even a lay brother, so they must lower themselves to find a woman to do it.' She was becoming more agitated, but Martin didn't think Edwin was in any danger. It was not him she was railing at.

'So, you took this habit last wash day. And to start with you hid it here? In your cottage?'

She nodded.

'So why did you move it? When we first went to the cave it was not there, I'm sure of it. We only found it the second time.'

Anabilia began to look more uncomfortable. 'I was afraid.'

'Afraid? Of whom? Of us?'

Anabilia looked directly at Martin, and he realised that she had known all along that he was there. 'When armed men come visiting, they don't often stop to ask what's what or who's done what. They just kill, burn and move on.' Her eyes bored into him, and it was he who looked away first.

Edwin was continuing. 'So, you were afraid of us, afraid we'd come back and find out about the stolen habit and about your visit. There's not much hiding place in your cottage, so you decided to move it elsewhere.'

She nodded. 'I didn't know about the cave until the day I took you there. All I'd ever seen was Brother Alexander disappearing several times after he'd been to visit me, and once on a moonlit night last week. But when I saw you going back and forth into it and calling to each other, I decided to go and look, so I waited until you were gone and then went to have a look myself. There was nothing there and Brother Alexander was dead by then, so I thought it was as good a hiding place as any. How was I to know you were going to come back?'

There was silence for a few moments.

'So, you're going to tell the abbot about this, are you? So he'll find an excuse to stop my corrody, throw me out to starve?'

Edwin shook his head. 'No.'

She looked surprised. 'No? And what's in it for you, this keeping silent?'

His voice was innocent. 'Does there have to be something in it for me?'

Even Martin wasn't fooled by that, so he wasn't surprised when the sharp old woman snorted. 'Just tell me what you want, boy, and have done with it. I have little enough to give you.'

'Your prayers for my success, perhaps. Oh, and tell me what you saw while you were in the abbey.'

Her eyes narrowed. 'All right.' She leaned forward again and whispered in his ear for some moments.

Edwin sat back with a slight smile on his face. 'Thank you. That knowledge may come in useful.'

She started to rise. 'All knowledge is precious. Now, if you've finished, go away and leave me on my own.'

She groaned her way to her feet and made her way inside the hovel. Martin looked at Edwin, who had not moved, and wondered why the smile had widened across his whole face.

Chapter Twelve

Edwin wasn't quite sure how he found himself outside the abbey gates again. Had he really ridden all that way without noticing? He dismounted and led the horse through the gate once Brother Thurstan had managed to open it, and then stood in silence while Martin took the animals to the stables.

'You've thought of something, haven't you?'

Edwin jumped. 'How did you sort the horses out so quickly?'

'I didn't. You've been standing here like stone for ages.'

'Really?'

'Yes.'

'Oh.'

'So, have you?'

'Have I what?'

'Thought of something. You've got that look on your face.'

Edwin considered. 'Actually … yes, I think I have. But I don't want to speak too soon. I'd rather think about it overnight to get it all straight in my head before I do anything about it.' He looked around him, belatedly aware of his surroundings. 'It *is* evening, isn't it?'

Martin clapped him on the back. 'Are you that far gone? It is. Now come on, let's go and find something to eat.'

Edwin roused himself enough to think that Martin didn't sound as cheerful as he might at the idea of an evening meal and the possibility of getting out of the abbey if he, Edwin, was right about his suspicions. Indeed, Martin was looking about him now, as if searching for someone.

'Who are you looking for?'

'Nobody.'

There was no point trying to get more out of Martin once he set his jaw like that and Edwin had plenty else to think about, so perhaps they were better just going back to the guesthouse and eating. He led the way.

Once inside they were greeted by Aylwin, who was still at the table with a much drier-looking set of pages.

Aylwin met Edwin's questioning glance. 'Oh, don't worry, I haven't been here all day. It was still too wet to look at this morning so I went to talk to the new master of the lay brothers – the abbot has finally appointed one – and I came back to it about an hour ago.'

Edwin and Martin sat down on either side of him. 'What is it?' Martin came out of himself long enough to be curious.

'A wool ledger.' Aylwin pointed. 'Look, it got very wet and now it's dry again some of the pages are stuck together in a big lump, and a lot of the ink has run, but you can still make out some of it, if you know what to look for.' He grew enthused as he indicated various aspects.

Martin's interest faded as quickly as it had appeared and he ran his eyes over the pages without much enthusiasm as he turned to Edwin. 'Is this important for what we need to find out?'

Edwin nodded slowly. 'If I'm right, then yes, it could be the key to the whole thing.'

Aylwin looked puzzled. 'Even though I can't find anything wrong with it?' He made a helpless gesture. 'I mean, of course, I can't see all of it, or anything like all of it, but from what I can see it just looks like a perfectly normal wool ledger.'

Edwin reached for the bowl which Brother Amandus had obligingly put before him. 'Oh yes,' he said, distantly, 'its very normality is what gives the whole thing away.'

It was like being behind a veil, away from the rest of the world. He ate without tasting; watched without really seeing as Martin reached for the bread and passed some to Aylwin; listened without hearing as Martin spoke. 'There's no point trying to talk to him while he's like this. I've seen it before. Just let him think it out and he'll be back to normal tomorrow.'

Edwin belatedly noticed that Sir Philip was also sitting at the table, although he was as far away from the rest of them as he could get. That awoke him from his thoughts and with some effort he pushed the veil aside. Now was as good a time as any to test one of his theories.

He addressed the knight directly. 'Good evening, Sir Philip.'

He received a reply which was not much more than a grunt – the bare minimum of civility which might be accorded to a fellow guest. Aylwin made a surprised noise. 'Come now …'

Without taking his eyes off the knight, Edwin reached into his purse, felt around for the metal chape, and placed it deliberately on the table in front of Sir Philip.

Aylwin leaned forward. 'What's that?'

Edwin felt Martin shifting into a position of readiness beside him. Perhaps he should have told Martin first what he intended to do. Too late now.

Sir Philip had already reached for his scabbard, so he evidently knew what it was. 'Where did you get that?'

'I found it in the lay brothers' range.'

'Well, you have my thanks, I'd been looking for —' he started to reach out for it.

'On the stairs which lead up to the parlour there.'

The hand froze in mid-air.

Edwin continued. 'A place you wouldn't expect to go, if you were just a knight who was staying here while his horse recovered.'

Sir Philip sat back and folded his arms. 'What business is it of yours where I go? Who do you think you are?' His tone was scornful.

Edwin had sometimes watched the earl and Sir Geoffrey playing a game called chess. He didn't know exactly how it worked – although he thought he'd quite like to learn – but he had seen the way that they stared at each other while they were absorbed in it. He felt the same concentration now, gazing intently at his opponent as Martin and Aylwin almost faded from view. It was his move.

He kept his voice soft. 'I am the man who is here to find a killer and bring him to justice.'

As he expected, Sir Philip lost his temper. He jumped to his feet and laid a hand on his dagger.

All was chaos. Aylwin cried out with shock. Martin threw himself between Edwin and the knight. Brother Amandus ran in and squawked as he saw the scene, rushing to try and placate anyone and everyone.

Edwin didn't move.

Sir Philip had not gone so far as to draw his dagger. He raised a pacifying hand to Brother Amandus and a threatening one to Martin before taking his seat again. Martin took up a position standing behind the knight.

Edwin looked in Sir Philip's eyes. 'I never said that killer might be you, sir.'

'Then what are you implying?'

'Brother Amandus here told me that there are two reasons why a guest, an outsider, might go up there. The first is that it is used as an office where business can be discussed.'

Aylwin, who was looking a bit shaken, chipped in. 'That's right. I have been up there myself on numerous occasions.' He frowned at Sir Philip. 'But you're not a merchant.'

'The hell I am!' If anything, Sir Philip looked more insulted by this than he had been at the thought that Edwin was accusing him of murder, but he didn't move.

'And the second,' continued Edwin as if nobody had spoken, 'Is that the brothers of the Order are allowed to receive guests there, so they can talk to them without disturbing the rest of the abbey.' He leaned forward. 'Visits from relatives, for example.'

Sir Philip's expression now resembled the earl's when Sir Geoffrey made a move and then said 'check'. He looked at the faces surrounding him. 'Very well,' he said, grudgingly. 'If it will put thoughts of murder out of your heads.'

Brother Amandus started to say that he should not listen to gossip, that he should clear the table and leave, but he didn't move.

Sir Philip gestured at Edwin. 'If you're so clever, you tell me.'

'Very well. You can correct me where I go wrong.'

'Fine.'

Edwin hoped to the Lord he wasn't about to make a fool of himself. 'You visit here regularly. This is partly because it is on the way between your manors and therefore it is a convenient place to stop.'

Sir Philip made an irritated gesture. 'Everyone knows this.'

'But it is also because one of the monks is related to you. You stop here so you can talk to him … and ask his advice.'

There was a flicker in the knight's eye and Edwin knew he was right.

He continued. 'Your estates are … not prospering. You're losing money.'

Sir Philip ran one hand through his hair. 'Yes! Yes, you're right. I'm a warrior, not a clerk – I need someone to manage my estates properly.'

Edwin nodded. 'And, of course, it would be better if that someone was from your own family. To start with I wondered – a son, a nephew – but when I worked out who it was and looked at your ages … he's your brother, isn't he?'

'Who?' Both Aylwin and Brother Amandus spoke at once, and then tried to look as though they hadn't.

Sir Philip sighed. 'It's not a secret. Or not particularly, anyway – I just don't like people prying into my business. Yes, Helias is my brother.'

Edwin nodded again as the others all exclaimed their surprise. 'And he'd make a superb steward for your estates. Just look at the work he does here as the cellarer – the abbey is prospering, there is food, drink, materials … and he organises it all.' He looked at the knight. 'But he doesn't want to leave, does he?'

Sir Philip's irritation started to show. 'No. He says he is *content* here, that he is *happy*. What is that when it comes to family honour and fortune?'

'So this time you thought you'd stay a while longer and try harder to persuade him. And to cover up the reason for it, you pretended your horse was lame.'

The knight threw up his hands. 'I concede.' He shook his head. 'How you can possibly have worked all that out, I don't know.'

Brother Amandus was looking at Sir Philip, at his dark hair and build. 'But – forgive me, my son – but you don't look in the slightest bit alike. Nobody could possibly have guessed you were brothers.'

'No, so we've always been told. Which is probably why not many people realise. We used to have another brother – dead, now – who was between us in age and who somehow managed to resemble both of us slightly. If you'd seen all three of us together then you might have guessed we were brothers. But Helias and I are different in looks, temperament, everything.' He surveyed the men around him once more, looking tired. 'So, now you know all, if you will excuse me I will go out and get some air.'

After he left, there was silence. Then Brother Amandus broke it, realising how late it was and that he had not yet cleared the dishes. He did so now, talking to himself under his breath. 'Never would have ... so unalike ... fancy Brother Helias having ...'

Edwin, too, was weary, and now his other thoughts crowded in on him.

Aylwin patted him on the shoulder. 'You're a very clever young fellow. I'll leave you to it now, but once you've solved everything else you have to tell me why the wool ledger is so important.' He too departed.

Martin, who had by now sat down again, finally spoke. 'For God's sake, next time you're going to do something like that, tell me!'

'Sorry. But I knew that if I was right then there was no danger.'

'And what if you were wrong, eh?'

Edwin felt exhausted to the very centre of his bones. 'But I wasn't. And now I need to think about the rest.' The veil was beginning to descend again, and this time he couldn't fend it off.

'I take it you don't think Sir Philip was involved?'

'No.'

'Then who?'

Edwin shook his head. 'Tomorrow.' He moved over to his bed and then hesitated. 'I don't think I'm going to sleep much. I was going to go to the church to sit and think, but you probably don't want me to, do you?'

'Not a chance. If you do then I'll follow you and you won't get much thinking done anyway, so you may as well stay here where it's warm.'

Edwin nodded and wrapped a blanket around himself. He allowed the world around him to fade. Soon Martin was asleep and Edwin stared ahead of him as the moonlight shone in through the window. He had to be right. There was no other possible explanation. He began once more to run over in his head the way events must have played out, and to plan the trap he would spring on the morrow.

When morning came he wasn't sure whether he had slept or not, but despite his sandy eyes and his pounding head he knew what he was going to do.

He shook Martin. 'Time to get up.'

Martin was normally a heavy sleeper but he evidently scented action in the air for he woke and rolled himself to his feet all in one move. 'Today's the day, isn't it? Tell me what to do.'

A short time later they were dressed and on their way to Chapter, for Edwin wanted to make sure that Brother Eugenius and the lay brother Sinnulph made their confessions as agreed.

Edwin installed himself in the same position he had occupied the other day, Martin a pace behind him. The one brown robe among all the white was very noticeable, and once the initial prayers had been said, the abbot indicated that Sinnulph should step forward.

There was – well, Edwin couldn't really call it a murmur of surprise, as the monks held their silence, but a kind of collective breath – as the abbot explained why Sinnulph was there, and invited him to confess.

The lay brother assumed the penitent position on the floor and began his tale. Edwin was pleased to note that it was full, but plain and unembellished. He told the facts about his sister and her family, about exactly what had been stolen to feed them, and about the pressure he had brought to bear on Brother Eugenius, but he did not claim to have threatened violence.

There was a profound silence as Sinnulph finished speaking and laid his head back on the floor.

The abbot's eyes swept the room. 'Before I ask the rest of the brethren for their thoughts, I believe we had better hear Brother Eugenius. Step forward, if you please.'

Nobody moved.

Edwin was immediately on the alert, looking at the backs of everyone's heads. He couldn't tell who was who from here.

The abbot sounded impatient. 'Brother Eugenius, it is your duty to step forward.'

By now the monks were craning their necks to look around the chapterhouse themselves, and it did not take long to confirm what Edwin already suspected: Brother Eugenius was not there.

Abbot Reginald allowed some of his anger to show in his voice. 'Brothers, this would appear to be unprecedented. It looks as though Brother Eugenius is too afraid to confess to his sin and has therefore evaded Chapter for that purpose. However, I will not judge him until I know what has happened – there is a possibility that he has fallen or is lying ill somewhere. Let us search the abbey for him.' He nodded at the prior, who moved swiftly among the monks allocating them places to look and giving them permission to call out his name and to speak aloud if they found the missing brother.

As the brethren filed out, the abbot was left in the chapterhouse with Edwin, Martin and the still-prostrate Sinnulph. The abbot looked down upon him. 'Rise, Brother, and go about your duties for now. By the time Brother Eugenius is found it will be time for the *lectio divina*, so this Chapter will reconvene tomorrow.'

Had Edwin detected a shade of sympathy in his voice? He could not be sure. Brother Sinnulph stood, bowed low, and left the room without speaking.

The abbot approached Edwin and Martin. 'What do you know of Brother Eugenius?'

Edwin shook his head. 'Only what Brother Sinnulph has already confessed, my lord. I taxed them both with questions yesterday and they told me of what had passed. It's true that Brother Eugenius was very upset at the thought of confessing, but I was sure that he was determined to do it.' He gestured at the empty room. 'I'm surprised he isn't here – and a little worried.'

A shadow crossed the abbot's face. 'Let us hope, for all our sakes, that he has simply tripped and fallen somewhere, and will be found with a swollen ankle.'

Martin's voice came from behind Edwin. 'Pardon me, my lord, but perhaps Edwin and I could help with the search? Not in the abbey itself, maybe, but out in the precinct or the other buildings. It would give us something to do, and the more searchers, the better?'

Edwin didn't think he'd ever heard Martin sounding so deferential to anyone except the lord earl, and he wondered if there was a particular reason. But the abbot was nodding, saying that they could go, and that he would remain in the chapterhouse praying and waiting for news.

Their way out of the abbey building led them across the cloister and then in the door to the lay brothers' grange and through the passage there. There were worried-looking monks both inside and outside, and Edwin wondered where on earth they should start.

He was glad when Martin took charge. 'He is obviously not in any of the places he is supposed to be, so let's start by checking the places he isn't supposed to be. The guesthouse, the stables, the outbuildings. They're all along this side of the precinct so we can move through them methodically.'

Edwin agreed, but they had barely reached the guesthouse when alarmed shouts came from the direction of the abbey building. They turned to see all the monks rushing in one direction, so they followed.

The crowd led to a flight of stairs and up to a part of the abbey Edwin hadn't visited so far: the monks' dormitory. A row of thin pallets was laid out on each side down the length of the room, all currently empty except for a neatly folded blanket. There was a crush of men towards the far end, talking, exclaiming, praying, and Edwin tried to get closer.

'Stand aside!' The raised voice was the abbot's, and the room fell silent immediately as the monks stood back with bowed heads to allow him a path. Edwin slipped behind him.

A monk was lying on the last bed at the end of the row. It was Brother Eugenius. His eyes were open, staring at the ceiling and away from the huge red stain seeping across the front of his white robe. A knife was protruding from his chest, and he was quite clearly dead.

Brother Richard woke up.

He opened his eyes but did not move. The blur in front of him eventually became a ceiling, but not the familiar rafters of the dormitory which had been his home for so many years. Where was he?

He attempted to move and was overcome by a wave of pain which left him gasping. The infirmary, he was in the infirmary. That was it. He had suffered from toothache, had some teeth pulled, and then after that it had all been a bad dream. He had a vague recollection of figures around his bed, of prayers, of bitter-tasting things being dripped into his mouth, of the sharp pain in his arm from the bleeding. And the agony, the ever-present agony in his face, his skin stretched and full to bursting.

Cautiously, he tried to move his right hand. It responded to him. He lifted it – heavy as lead! – to his face. His face was still there. It felt like a normal face. There was pain in his mouth but he could bear it.

He put his hand back by his side and listened. It was quiet. With a great effort he turned his head a little and saw that he was behind a screen, on his own. He laid his head back again. He would wait, and eventually someone – Brother Durand – would come.

Yes, Brother Durand had been there, hadn't he? All through the dream, the nightmare, through the darkness and the light. Brother Durand had hurt him, trying to smear something on his face and get liquid into his mouth. But Brother Durand had done this to save his life. He was alive.

Other figures in white robes had been there. He had heard them praying. He had survived because of their prayers.

Something troubled him, but he didn't know what it was. Some fleeting recollection that he could not pin down. He would lie still until it came back to him. He should pray and give thanks. *Pater noster, qui es in …*

He had it. One of the figures who had been around his bed had not been in a white robe. Someone who was not a monk had come to see him. He moved his fingers as he remembered the pressure on his hand. A man he didn't know had come to speak to him. He couldn't remember what it was about.

He might have dozed again, or he might just have stared at the ceiling. Brother Alexander. He must speak with Brother Alexander. He opened his mouth, unsure if he would be able to make a noise.

And then it came crashing in on him and he thought he would be sick. Thank the Lord he wasn't, for that would have caused much pain in his mouth and to his face. He could feel his heart pounding faster. Brother Alexander was dead. He was dead and he, Brother Richard, needed to talk to the man who had visited him. He didn't know why, he couldn't remember, but it was important. He wanted to cry but his eyes were too dry and he felt them stinging.

He tried to move his legs. They shifted a little, but strangely, as though they weren't part of him. He rolled and leaned over. He fell out of bed and let out an involuntary cry of pain. He lay on the floor, waiting for the stars to stop moving around his head.

Hands were helping him up. A white robe. Was it the infirmarer? No. A voice was speaking.

'Brother Richard! Surely you should not be out of bed! Please, let me help you. Then you must lie still while I go to fetch Brother Durand.'

Brother Richard took some time to focus his eyes and realised he was looking at the novice, Benedict. What was he doing here? Never mind that now. Benedict was not strong enough to lift him and put him back into bed, and neither could Brother Richard manage it himself. They ended up in a heap on the floor, but eventually the room stopped spinning enough for him to realise that he was sitting more or less upright with his back against the bed.

He waved for Benedict to calm down. He opened his mouth and made an incoherent sound. Please, Lord, give me strength. He tried again. 'Up.' The novice did not seem to understand. 'Help?'

Benedict's face cleared. 'Yes, Brother, I will help you up into your bed. Just let me draw breath for a moment.' Brother Richard looked at him again and belatedly realised he was seeing a skeleton covered in skin. He tried to wonder what had happened to the boy but he could not get the thought to sit still.

He made a gesture with his arm and managed to get out a word which he hoped sounded a bit like 'Durand'.

Benedict seemed to understand. 'He is not here, Brother. He has gone to look for Brother Eugenius, who is missing.'

Brother Richard felt his mind coming back to him a little as he sat still. He made a circular motion with his hand to encourage Benedict to keep talking.

The novice now sounded unsure. 'I know the Rule is relaxed a little in the infirmary, but I'm not sure I should gossip ...'

Brother Richard intensified the circular motion and also grasped hold of Benedict's sleeve. How white his hand looked. He hardly recognised it as his own.

Benedict spoke slowly. 'You have been ... away from us for quite some time, Brother. There has been upheaval. Brother Alexander is dead, murdered. Some men are here to find out who did it. And I don't know what has happened to Brother Eugenius: Brother Durand went to Chapter but then came back to ask if he had come here, as he could not be found anywhere else. I hope nothing has happened to him.' He crossed himself.

Brother Richard sat in silence for a while, but then became aware that somewhere on the other side of the screen there was a whispering. He gave Benedict a questioning look.

'That will be the other brothers who are in here. I will see what they are about.' He stood and disappeared, before returning a few moments later looking, if anything, even paler and more frail than he had before. '*Requiescat in pace.* They say that Brother Eugenius is dead.' He held on to the screen for support.

Something needed to be done. He, Brother Richard, needed to talk to the man who had visited him. He would remember what it was about when he got there. But he had to go. Brother Alexander was dead.

He stretched his mouth a few times and managed to sound more coherent. 'Help. Up.' He held both his arms up in an unmistakeable gesture. Benedict started to shake his head. 'Now.' There was no way he was going to be able to say the word 'obedience', but he hoped the novice understood.

Benedict evidently did, for he nodded and, with some effort, hauled Brother Richard to his feet. He held on tightly to the novice for a few moments until he was sure he wasn't going to fall over again, and then carefully straightened. He could stand. Could he walk? He put one arm around the bony shoulders and pointed towards the infirmary door. 'Go.'

———

Edwin looked down at the corpse. The guilt was overwhelming. If only he had said or done something last night, instead of stupidly taking all that extra time to think. Why hadn't he acted on his convictions? His inability to do so had led to the death of an innocent man.

Most of the monks had been sent away to their reading – the abbey schedule was not to be affected, even by such an event – and the dormitory now contained only the abbot, the prior, the infirmarer, Edwin and Martin. And the body of poor Brother Eugenius, now with his eyes decently closed.

The abbot finished intoning a prayer for the dead, and everyone said 'Amen'. Then he turned to Prior Henry and Brother Durand. 'We will have to see what we can do with the body. Clearly it cannot lie in our graveyard.' They nodded.

Edwin cleared his throat.

'Yes, my son?'

'Why can Brother Eugenius not be buried with the other monks?'

The abbot explained as though to a child. 'Because he has committed the mortal sin of suicide. He is therefore not in a state of grace and cannot lie in consecrated ground.'

Edwin was confused. 'Suicide?'

'Yes, for what other explanation is there? He was too afraid to confess his sin, so instead of joining his brethren at Chapter he came up here to kill himself.'

Edwin shook his head. 'Please excuse me for contradicting you, Father, but I don't think that's the case.'

'Why not?'

'Look here,' Edwin leaned over and pointed. 'He has been stabbed in the heart. If he had done that himself then his hands would be covered in blood, surely?' He mimed a demonstration but stopped when he saw the revulsion on the faces of the three monks. 'Sorry. But there is no blood at all on his hands, and his arms are by his side. And there is blood on the floor over here, away from where he lies.'

The prior broke in. 'You think – pardon me, Father Abbot – you think someone else might have done this?'

'Yes. And I'm not sure, as I don't have a great deal of experience at this, but is that bruising around his mouth?' He hovered his left hand above Brother Eugenius's mouth, as though he would press down on it, and the pattern of the marks became clear. 'I think someone came upon him, face-to-face, stabbed him with that knife – that is another one from the scriptorium, isn't it? – and then when he was weakened by the wound, pushed him down and put his hand over his face to stop him making a noise, and kept it there until he was dead.' He stood back.

The abbot looked at the infirmarer, who nodded thoughtfully. 'I think he may be right, Father. But if so, then whoever killed him would have tell-tale marks of blood upon him? And there were none such at Chapter.'

Martin had walked off while Edwin was talking, and now he spoke from halfway up the room. 'Like this?' He held up a white robe, indicating the red splatters all over the sleeves.

'Where did you find that?' The abbot's voice was sharp.

'Here, under this mattress. I noticed it wasn't quite as straight as the others. Whoever killed Brother Eugenius looked at himself, realised he was covered in blood, and changed his robe. Do you keep spare ones up here?'

'Yes, each brother has two so he can change if the other gets too soiled at his labours, for it is not fitting to praise the Lord during the services while filthy. Whose bed is that?' This last remark was addressed to the prior.

Brother Durand broke in. 'It's mine, Father Abbot, although I can assure you that I am not the culprit.'

Edwin looked at the tall form of the infirmarer. 'I can hardly believe you would hide it under your own bed. And besides … Martin, can you bring that here and hold it up next to Brother Durand, please?'

Martin did so, and they could all see immediately that the robe was too short to belong to the tall infirmarer.

The abbot sighed. 'So. This is better for the soul of Brother Eugenius – we will make it clear that he did not kill himself, so that no taint can attach to him or to his memory. But it means we have a *second* killer here among us? I cannot credit this.'

'No.' Edwin had known since the moment he saw the body that his theory had been confirmed rather than disproved, although he would bear the guilt until his own dying day that he had waited long enough for a second murder to be committed. He knew why he had done it – it was because he did not want to act hastily and risk making a fool of himself in public, but what was that compared to an innocent man's life? He glanced around at all the faces looking at him. 'It means we have one killer who has struck twice.'

'Who?'

'If I tell you now, I have no way of proving it and it will just be my word against his. But I think I know a way to catch him.'

Martin stepped forward. 'Oh no. You're not going to go using yourself as bait or anything foolish like that. The lord earl would never forgive me if I let you get killed too.' He folded his arms and looked belligerently at the abbot, as if to face down any arguments.

But the abbot was agreeing. 'I cannot let you risk your life, my son. Just tell me who you believe to be the culprit and why, and we will move from there.'

Edwin shook his head. 'It's all right. I am not going to risk my life. If I can get going now then I can set up what I need to do and then get well away before he comes near.' He pleaded. 'Please, my lord. It's important that everyone knows the truth, without a doubt, and it will be better this way.'

The abbot nodded. 'Can you tell me, solemnly and in the presence of God and the body of Brother Eugenius, that your life will not be in danger?'

'Yes.'

'Very well then.' The abbot addressed Prior Henry and Brother Durand. 'Cover him now, and send some of the lay brothers to carry him to the infirmary. He may lie there until his interment.'

The prior unfolded a blanket and the two of them placed it over the body before bowing and leaving. The abbot made the sign of the cross over the body one final time and also departed.

Edwin forestalled Martin just as he was opening his mouth. 'You are not coming with me.'

'Oh, I am.'

Edwin walked out of the dormitory, down the stairs and then made his way out of the building, striding across the precinct.

Martin stepped ahead of him, turned, and put out a hand flat on his chest to stop him. 'What are you going to do?'

'Something I don't need you for. Now leave me alone.'

'You have to tell me more than that.'

'No, I don't. It is my fault that Brother Eugenius is dead – I could have stopped this happening if only I'd acted last night and not started worrying about looking like a fool. I need to put things right. And besides, I think there's someone you need to talk to.' He pointed.

Martin turned to see Brother Guy coming out of the stables. As Edwin expected, he was struck dumb and immobile by the sight of him – Edwin had no idea what was between them but this was his opportunity.

When Martin turned round to argue again, Edwin was gone.

Martin cursed as he looked around him wildly. He ran over to Brother Guy and skidded to a halt before him, kicking up a cloud of dust. 'Did you see where he went?'

Brother Guy made a 'who?' gesture.

'Edwin, my friend … he's just … I need your help.'

He was met with a troubled look.

Martin was agonised. He didn't know what to say, how to confess, but he had to say *something*. Brother Guy took a step back.

'No, wait,' said Martin. 'I do need your help, but I also need your forgiveness.' He lowered himself to his knees in front of the lay brother, despite the odd looks he knew he was attracting. He bowed his head and spoke to Brother Guy's boots. He was aware that his hands were shaking, but he had to get this out before he could ask for help.

'Since I arrived I have treated you with disdain. With contempt. I ask forgiveness for this.' He felt a hand touching the top of his head. 'If I had only known that you were a knight, I would have spoken with more respect, I would have …' He tailed off, conscious that the hand was lifted again. He looked up to see Brother Guy shaking his head, a stern expression on his face. 'I mean, I know you're not a knight any more, but your rank, your background …' The head-shaking intensified, and Martin was at a loss. He stared for a long moment. Then he understood.

He bowed his head again. 'What I mean is, I should have treated you with more respect, as I should treat any man, regardless of his rank. Even were you a lay brother who came from a local village family, I should have demonstrated my worthiness by acting courteously.' He waited, and was rewarded by the touch on his head again. This time it was a benediction.

Brother Guy sketched the sign of the cross in the air over Martin's head and then helped him to rise. Martin's heart felt lighter. 'Thank you.'

Brother Guy stood waiting expectantly and gestured for Martin to speak. He poured out the story of Brother Eugenius's death, of how Edwin thought he knew what had happened and had gone off to set some kind of trap. 'And he's in danger, Brother, I know he is, despite what he said. It's my duty to protect him – please, please help me.'

He received a nod and a gesture to keep talking. He realised he hadn't said anything which would help right now, for he had no idea what Edwin was thinking or where he had gone. He tried to think his way through it, aloud.

'It must be one of the choir monks, for both the dead men were killed in places where nobody else is allowed to go. But they're all so alike, I can't tell them apart. And how could the killer even know who he was killing? Brother Eugenius, maybe, for he was on his own. But Brother Alexander, he was surrounded by others and they all had their hoods up, so how could anyone tell him from anyone else?'

As he spoke his eye fell on the twins, Brothers Godfrey and Waldef, who were crossing the precinct. How long had he been here, talking to Brother Guy? Was the reading over? He pointed. 'For all I know, all the monks could be as indistinguishable from each other as they are. And nobody can tell *them* apart.'

Martin knew he was starting to panic. In God's name, how was he going to face the earl if something happened to Edwin? And where the hell was he?

He felt a hand clamp his arm and he looked into a pair of eyes which had seen danger and death many times, and had survived. They were urging him to do something, but he didn't know what. 'Please, *say* something. Tell me what to do.'

Brother Guy looked pained, but he did not speak. Instead he turned Martin round and pointed very firmly at the twins.

'What? I'm sorry, Brother, I just don't understand. Please – Edwin's life might be at stake. Help me.'

Finally Brother Guy nodded, looked to the heavens, and opened his mouth to speak.

———•———

Edwin looked at the wool ledgers before him in the lay brothers' parlour. He had made it into the building and up the stairs unseen; nobody challenged him and nobody followed. Like the rest of the abbey the parlour was a plain space: a table, some stools, a storage kist, and the shelves in front of him on which sat the ledgers. Unlike the books in the library these were stored upright, and there were three rows of them. All the spines were towards him, and all were neatly labelled with dates. He started with the one with the earliest date, the leftmost one on the upper shelf, and methodically began to take them down and look through them.

It was the fourth one on the second row. As soon as he lifted it off the shelf he knew that it felt different, loose, so when he laid it on the table and began to open it he was unsurprised to see a flash of colour.

He opened the book fully, laying the hard cover as flat as he could and smoothing down the plain binding page. It was glued to the cover and was evidently part of the original ledger, as was the matching page at the back, but all the rest of the inside had been torn out, and bound manuscript leaves from another work had been placed inside to fill the space. The inner manuscript was the same thickness as the removed part, so when the ledger had been on the shelf with its spine facing outwards nobody could have noticed any difference. The label indicated that the accounts were from some years ago so there would have been no real occasion for anyone to take the book off the shelf in the normal course of things. It was a good hiding place.

If Edwin was right, then this was what someone had killed Brother Alexander for. *All knowledge is precious*, that was what Anabilia had said, in a throwaway remark. And knowledge was to be found in books. And books were valuable. The fabled 'treasure' which Brother Alexander had brought back from the East was neither gold nor jewels, but a book. But why? Why would someone kill for this?

And then he opened the manuscript and he understood, for all the wonders of the world were contained inside.

Edwin had no idea how long he stood there, staring, unable to take his eyes away from the most beautiful thing he had ever seen. He drank in the words, the pictures, the decorations, the thoughts, the experiences. It might have been an hour; it might have been a year. Time was immaterial. The world stopped. He could look at this for the rest of his life. Every page contained not only the words of Holy Scripture, but the most wonderful images, pictures which told stories of their own and which were decorated to the last, tiniest detail. He could see every link on the armour of Goliath as he was slain by the boy David; he stared in horror at Adam and Eve being expelled from Eden; he flinched despite himself at the vivid depiction of blind Samson bringing a building crashing down to destroy the Philistines; he drank in the sight of God the Father creating the world, running his finger in awe over the image as many others had evidently done before him; he could not take his eyes off the intricate interwoven decorations which filled every space on every page. He gazed at the red, the gold, the *blue*.

He was disturbed by a sound behind him.

Edwin turned to see Brother Octavian standing in the doorway. Oh dear Lord – he'd spent too long entranced by the book and the *lectio divina* was finished. The *lectio divina* which was to keep all the choir monks occupied until he had dragged this book out and left it in public so he could watch the librarian's reaction. And now here he was alone with him. What a fool. He'd have to make the best of it. Maybe he could stall long enough for Martin to find him.

Or maybe he would die, for really, what difference was it going to make? He was going to die in the earl's service at some point anyway. Perhaps here, in this room, with the most stunning object he'd ever seen, was as good a place as any. A quick thrust to the heart and it would all be over. He would be at peace.

And then, in a moment of blinding clarity, he realised that he had been driving himself towards this moment ever since he had arrived at the abbey, ever since the earl had sent him here – ever since he received word that Alys was already married. For his life was worth nothing, and would be better ended. Why else would he have gone to so much trouble to elude the man who was sworn to protect him? His life was over. He *wanted* it to be over. He should accept his death calmly.

But.

If he were to die then the killer might go on to murder again. Edwin thought of Brother Eugenius's body, of the blood pooling on his chest. Of others who might suffer. He had to do something, he had to do just enough to let the killer be identified before he gave in and let himself step into the welcoming arms of death.

'Brother —' He felt the unsteadiness in his voice and cleared his throat before trying again. 'Brother Octavian. I was just going to come and fetch you. Look what was hidden here, hidden inside one of the ledgers. It's a Bible, Brother, the most incredible thing I've ever seen.' But if he wanted to die, if he truly desired it, why was he looking past the monk at the door? Why was he hoping that Martin would arrive? Martin would be sad if he died, and so would Mother. Could he do that to them?

Brother Octavian moved towards him, almost staggering as he looked at the book on the table, now open on a page depicting a battle which was so vibrant it almost jumped up off the parchment. He approached with one shaky hand held out in front of him, his mouth open but incapable of speech as he stared at the riches before him. Edwin knew how he felt.

Perhaps he could escape after all, using Brother Octavian's disorientation to his advantage. But it was too late: by now the monk was standing right next to him, his robe brushing Edwin's tunic, and Edwin felt the point of the knife in his side.

Chapter Thirteen

Martin stood with Brother Guy as the lay brother continued to point to the twins, now almost across the precinct and oblivious to the scrutiny.

And finally Brother Guy broke his vow of silence. His voice was low and rumbling. 'Think. Who can tell them apart?'

Martin's mind ran back over the last few days. Nobody could, could they? He hadn't … oh, wait. He remembered the end of the *lectio divina*, when he'd been so bored watching the monks read. Brother Guy had entered from the lay brothers' range just as the monks were giving their books back. And Brother Octavian, the librarian, knew which twin was which because of the book each was reading. And if he could tell *them* apart, he could identify any of the brethren from their reading material. He could, for example, see which reader was Brother Alexander. He could creep up and stab him.

He was crossing the precinct now.

Martin had no idea why Brother Octavian should do any of these things, but he didn't care. He drew his sword and sprinted across the open space as he saw the monk entering the abbey building through the door in the lay brothers' range. Martin followed, but he was a way behind and when he skidded to a halt inside he couldn't see his quarry. There were doorways to the left and right of him. Where had the guestmaster told them they led, on that first day? If only he'd been paying more attention! There was a passage ahead which led into the cloister. He felt his sweaty hand starting to lose its grip on the sword hilt. Dear God, if he'd slipped in among all the other white monks …

Martin looked wildly around him. He was standing at the bottom of a flight of stairs. The stairs! That was where —

A voice came floating down. Edwin's. Martin tore up the steps and burst into the room.

Two figures swung round to face him. One was Edwin, looking pale and shocked. The other was Brother Octavian, who was holding a knife to Edwin's ribs.

'Stop!' The monk was wild-eyed. 'I can kill him before you can get near enough to hurt me with that.' He pushed the point of the knife further into Edwin's side, and Martin saw his friend give a start of pain as the sharp point pricked into him.

Martin raised his left hand in the air and took a careful step back. 'Put the knife down.'

'Put your sword down first.'

Martin hesitated and the knife pressed further into Edwin's side. Edwin gasped and a small bloodstain appeared on his tunic. 'All right, all right!' He carefully placed the sword on the floor and stood. The hilt was towards him and he began to calculate how quickly he could pick it up again if he needed to.

A sound came from behind him and he knew that Brother Guy had followed him up and was in the room. Good. Numbers were now in their favour, though Brother Octavian was still holding the knife far too close to Edwin's body. It was a small, sharp-looking thing, similar to the one which had been used to kill Brother Eugenius, and Martin knew that it would slide into Edwin's unarmoured body like butter, leading to a swift and inevitable death.

Brother Octavian looked about him, and Martin could see him weighing up his options. There was only one doorway. Both he and Brother Guy stood between him and it, but the monk had the knife and the hostage. Martin glanced down again at his sword.

Brother Octavian caught the direction of his gaze. 'Brother Guy. Step forward and kick that sword over towards me.'

Martin exchanged a glance with the lay brother, who did as he was bid and then moved to stand level with Martin but apart from him, so that there was a gap between them and the way to the door was open. Martin cast him a questioning look and received a barely perceptible nod. Did he have a plan?

'What is it you hope to achieve?' Martin tried addressing Brother Octavian directly. Negotiation was not going to be his strong point, but he had to try something. And why, in the Lord's name, was Edwin not saying anything? Surely he was clever enough to talk his way out of this, if he tried? But he was just standing there. Admittedly he had a knife held to him – the bloodstain didn't appear to be getting any bigger, thank God – but he looked … blank. As if he wasn't there at all, in his mind.

'This young man and I are going to walk out of here with the book.' Martin belatedly noticed that there was some kind of brightly coloured volume open on the table. Was this what it had all been about? A *book*? What was wrong with these people?

Brother Octavian was continuing. 'Nobody will see the knife, and we will look as though we are simply walking together and discussing the work. If you try to stop me leaving, I will kill him.'

'And then what?'

'I will tell Father Abbot that you both came here and threatened to kill me, and that I struck out in self-defence. Edwin will be dead, Brother Guy cannot speak, and nobody will take your word over mine.'

He was never going to get away with it, but he still had the knife, and Martin knew he would use it – after all, it looked like he had already murdered two others. The safest thing to do for now would be to allow him out and then follow at a safe distance until he could somehow get the blade away from him. Martin nodded to Brother Guy, who was no doubt thinking along the same lines. They both moved aside to make the path to the door wider.

'Pick up the book. Carefully!' Brother Octavian was addressing the still-silent Edwin, who obeyed. 'Now move.' They started to walk towards the doorway. 'You two – stay well back.'

Martin kept his eyes on Brother Octavian's face. He was mad, and mad people were unpredictable. His fingers itched to try and tackle the monk as he went past, to try and wrest the knife from him, but he couldn't risk it.

And then Brother Octavian stopped and turned whiter than his robe. Martin actually saw the colour drain from his face as it assumed an expression of profound terror. He was looking past Martin, and Martin risked a glance behind him. Two monks had appeared at the top of the stairs – the novice Benedict, gaunt and skeletal, and another whom he was supporting who looked like death. Martin had to look twice to check that Benedict wasn't hauling a corpse around with him, but the man was apparently breathing. Martin didn't recognise him – older, tallish, blond hair going grey. He'd never seen anyone so ill standing up.

But the effect on Brother Octavian was astounding. He stopped and stuttered out some words. 'Brother Alexander … dear God, you've come back …' He started to back away, still keeping hold of Edwin. 'You've come for your book … take it, take it!' His voice rose to a shriek as he shoved Edwin's arms forward to proffer the book.

And in doing so, he moved the knife away from Edwin's side.

Martin threw himself forward, forcing the monk's arm up and away. Then he grabbed Edwin and pulled him hard, turning them both so his own body was between Edwin and Brother Octavian.

He looked up, expecting the knife to descend at any moment, but Brother Guy had reacted almost as quickly: he took two paces forward and then landed such a huge punch to Brother Octavian's head that the *smack* noise echoed around the room. The monk crumpled silently into a heap with the lay brother standing over him.

There was another movement from the door as the corpse-like monk fainted and Benedict failed to take his weight properly – Brother Guy caught them both and lowered them safely to the floor. Then he sat down heavily himself.

Martin was in the corner, still shielding Edwin with his body. He put his hand down to the wound in Edwin's side but it came away only with a small brownish stain on it, thank the Lord. He looked at the chaos and the bodies around him and had no idea what was going on. Perhaps one day someone would explain it to him, but right now nobody else seemed capable of speech or movement. He lifted his head and bellowed as loudly as he could, sure that the sound would carry out the building and across the silent abbey. 'Help! Someone! Help!'

Edwin realised that he wasn't dead.

He had been in some kind of daze, the voices washing over him and even the sharp stabbing in his side not waking him completely. Now he came back to himself, piece by piece. He was on the floor. Someone was cradling him – Martin. He was still clutching the book to his chest. His side hurt. He could move his hands and feet. He was alive. He wasn't yet sure whether he was pleased about this or not, but it was undeniable.

Brother Helias made a breathless entrance into the room. 'What is —' He looked around him in horror. But then, as Edwin watched, he took charge. He issued orders to those crowding in behind him to fetch the abbot, the prior and Brother Durand, while he himself crouched to check on the condition of the three prone monks.

'Can you stand?' The voice in Edwin's ear was Martin's, and he nodded. He felt himself being lifted to his feet and then he stood with Martin's steadying hands still on his shoulders. The pain in his side briefly prickled as he stretched himself upright, but it soon subsided.

Brother Guy was also now back on his feet, and he stood over Brother Octavian. When the cellarer tried to approach he held up one hand. Surprised at being thus impeded by a lay brother, Brother Helias stopped. 'What is it?' Brother Guy pointed firmly at the unconscious monk, then at Edwin, and then made a downward stabbing motion with his hand.

'He did what?' Brother Helias strode over to Edwin and Martin and noticed for the first time the stain on his tunic. 'You are wounded? Badly?'

Edwin shook his head, wondering if he could take a vow of silence, starting now. He did not have the energy or the heart to start explaining everything, though he knew he must in due course. But he had to keep his dark secret to himself, for if any hint of his wish for self-slaughter were to become public knowledge he would be forever condemned.

By this time Brother Durand had appeared and he was speaking to the novice Benedict, who had managed to sit up. The other monk was still unconscious – good God, was that Brother Richard?

Edwin hadn't seen him since the huge swelling had gone from his face, so he couldn't be sure it was the same man to whom he had spoken and over whose bed he had prayed, but the prone man was about the right age, and surely there was nobody else in the abbey who was that ill. Something else fell into place and he stepped forward, shaking off Martin's arm. He did not let go of the book.

The abbot had also appeared and he was issuing brisk orders for the sick and injured monks to be taken to the infirmary. Brother Guy did not dare to stop him but he did attract the cellarer's attention and pointed from the abbot to Brother Octavian.

Brother Helias murmured to the abbot, words Edwin did not catch, but from the gestures he worked out the gist of it.

The abbot stepped over to Edwin. 'Is this true? Brother Octavian made an attempt on your life?'

Edwin nodded.

'And you think he is also responsible for the deaths of Brother Alexander and Brother Eugenius?'

Edwin nodded again.

The abbot looked down at the still-unconscious monk with an expression of anguish. 'Very well. But he still needs to go to the infirmary.' He looked around at the various options available, at the monks and lay brothers of varying degrees of age and fitness who now filled the room. 'Brother Guy. Please take Brother Octavian to the infirmary and place him in a bed away from other brethren. Stand by him and, if he wakes, do not let him leave or even rise from the bed. You may take another brother with you to help carry him.'

Brother Guy bowed low, then bent down and easily scooped up the librarian in his burly arms. With another respectful inclination of the head towards the abbot he left the room.

'Or not, if you don't need any help,' the abbot murmured under his breath. 'Don't go anywhere,' he said to Edwin and Martin, before moving to consult with the infirmarer. Edwin remained silent as he watched. Benedict was now on his feet and was being supported by another brother who was instructed to accompany him back to the infirmary.

'And Brother Richard?' the abbot was asking, which confirmed to Edwin the man's identity. The stricken monk was also starting to come round, and as his eye fell on Edwin he pointed and tried to sit up.

'He has not helped himself, Father, but I think he has not hindered his recovery too seriously.' Brother Durand surveyed the room. 'I have no idea how he got here, Father, or what his intention was, but with your permission I would prefer to get him back into bed before any further inquiries are made.'

The abbot nodded. 'Yes, do so. Should we fashion a stretcher?'

'I'll carry him, if you like.' Martin stepped forward.

Brother Durand initially looked as though he would snap at the offer, but he stopped himself after a warning glance from the prior. 'Thank you. That would be most welcome. But please – carefully.'

Martin settled Brother Richard in his arms and nodded at the infirmarer. 'Lead the way.'

The prior now shooed any remaining stragglers out of the room, and Edwin was left alone with the abbot.

Abbot Reginald looked about ten years older than he had when Edwin had first met him. He rubbed a hand across his face and moved to half-sit on the edge of the table. 'And so.'

Edwin looked after the departing party. 'I believe I now have everything straight, my lord, but as there is no longer any danger to anyone, might I take just a little more time? I can explain everything, but I need to talk to Brother Richard first.'

'Brother Richard? What does he have to do with all this?'

'More than you might think, my lord. So may I?'

'You may. Please come and see me in my parlour when you have finished. I shall go there now to await you and to pray.' He hesitated. 'Incidentally, why are you holding one of our wool ledgers?'

Edwin had almost forgotten he was still carrying the book. His arms were stiff as he held it out. 'Please take this with you, my lord. Keep it shut for now, but when you get back to your parlour, open it and look inside. And when I get back I will tell you everything, I promise.' He turned towards the door, leaving the abbot gazing in puzzlement at the perfectly ordinary-looking volume in his hands.

By the time Edwin reached the infirmary all the men had been settled. A bed had been moved right into one corner of the room, away from the others: this contained Brother Octavian, now beginning to come round. He had the makings of a huge bruise on his jaw. Brother Guy stood in silence, unmoving, his arms folded, watching him. Edwin remembered the noise of his fist striking flesh and bone and had no doubt that Brother Octavian wouldn't be able to escape.

Benedict was sitting up in another bed, with the ancient novicemaster next to him holding a bowl of broth and a spoon. He nodded to Edwin as he passed.

The screen was still in place at the far end of the infirmary. Martin was standing next to it and he made room for Edwin so they could both see round. Brother Richard was in bed but sitting, supported by pillows, and he looked a little more alive. Prior Henry and Brother Durand were praying by his bedside; as Edwin watched they crossed themselves and Brother Durand gestured that Edwin could speak with the sick man.

Propped in his sitting position, Brother Richard was still pale, his face drawn with pain, but the terrible swelling was now gone and he was able to raise his hand and even offer a tired smile of greeting.

Edwin saw that there was a stool by the side of the bed. 'May I sit and speak with you?'

Brother Richard gestured his permission.

'I'm sorry to disturb you when you need to rest, but it would be very helpful if I could ask you a few questions. I'll try not to tire you out, and as far as I can I'll make them questions you can answer with a yes or a no.'

Brother Richard nodded his head, moving it as little as possible.

'You travelled with Brother Alexander, didn't you? When you were both younger?'

A nod.

'To start with you went to Paris, but after that you travelled south, to the lands of the Moors?'

Nod.

'Where you studied with masters? You, Brother Alexander and another man called Daniel of Morley.'

Nod.

'The prior was confused when he mentioned the name to me. It wasn't the *writings* of Daniel which had a great influence on Brother Alexander – it was the man himself.'

A slight shrug. Edwin got back to his point.

'And then you all came back, what, twenty, twenty-five years ago? And you all became monks.'

This time Brother Richard shook his head.

Edwin was confused. 'You didn't all come back? Or you didn't all become monks?' He realised what he was doing. 'Oh, sorry, that's not very helpful, is it. You all travelled back to England together?'

Nod.

'And you all joined religious orders?'

Brother Richard put up his hand to stop Edwin. He opened his mouth and shut it a couple of times, as if unfamiliar with the feeling. He cleared his throat, tentatively. Then he managed a few words, his voice rusty and the words unformed. 'Daniel – Aug-us-tin-i-an. Me – here. Alex-ander went to teach. At the school at St Al-bans. Took the cowl later – came here.'

This time it was Edwin's turn to nod. 'And he came here because of you, didn't he? That's why he travelled across more than half of the kingdom to join the Order here, rather than taking orders at a monastery nearer to where he lived?'

'Yes.'

'Because he was your brother, wasn't he? I mean, not just your brother in the Order, but your actual brother, your blood brother.'

Brother Richard's eyes filled with tears and for a moment he couldn't speak, then he forced some words out. 'Yes. We went … ever-y-where toge-ther when we were younger.' Pause. 'Then he tra-velled and I missed him, so when he went a-gain I … went too.' He put his hand up to his jaw, the effort of so much speaking obviously paining him.

Edwin looked on in sympathy. 'I am sorry, Brother – sorry for your loss and also sorry that I'm hurting you. Just one more thing, please?'

Brother Richard nodded, wiping away a dribble from his mouth with his sleeve.

'When you came back, Brother Alexander had a book with him, didn't he? A very precious book that he treasured.'

Brother Richard took a deep breath and made a huge effort to speak as clearly as he could. 'I told him that would be trou-ble. It was a Bible – ill-um-in-a-ted – a Chri-stian book, and he said it should-n't be in hea-then hands, how-ever good their masters were.' He sat back on his pillows, exhausted.

'So he stole it?'

A shake of the head.

'He bought it?'

Nod.

'How?' Edwin realised he wouldn't get any more words so he held up his hand. 'No, wait. I will work it out. Before he travelled he had sold his lands and goods?' There was no shake of the head. 'So he had money, gold, the gold which was meant to keep you both while you were away and then set you up when you got back?' Still no disagreement. 'And he used every last penny to buy the book.'

Brother Richard nodded, but Edwin was talking to himself now. 'Which is why he took a job when he got back and why you joined the Order. And it is also why he would not part with it even when he took the cowl, even when he was supposed to give up all his worldly possessions. And someone knew, and someone didn't like him breaking the Rule. And that person killed him.'

He looked at the man in the bed, but Brother Richard's eyes were closed; he had dozed off from the effort of trying to communicate. Edwin asked the Lord to guard him, and then stood. As he rounded the screen he exchanged a glance with Brother Durand and Prior Henry, who had been standing there the whole time to act as witnesses.

Edwin stood in the abbot's parlour, in exactly the same spot he had occupied on the day he arrived. The abbot sat in his chair, the manuscript of wonders spread open on the table before him.

How Edwin wished he could take it away and look at it in solitude for the rest of his life. But that way madness would lie.

He stumbled over his words at first, too tired and unwilling to speak, but he gained fluency as he went along and eventually communicated to the abbot Brother Alexander's travels, his bringing back of the book, his reasons for joining Roche rather than another abbey, and his relationship with Brother Richard.

The abbot shook his head. 'I never noticed. Of course, two men in middle age may well bear a slight resemblance without being related, but I never considered that they might be brothers. And they never spoke of it.'

'Not all brothers are as close as Brothers Godfrey and Waldef, my lord.' As with Helias and Sir Philip, thought Edwin.

He continued. 'And so, once I had worked out that the "treasure" was a book, that naturally threw suspicion on Brother Octavian. But how could anyone know how much he coveted it – that he would be willing to kill for it?'

The abbot sighed as he looked down at the manuscript. 'It is beautiful, yes, and it contains the word of God, but how could anyone …? Evidently I do not know some of the brethren as well as I should. If I had been a better father to them all, this might not have happened.' He shook his head sadly.

The prior, who had been standing silently in the corner all the while, interjected. 'May I speak, Father?' The abbot gestured his permission, still lost in his own thoughts.

Prior Henry turned to Edwin. 'If, as you say, Brother Octavian did kill Brother Alexander – and everything does seem to point that way – what possible reason could he have for doing away with poor Brother Eugenius?'

Now it was Edwin's turn to sigh, weighed down as he was by guilt. 'I think that he just said the wrong thing at the wrong time. Brother Octavian was no doubt scared that someone might find out what he'd done. By that stage he'd hidden the book – and where better to conceal it than among other volumes? Perhaps he meant at some point to bring it into the abbey library, but someone would notice it and ask where it came from, surely?

And he'd have to share it. So he put it where nobody would think to look, and where he could access it in secret whenever he could.'

The prior was shaking his head. 'But I still don't see what this has to do with Brother Eugenius.'

'He probably mentioned wool ledgers in front of Brother Octavian. He was upset at what had happened at the lay brothers' grange, and he must have said something about confessing at Chapter. Brother Octavian, already in a heightened state, would have been terrified in case he was going to be unmasked. So after the service this morning he either found Brother Eugenius alone in the dormitory or lured him there, and stabbed him.'

'Cold-bloodedly?' The abbot managed to sound both disbelieving and horrified.

'Yes. For it is a sad fact that once a man has killed, he is more likely to kill again.'

The abbot and the prior looked at each other. 'I have heard this,' admitted the prior.

'But what actual proof do we have?' The abbot pointed to the book. 'This, yes, but does it show that Brother Octavian committed murder? What you say sounds very plausible but I would not like to condemn one of the brethren unless we are sure.'

'I thought you would say that, my lord, which is why I wanted to find Brother Octavian and the book together before I said anything. Although that ended up leading to the death of Brother Eugenius, an innocent.'

'An innocent, as you say. *Requiescat in pace.*' They all crossed themselves.

'But if …' He tailed off.

'What is it?' The abbot had caught the tone of Edwin's voice.

Edwin swallowed. 'You're not going to like this, my lord.'

'Not going to like what?'

'From what I have gathered so far, I think Brother Octavian may have thought that in some way he was justified in killing Brother Alexander. But even he will harbour doubts in his soul about Brother Eugenius. Could we … might you give your permission for Brother Eugenius's body to be brought to Chapter tomorrow morning when Brother Octavian comes before it? I think that might sting him into a confession.'

The abbot closed his eyes. 'What you suggest is … distasteful.' He opened them again and looked directly at Edwin. 'But do you truly believe that this will bring an end to all this? Everything? We can be sure that the killer is found and we can return to our normal lives?'

Edwin squared his shoulders. 'Yes, my lord.' He hoped desperately that he was right.

'Then so be it.'

The abbot looked down at Brother Octavian, prostrate on the floor. 'You will endure your earthly punishment regardless of whether you tell us or not. But for the sake of your immortal soul, your peace with Almighty God, you must make a full and frank confession.'

Brother Octavian sobbed on to the flagstones. Edwin watched as the tears made darker patches on the floor as they dripped from his face.

The abbot was relentless. 'Speak.'

The shivering monk mumbled something which Edwin didn't catch.

The abbot looked at the prior and nodded. 'You may raise yourself to your knees while you confess.'

Brother Octavian pushed himself up into a kneeling position. He looked around at his audience, his face streaked with tears, and then lowered his head again before beginning his tale.

'Brother Alexander was a learned man, a travelled man. I enjoyed speaking with him about our books and about others he had read while he was abroad. One day he told me of the most exquisite treasure he had ever seen – a holy Bible illuminated on every page with gold and coloured illustrations. He said that the mere sight of it made him want to drop to his knees and praise God for the beauty of His creation. He told me that while he was in the southern Moorish kingdoms he would spend hours every day studying it. I asked him to tell me of it again and again, until I felt that I knew it almost as well as he.'

He took in a great shuddering breath and looked directly at the abbot. 'And then, Father Abbot, one day he told me something he said he had never told anyone. When he returned from his travels, he had brought the Bible with him.'

Edwin heard an intake of breath from the silent monks around him.

'I asked him why he had not given it to the abbey, Father, for surely such a treasure should be shared, should be available for all to study? Such a book should be kept in safety in the library here, and I would have guarded it with my life. And when Brother Alexander took the cowl he swore to forsake his earthly goods. But he would not answer me, would not show me the book.' His voice rose into a howl of anguish. 'He would not tell me where he had hidden it! Such a treasure almost within reach, one of the wonders of the world, and I could not see it for myself!'

He stopped as another huge sob overtook him, and buried his face in his hands. Edwin looked around the silent room at the tension on the face of the brothers. Some of them were leaning forward, others gripping their robes in clenched fists.

Brother Octavian managed to slow his breathing and choke out his next words. 'I took to following him, Father. I knew he would not be able to hide the book anywhere without wanting to go and see it, so I followed him. And when I saw him disappear into the side of the cliff I knew that had to be it. By the time he came out it was too late to go in – someone would have missed me if I had not come to vespers – so I resolved to steal out in the night. Once compline had finished and the brethren were asleep I slipped away out of the abbey. I had no problem getting past Brother Thurstan, and I left the small gate unbarred. It took me a long while to find my way there in the moonlight and even longer to find the cave, but at last I was there.'

Edwin knew how this was going to end, but he found himself on the edge of his seat along with everyone else.

'And there it was.'

All the monks gasped, as one.

'I could not see it properly as it was dark, but I knew what it was. I took it out of the box and bag which held it, as I thought it would be easier that way: anyone who saw me carrying a bag would no doubt ask me what I was doing, but who would think to question me holding a book? I brought it back to the abbey. I was going to put it in the library, but that would not do. So I hid it: I went to the lay brothers' parlour, removed the pages from one of the wool ledgers, put the manuscript inside, and threw the ledger pages into the beck.'

There was a shocked silence in the room. What struck Edwin most was that Brother Octavian seemed to be feeling no guilt; such tears as he had shed were for himself.

The abbot looked down on him with no pity. 'Continue, Brother Octavian. You have told us a tale but you have not yet confessed your greatest sin.'

Brother Octavian spread his arms wide. 'The rest is simple, Father. Brother Alexander would soon find that his book was gone, and he would know who had taken it. He had to be silenced. So while the brethren were at *lectio divina* I took one of the knives from the scriptorium and stabbed him with it.'

The uproar that this produced in the room was all the more forceful for its lack of volume. Monks were raising their arms to the heavens and groaning, wailing, praying … all in contrast to the kneeling figure in the middle who remained immobile.

Brother Octavian was continuing, now in a flat, emotionless voice which was in contrast to his earlier passion. 'I knew it was him as he had the work of Aelred of Rievaulx which he had been reading since Lent. I was careful to stab him in the heart through the back of his robe so that no blood would spill on to the text.'

He looked upwards before continuing. 'But I had misjudged my punishment. I knew that I would burn for eternity in hellfire, but I thought it would be worth it for the study of the book. How was I to know that my punishment would be to live in constant fear that someone would find it and take it away?'

Edwin was jolted as an accusing finger emerged from the sleeve of the monk's robe and pointed straight at him. 'Him. Who was he? Some upstart villager from somewhere who thought he was interested in learning. But he was cunning, and I knew he would find it eventually.'

The abbot spoke again. 'But in the event, it was not Edwin who frightened you the most, was it? It was poor Brother Eugenius.'

Now the first signs of agonised guilt started to show on Brother Octavian's face. 'He came back from the grange – I knew he had been talking to Edwin – he spoke in a confused way so I didn't understand everything he said, but he mentioned wool ledgers and said that he must make a confession before Chapter – it wasn't all his sin, but he needed the truth to be told – I was sure he was looking at me.'

He faltered into silence. The abbot locked his gaze with Edwin's and Edwin felt himself nodding.

The abbot's voice was like stone. 'Look, Brother Octavian. Look upon the face of the dead.' He pointed to where a shrouded body lay in the back corner of the room. It was behind the abbot and the prior and was covered in a plain cloth, so neither Brother Octavian nor most of the other brethren had noticed it before. But now the prior removed the cloth to reveal the body.

Brother Octavian started to his feet with a shriek and began to move backwards. But brothers Durand and Helias caught his arms.

The abbot was grim. 'Bring him closer.'

They forced him to move forward until he was looking down at the body. He writhed in their grasp, trying to turn his face away.

The voice was like stone. 'Look at him. Gaze on the face of your murdered brother and tell me what you had to do with his death.'

'Look!'

It was the prior who had exclaimed. Every man in the chapter-house, including Edwin and Martin, craned forward to follow the direction of his finger. Brother Eugenius had been washed and was dressed in a clean robe, a linen bandage tied around his jaw. The robe, the band, his face, all were white. But a crimson stain was erupting from the site of the wound on his chest, spreading across the robe, accusing the killer in his presence.

Brother Octavian screamed and fell limp in the arms of his captors. 'Yes, yes, I killed him!' he sobbed. 'Please, cover him up – take him away – please!'

At a nod from the abbot the prior replaced the cloth over the body. Edwin kept glancing back at it, and sure enough, eventually a red stain made its way through.

Brother Octavian was back kneeling on the floor. Now he could hardly speak through his sobs. 'I had already taken a knife from the scriptorium. The service had finished and we would soon be on our way to Chapter. As ever some of the brethren wished to visit the latrine so I followed them up to the dormitory as if I was one of them, signing to Brother Eugenius to ask if he would come to help me with something. He followed.'

Edwin surveyed the room. Every single eye was on the man on his knees.

'I waited until the others had gone. Once we reached his place at the end of the dormitory he turned to face me, and God forgive me, I plunged the dagger straight into his heart.'

Many of the monks had tears streaming down their cheeks. Edwin was taken back to a place and time where he, too, had plunged a knife into another man's body, and for a moment he staggered as he remembered the feeling, the awful sensation.

Now that Brother Octavian had started, it seemed he couldn't stop. 'It was sharp and I thought it would kill him straight away, but it didn't! His eyes looked at me in such pain, and a great groan began to escaped him. I pushed him down on the bed and forced my hand over his mouth until he had stopped breathing.'

The abbot's face could have been the model for a carving of a man enduring the torments of hell.

Brother Octavian's shoulders shook as he forced out his last few words. 'I realised that my habit was covered in blood so I took it off and hid it under one of the beds – I can't remember which one. The I took a spare and put it on and came to Chapter. And I heard Brother Sinnulph's confession, and I knew I had been wrong …'

Brother Octavian faded into an agonised silence. After a long moment during which he locked eyes with the abbot, tears streaming, he lowered himself back to his penitent position, face down on the floor, and spoke no more.

The abbot let the silence grow longer, trying to compose himself and waiting until the agitated monks had settled themselves and peace reigned in the chamber once more. Then he addressed the wretch on the floor.

'You have confessed to the most heinous crime, the murder in cold blood of two men, God's chosen creatures, and also your sworn brothers. You have offered no justification – your talk of sharing the book for all is just a mask for your own greed and selfishness. You coveted this treasure, you wanted it for yourself, and you were willing to kill to get it. You murdered Brother Alexander for it. And then, to try and hide your crime you killed another, an innocent. His spirit has accused you in this very room.' Edwin couldn't help looking at the shrouded body again.

'THOU – SHALT – NOT – KILL!' thundered the abbot suddenly, making everyone in the room jump. The abbot pointed with a shaking finger to the shrouded and bloodstained figure. 'For this you have shown no repentance and therefore *there can be no forgiveness.*' He fell silent as he tried with a mighty effort to compose himself. When he spoke once more his voice was level. 'You will be cast out and exiled from us.'

Edwin felt Martin move impatiently next to him. He put a steadying hand on his arm to forestall the outburst he knew was coming, about how the monk should be turned over for hanging, because he had an idea of what was coming next. Martin swallowed his words before they came out of his mouth and Edwin turned his attention back to the abbot, who was continuing.

'You will be as one dead to us, and you will spend the rest of your days in a living tomb, praying for the souls of Brother Alexander and Brother Eugenius and praying that your suffering and repentance might be so great that some measure of mercy might be extended to you during your time *in hell.*'

He looked around at the rest of the monks. 'As of now, Brother Octavian is dead to us. None of you will ever speak one word to him again. Now come.' He swept past the prostrate man, making sure that the skirts of his robe did not touch him, and out of the room. One by one the other brothers stood and followed him, until Edwin, Martin and Prior Henry were left alone in the room with the condemned man, lying perfectly still on the floor.

Martin walked over to the shrouded body. 'How did you make it bleed like that just when he was looking?'

The prior looked surprised. 'I didn't.'

Edwin saw both faces turn to him. 'Don't look at me!'

They all gazed at the corpse. Prior Henry crossed himself. 'A second miracle?'

'God's work, Brother,' Edwin heard himself saying. 'In case my word wasn't enough.' He muttered the rest under his breath. 'This time the killer of an innocent shall not go free.' He unclenched the fist he hadn't realised he'd made.

Prior Henry expelled a long breath and turned his attention to the condemned man, still unmoving. 'While we wait for the cell to be built he must be kept alone. We will put him in one of the cellars and lock the door.'

Martin nodded. 'I don't think he'll be trouble but I'll help you take him.'

Prior Henry inclined his head, his face still pale from the wonder he had witnessed. 'Thank you. But please, as Father Abbot said, take care not to speak to him. Not now, and not later.'

Edwin watched as the two men lifted the unresponsive Brother Octavian to his feet, took one of his arms each and started to move towards the door. As they passed Edwin, the condemned man suddenly came to life and he lunged forward. He could not reach Edwin, of course, not with Martin and the hefty prior both holding him, but Edwin took a step back nonetheless.

Brother Octavian's voice was pleading. 'Of all people, surely you can understand? You saw the book, and I saw you – I saw how deeply you felt about it. You wanted it – you wanted to spend the rest of your life looking at it – I *know* you did. Surely you can understand?' His eyes bored into Edwin's soul.

Edwin closed his eyes and slowly turned his back. He folded his arms to quell the shaking in his hands, and remained in silence until he heard the others leave the room.

Chapter Fourteen

A movement from the doorway caught Edwin's eye and he turned to see that Brother Helias had re-entered the chapterhouse.

The cellarer's voice was full of sympathy. 'You look as though you need some time for peace and reflection.'

Edwin nodded. 'Not to mention sleep.' He ran his hand over his face.

'I don't think you'll get much rest in here – you'll just sit thinking about everything which has happened. Come to my office, where it's quiet, and I'll find you a cup of something.'

'Aren't you supposed to be reading, with all the others?'

'I am often excused on account of the duties of my post. And now that I have no assistant …' he trailed off.

Edwin touched his shoulder, briefly. 'I am sorry, truly sorry, about Brother Eugenius. If only I had acted earlier.' To his shame he felt tears stinging his eyes and he buried his face in his hands.

Brother Helias spoke soothingly. 'Come now.' He put an arm around Edwin's shoulder and led him out of the chapterhouse. They went around the long way to avoid walking through the cloister where all the other monks were, and eventually found themselves in Brother Helias's office. Edwin felt himself being lowered on to a stool, and he inhaled the room's scent of spices. A cup was put into his hand and he took a sip of cool ale. He opened his eyes, sat back against the wall and said nothing, watching the cellarer bustle about his tasks.

After some time Brother Helias paused and looked at him. 'Are you ready to speak now? You might feel better if you just let out whatever is bothering you.'

'A confession, you mean?'

'No, no – for you have nothing to confess and I am not a priest like some of the brethren.' He drew up another stool, set it next to

Edwin and sat down. He took both of Edwin's hands in his own. 'But I can see that you are burdened with something, something which is weighing heavily upon you. If you don't wish to speak of it, then that's fine. But if you do, then I am listening.'

There was silence. Edwin's eyes wandered over the room, the stores, the parchments, the monk in front of him, the colour of the hair around the tonsure, so like his own. He stared at the weave of Brother Helias's robe, noticing a small patch of grey where there was an imperfection in the wool. He wondered if Brother Sinnulph would have been allowed to class that as a high grade.

And then he talked. He spoke of his life in the earl's household, the ever-more impossible tasks he was given, the way people kept dying violent deaths around him. He spoke of his hasty actions of the previous month which had almost resulted in a number of deaths, including his own; he spoke of his subsequent inability to act here at the abbey which had left another corpse on his conscience. He spoke of losing the only woman he thought he would ever love, and his despair; he spoke of the abbot's offer and his feeling of being torn about staying or going.

Once he had faltered into silence he realised he was on his knees clutching the hem of Brother Helias's robe. He uncurled his fingers, wiped the back of his hand across his wet face, and hauled himself back up on to the stool. He looked at the floor.

At first he couldn't work out what Brother Helias was saying to him, but then he realised it was a prayer, Latin being pronounced in a soothing voice as the monk asked the Lord and His saints to help Edwin and to watch over him. Edwin let it wash over him as he wondered miserably if the Lord was listening.

Brother Helias finished his prayer. 'Amen. And now, let us address more practical matters.'

'Which ones?'

'One thing at a time, my son, one thing at a time. You speak of the dangers of your life in the earl's household. But consider that they are also challenges for you and your mind. Ask yourself: would you really, truly be happier labouring in the fields day after day?'

Edwin was tempted to answer that yes, he would, if only because it would be less dangerous, but he knew it was a lie. He would go mad from the boredom. He said as much.

Brother Helias nodded. 'You are not suited for work in the fields so God's plan for you must lie along a different path. It looks as though you have three choices.'

'Three?'

'You can return to the lord earl and continue in his service. Or you can stay here and join the Order, as Father Abbot has invited you to do. Or you can do neither of those things but instead leave and do something else.'

'Do what?'

Brother Helias chuckled. 'That I cannot answer, not on so short an acquaintance, but there are many opportunities for a man who wishes to travel and who is not afraid of the attendant hardships.'

'Only if he is a man with money.' And that was the crux of the matter. He was not a lord, not a knight, not a merchant, not a man of means. He must learn to know his place. 'Which reminds me,' he sat up straighter and tried to get his tongue not to fall over the words as they came out of his mouth, 'in all this talk of me joining the abbey, surely we are all forgetting: I would have to be a lay brother, wouldn't I?'

'How so?'

'You think that because I've come here from the earl that I'm from a great house – well, I'm not. I'm only in his household by accident; I come from a family which has lived in the village of Conisbrough since as long as anyone remembers.'

Now Brother Helias looked confused. 'But – you are educated? You read, you understand Latin?'

'My father was the bailiff on the lord earl's Conisbrough estate, which raised him a little above the village. He sent me to be taught by our priest, and that's how I learned. But I am by no means from a noble family, not even a minor one. I would bring no donation to the abbey. And so I would end up labouring in fields all my life anyway, would I not?' He was aware that his voice sounded bitter, and he made no attempt to disguise it.

Brother Helias looked thoughtful. 'I don't think the situation is quite as you paint it.'

'Why not?'

'As you may be aware, Father Abbot goes to great pains to ensure that each of us serves God and the Order in the way best suited to us. He knows that you are intelligent and lettered. He knows that you would be of more worth to the abbey as a monk who could eventually become one of the obedientiaries, so he would surely admit you as a choir monk. There are many who would make good labourers, but few who would make good cellarers. Or, for that matter, good scholars.'

Edwin jerked his head up. 'Scholars?'

'Yes. Don't forget, once you are a monk you will be obliged to undertake the *lectio divina*. You will read every day, and deepen your faith and understanding.'

Edwin licked his lips. 'Read? The books in the library here?'

Brother Helias inclined his head and watched Edwin for a moment. 'But there is one more thing we must speak of. This woman you mentioned, whom you love.'

Misery returned. 'She is in Lincoln, she is married to another, and I will never see her again.'

'I know very little of these matters, my son, as I've been in the cloister all my adult life. But tell me, is it likely that you might ever love another?'

'I – how can I know that? But in all honesty, I don't think so.'

'So you will not pine for a different life? One with a wife and children?' He sighed. 'I went through a period, many years ago, when I questioned my own life here and wondered how things would have been different had I married and had sons and daughters.'

'How did you overcome it?'

'I realised that I was in the right place. Had I been a married man with a wife and children, I would no doubt be yearning for the life of the cloister and of quiet contemplation. I prayed and I understood that we need to recognise that we will always dream that something else is better, when in fact it is not.'

'So, you have been happy here?'

'Yes.'

'So your brother said – and I don't think he's very pleased about it.'

Brother Helias stifled a movement of surprise. 'Ah. So, you know about that, do you?'

Edwin nodded. 'I wasn't trying to pry, but I found out while I was looking into Brother Alexander's death. Sir Philip told me all about it because he thought I suspected him of being the killer.'

'Philip would never kill a man in cold blood. In battle, yes, or maybe even if he struck someone during the heat of an argument, but he would never plan and carry out a murder like that.'

'A true knight, then.'

Brother Helias sighed. 'Yes, albeit one who prefers a knight's martial duties to his administrative ones. But that book is closed, and we shall speak of it no more. I am happy here, and I intend to stay in the Order, in whatever capacity God and Father Abbot see fit, until the day of my own death.'

'Happy …' Edwin couldn't even start to comprehend what that might mean.

Brother Helias raised a finger. 'But.'

'But what?'

He had a thoughtful expression on his face. 'The Lord grant that the words come out in the way that I intend them. But – when you are making your choices, you need to remember to be running *towards* something, not just away from something else.'

'I … I don't think I understand what you mean.'

'Do not choose to enter the Order only because you wish to get away from your position in the lord earl's household. The life here can be hard – the lack of sleep, the restricted diet, the obedience, the labour – and it is not to be undertaken lightly. Do not join us because you think you have nothing else. Join us only if you *want* to join. Ask yourself in your heart, do you *want* to live here, within these walls, for the rest of your life? Do you *want* to spend a large part of each day in prayer? Do you *want* to study and learn? Then, and only then, will you know where your path lies.'

Edwin stared ahead without speaking, and after a few moments Brother Helias stood and went quietly about his duties. Edwin watched him without seeing as he let all the thoughts in his mind crash against each other and fight their way through to the front. He closed his eyes, but that just made him feel as though he was falling from a high place. Better to stare straight ahead.

It was some while later when he stood. He brushed the front of his tunic down with his hands, ran his fingers through his hair to try and neaten it, and wiped his sleeve on his face. He took a deep breath. 'Brother, do you think it would be possible to speak with the lord abbot? I have made a decision.'

———

Martin hummed to himself as he brushed the courser's coat until it shone. It was all over, they would be out of here by noon, and he could go back to where he belonged. His saddlebag was packed and lying in the corner, and he had already lugged over from the guesthouse the bag containing his mail hauberk. He hadn't needed it in the end, although perhaps he should try to persuade Edwin to wear one in future.

He looked over the horse's back to see Brother Guy approaching, so he waved and beckoned him over. He was still a little ashamed of his earlier behaviour, but he seemed to have been forgiven, and he had certainly appreciated the lay brother's presence during the scene the previous day.

Brother Guy picked up a second brush and looked enquiringly from Martin to Edwin's palfrey.

'Please do, Brother. I'm just getting everything ready to leave. No doubt Edwin will be here soon.'

He watched as Brother Guy made swift, practised strokes and soothed the horse with calming sounds without actually speaking. Martin's own stokes grew slower and then stopped. 'Brother, may I ask you a question?' He received a nod so he stepped round into the other stall. 'How did you hit Brother … you know, *him*, so that he was knocked out straight away? He just went straight down after one punch and I've never seen that before.'

Brother Guy started to frown and shake his head so Martin rushed on. 'I know, I know you're a brother now and you don't do that sort of thing, but it would be really useful for me to know, and it actually prevented more violence, didn't it?'

A conflicted expression crossed Brother Guy's face but eventually he nodded. He came to stand next to Martin, looked at the horse, pulled Martin out of the stall into the path through the stable where there was more space, then pointed to himself. He placed his left leg forward, right leg back, and then bounced a little to show he was loose. He indicated to Martin that he should do the same. The he started to bring his right arm back, low down, while twisting at the waist. Martin followed. Brother Guy gave him a considering look and then indicated that he was too tense. Martin tried to make his movements more free and Brother Guy nodded.

Next Brother Guy took up a position opposite Martin. He took Martin's arm and clenched fist, then squeezed to show that he should now tighten it. Martin braced himself, feeling the muscles in his arm harden. Then his fist was pulled round and placed on an exact spot on Brother Guy's face, on one side of the lower part of his jaw. Martin's eyes locked with the other man's even as his knuckles were pressed into his face.

'I have to hit here? Exactly right here?'

Brother Guy nodded. He mimed his head snapping to one side away from the blow, and then rolled his eyes and made as if to fall backwards.

'That will knock him out? If I make his head do that?'

Brother Guy nodded again. This time he took Martin's fist again and pulled his arm until it had gone past his head.

'What ... oh, you mean I need to make sure I follow through? I don't just stop once I've hit him?'

'You also need to make sure you turn your hips a bit more.'

The voice had come from behind Martin and he turned in some embarrassment to see that Sir Philip had entered. The knight was carrying saddlebags which he dropped in another stall containing the bay Martin had seen previously, which now didn't have any sign of a bandage.

Sir Philip came towards them. Martin was acutely aware that he still had his fist in Brother Guy's face. 'I'm setting off imminently. I didn't get the chance to talk to you last night but I heard what happened.' He looked from one to the other. 'Heard about both of you.' He bowed deeply to Brother Guy. 'My lord.'

Brother Guy shook his head with a sad smile and indicated his robes.

'I know, I know. But what a man is now does not erase what he has been.' He looked up at Martin. 'Or what he will be. You'll make a fine knight one day – just make sure you never stop learning. May I?' This last was addressed to Brother Guy, who inclined his head. 'You're doing your arm exactly right, but don't stand there like a stone while you're bringing it round. If you twist your hips while you're doing it you'll be able to put more force behind it.'

Martin tried it and could immediately feel the difference. He stepped back so they could both see him, and then made the exact sequence of moves they had outlined between them.

'Yes, good,' said Sir Philip, and Brother Guy nodded his approval once more.

The knight clapped them both on the back. 'I might not know how to manage an estate, but I can still hit a man effectively. But now I must depart. Perhaps our paths will cross again.'

Martin watched him saddle the bay and lead it out of the stable before he turned to Brother Guy. 'Do you think I'll make a good knight?'

The lay brother thought carefully for so long that Martin started to feel the first fingers of worry. Then Brother Guy nodded. He took Martin's right arm, held it up, and pointed to his sword. Martin understood. 'I need to know how to use this.' Brother Guy indicated agreement, and then pointed to his head, tapping his temple with one finger. 'And I also need to use my head. Well, I'm not quite so good at that, but I'll try. Sir Geoffrey is always saying that.' Brother Guy nodded once more but then held his finger up to show he hadn't finished. 'Something else? What is it?'

Brother Guy pointed to his heart.

Martin bowed his head, and then knelt. 'I will try, Brother, I really will. Please, will you bless me before I go?' He felt a hand on his head and looked up to see Brother Guy's lips moving silently in prayer. Then the hand was lifted and Brother Guy made the sign of the cross in the air over him before helping him to his feet. Then with one last pat on the shoulder he was gone, and Martin turned back to his horse.

He spent a long time at it – after all, he wanted them to look their best when they arrived back at Conisbrough in front of everyone – but eventually he found he had brushed, saddled and packed and there was still no sign of Edwin. Where in the Lord's name was he? Were they leaving or not?

———————

Edwin stood with his hands behind his back so the abbot would not see him twisting his fingers. He felt obscurely as though he had been summoned to answer for some misdemeanour, although it was he who had asked for the meeting and he hadn't done anything wrong.

The abbot came as near to smiling as Edwin had ever seen. He was seated, his long fingers intertwined as he rested his hands on the table. 'You wished to speak to me, my son?'

'Yes, my lord.'

'On the subject of your decision on joining the Order.'

'Yes, my lord.'

'You have considered carefully?'

'Yes, my lord. And this morning I spoke at some length with Brother Helias, which helped me to get a number of things straight in my mind.'

'Yes?'

'He helped me to see, my lord, that a life here would mean many things. It would mean peace and seclusion, it would mean work and prayer, and it would mean studying and learning, so I could have a greater understanding of God and the world.'

The abbot nodded. 'Very well put. Brother Helias sees things very clearly. And are these things attractive to you?'

'They are, my lord.'

'I am glad to hear it. We can ...'

'But.'

The abbot, probably unused to being interrupted, looked up in surprise.

'Pardon me, my lord, but there is more. The other thing Brother Helias made me realise was that, however much I might think I want that, it is not for me.'

To Edwin's surprise, the abbot's voice was understanding rather than angry. 'Can you explain to me why that should be?'

'I – I just – it's difficult to put into words, my lord.'

'Please, try. The Lord knows what is in your heart without the need for verbal expression, but I am not so fortunate. Please help me to understand.'

'Well. To start with, I don't feel that I have a great *calling* to be a monk. I know that perhaps others may join religious orders without such a vocation, but if I was going to dedicate my life to something, I would want to *want* it more. As it is, to use Brother Helias's words, I would be running away from my old life, not running towards a new one.' Edwin started to pace up and down, enumerating his points on his fingers. 'I do want peace – more than anything. And I do want to work: I have no fear of that. But I'm not sure I could trust myself to be content if I didn't think that I was suited to the work I was bidden to do. I realise that's prideful of me, but I have to think of it. And I do want to study – I was overwhelmed by all the books you have here and the possibilities they contained – but who is to say that I wouldn't begin to covet them, to want more, as did Br— you know who I mean. I would be doing it for my own purposes, not God's. And then there is my duty.'

'Your duty?'

'To the earl, my lord. I will be honest and admit that I don't particularly like some of the things he asks me to do, but I owe it to him.' He looked at the abbot, but he could find no expression to help him work out what he was thinking. 'If he hadn't sent me here, for a task I didn't really want to do, then I wouldn't have had this opportunity in the first place, would I? Would it be fair to repay him for his trust in me by asking to leave his service? Or worse, staying here and cowering behind the walls while another tells him in my place?'

He stopped pacing. 'And finally, there is my family. My mother is a widow with no other children, my lord, and what would she do without me? And …'

The abbot was looking at him in sympathy. 'Peace, my son, peace. I have heard enough to know that our life here is not for you, and I will not press you further. But you should know that this is our loss, not yours. You are a good man, and perhaps without knowing it you have demonstrated adherence to some of our most important rules.'

'I have?'

'Many of them. For example, precept eight: to respect all men; eighteen: to come to the help of those in trouble; thirty-four: not to be proud. And forty-nine: to know for certain that God sees one everywhere. He will guide and protect you in the life you choose.'

'I hope so, my lord.'

The abbot stood and came round the table to face Edwin. 'You may not believe it, my son, but He will. Your fidelity to your lord and your devotion to your duty will have their reward.'

Edwin could feel the weight of sadness threatening to crush him. 'Maybe in the afterlife, my lord, but good things don't tend to happen to me in this one.'

Abbot Reginald put one hand on his shoulder. 'Careful, Edwin. Despair is also a sin. Now, kneel and I will give you my blessing before you go.'

Edwin did as he was bid and tried to swallow back his tears as he listened to the words of the prayer. Then he kissed the ring on the abbot's finger and stood.

'Thank you, my lord.'

The abbot's parting words followed him as he left the parlour. 'Remember the final precept on our list and keep it with you, my son: never despair of God's mercy.'

Martin was kicking his heels outside the stables when two white monks passed by. They stopped to incline their heads and he saw that they were Godfrey and Waldef, the twins. Martin didn't know which one was Brother Godfrey who had come to Conisbrough, but whichever he was, he had lost the expression of pain he had once carried: they both looked content. Martin bowed to them, for without knowing it they had helped him to save Edwin's life. One of them made the sign of the cross in the air and they moved on.

Another white monk approached, the one whose hair looked a bit like Edwin's, though Martin couldn't remember his name. '*Benedicte*, my son. Are you waiting for Edwin?'

'Yes, Brother. Do you know where he's got to?'

'I spoke with him at some length this morning, and he has gone to see Father Abbot.'

'Oh.' Martin couldn't think what that might be about, but he didn't care as long as it was over quickly. 'Do you know how long he will be?'

'I'm afraid not. You are welcome to sit in my office while you wait, or you could go back to the guesthouse …?'

'Thank you, but I'll wait here. I'm sure he won't be long.'

The monk looked as though he was going to say something else, but instead he inclined his head politely and moved on.

Martin had a sudden thought. 'Wait!' The monk stopped. 'Do you happen to know if Benedict – you know, the novice – is still in the infirmary?'

'I think that he is, yes.'

'Thank you.' Martin watched the monk walk away. It would mean braving the temper of the infirmarer again, but he should probably say goodbye to Benedict before he left, and it was better than hanging around.

When Martin arrived at the infirmary building he found that the door was already open, letting in some air and light to those inside. He peered round. Brother Durand was bending over one of the beds, spooning something into the mouth of one of the aged monks, and Martin thought he might get away with it. But of course as soon as he stepped inside the doorway he cast a shadow and the infirmarer looked up and saw him straight away. His lips set in a thin line.

Martin didn't want to be prevented from entering, but he didn't want a scene either. And then, bizarrely, he remembered something the old hermit woman in the woods had said, and it gave him an idea. Looking straight at the infirmarer, he deliberately unbuckled his sword belt, removed it, wrapped the belt around the sword in its scabbard, and placed the whole lot on the ground outside the building. Then he took a deep breath and walked in.

Brother Durand stood and walked towards him until they were face-to-face. Martin felt again the unusual sensation of looking at someone who almost matched him in height, and they stood for a moment in silence.

It was the infirmarer who spoke first. 'Thank you.'

Martin nodded. 'When men with swords come calling …' He saw the surprised look on the monk's face. 'Someone said that to me recently. And I thought about all the things you've said to me since I've been here and I wondered if maybe it wasn't me, it was the sword?'

Brother Durand nodded slowly. 'I think you may be right.'

'What happened?'

'It was a long time ago.'

'But something happened?'

'Yes. There were wars throughout my youth. The old King Henry against his sons, then his sons among each other, and then Count John against his brother, or in his brother's absence. Men from both sides would ride across the countryside, stealing and destroying. My own family was safe behind our walls, but more than once I woke to see smoking ruins and had to ride through villages of the destitute and dead. I had played with some of those boys when we were children, and what had they and their mothers done to deserve death? Nothing.'

'I'm sorry.'

'I'm sure you are, but if your lord ordered you to do the same then you would, wouldn't you?'

Martin didn't know what to say, so he said nothing.

Brother Durand held up his hand. 'But I should not judge you for actions you have not yet committed and may never commit. Instead I should treat you with respect as I would any man – and thank you for the help you have given me and the brethren while you have been here.'

'You're welcome, Brother.' Martin looked at the empty bed, still in the corner, where Brother Octavian had been brought after the scene in the parlour. 'But I can't help thinking that you're all a bit too lenient. He killed two men – two monks – and yet he won't face a trial? He won't hang?'

Brother Durand was shaking his head. 'I don't think you quite understand what will happen to him, how he will spend the rest of his life. If you did, I think you would see it as a far harsher punishment than death.'

Martin had no idea what he was talking about, but the last thing he wanted right now was to get into an argument with Brother Durand just after they had apparently made peace.

The infirmarer resumed his normal brisk tone. 'Now, did you come to see me in particular?'

'I wondered if I might be allowed to speak with Benedict before I go. Please.'

'That will be fine as long as you do not disturb the others. He's there.'

Martin followed the direction of the pointing finger and spotted Benedict a few beds further up the room. 'Thank you.'

Benedict was awake and struggled up into a sitting position when he saw he had a visitor. Martin shoved a pillow behind his back.

'How are you?'

'I am well, thank you. I believe it was you who carried me here when I …'

'I did. But don't worry, I would do the same for anyone.'

Benedict allowed himself a smile. 'I was not trying to put myself above others. But please allow me to thank you anyway.'

'You're welcome.' There was an awkward silence. Martin was aware he wasn't very good at this kind of thing.

'How lo—'

'When are y—'

They had both spoken at the same time. Martin gestured. 'You first.'

'When are you leaving? I understand that your business here is finished.'

'It is. And we're already packed – I'm just waiting for Edwin to finish talking to the abbot and then we're off.'

Benedict looked sad. 'And you're pleased about that, aren't you?'

'You bet I —' Martin caught himself just in time. 'I mean, yes, I am. For I need to get back to my lord, to my service.'

'And I to mine.'

'That was what I was going to ask you. How long must you stay here? In the infirmary, I mean?'

'Another two days, Brother Durand says. Until my fever has completely gone. And in the meantime I must eat the infirmary food, which means eating more. And there is *meat*.'

Martin almost laughed at the shock in Benedict's voice. 'Well, don't get too used to it. You'll be back on beans and vegetables soon enough.'

Strangely, this made Benedict look more cheerful. 'Yes. And back to the usual round of offices and labour.'

Martin looked at his weedy arms. 'Just remember – chopping wood is all about getting the rhythm. Do it like I showed you and it will get easier.'

'Thank you.'

There was another silence.

Benedict broke it this time. 'I will pray for you.'

'For me?'

'Yes. I was just thinking selfishly – thinking that I would miss you and that it was a shame you were going. But I see that you would be unhappy here, just as I would be unhappy if I went where you were going. We each have our own path and we must be content.'

Martin nodded. 'Do you know what? I think you'll make a very good monk.'

'Really?' Benedict looked like he'd been given a bag of gold. Or perhaps that was the wrong thought. He looked as though he'd been given a plate of beans and vegetables. Martin smiled to himself.

'Yes. And when I turn eighteen next spring I will remember that you are doing the same and taking your vows. And I will think of you and wish you well. But now …'

He held out his hand. Hesitantly, Benedict did the same, and Martin shook it firmly before he stood. There was something in his eye and he rubbed it hard as he walked out without looking back.

———•———

Edwin watched the countryside go past as he sat on the horse. Villages, houses, fields, people, animals, crops … even the thought of a good harvest didn't rouse him. Martin had tried to make conversation with him once or twice, but he'd just grunted so Martin had given up. Martin himself seemed quite happy – stretching his limbs as if he'd been in a cramped cell for a week, and looking as though he'd rush off in a whooping gallop if he didn't have Edwin and the packhorse slowing him down. Edwin was half-tempted to tell him to go and get on with it.

He had done his duty. That must be its own reward. He had been sent by the earl to Roche to find out who had killed Brother Alexander, and he had done just that. Moreover, he had survived the experience and could therefore expect to be given something even more difficult to do next time. He would not starve even if the harvest was bad one year, and he could afford to keep his mother in comfort so that she need not be forced to marry again if she didn't wish. He must keep thinking of that. His own life, his own happiness, was incidental.

Martin pointed out the castle which had now appeared in the distance, and urged his mount into a trot. But the castle could be seen for miles around and they were nowhere near Conisbrough yet, so Edwin continued to let his horse amble at its own pace. Martin realised he was getting too far ahead and came back.

They were overtaken by a rider heading in the same direction who was making good speed.

Martin reined in next to Edwin. 'What in God's name is the matter with you?'

'Nothing.'

'Oh yes, very nothing, I can see that. You've been looking like you're on your way to a funeral ever since we left. Aren't you glad to get out of there? Didn't you find it even slightly ... suffocating?'

Edwin made a noncommittal noise.

'And that reminds me – what did you need to talk to the abbot about this morning? I thought we were all finished so I started packing. Did I miss something?'

A little bell sounded in Edwin's mind. This was something else he needed to keep buried, along with the awareness that he had not cared whether he lived or died when the moment had come. Nobody would understand – it would just cause puzzlement and distress. He needed to come up with something. 'Oh, I just wanted to ask him about that book – the one that caused all the trouble.'

As he had expected, mention of the word 'book' caused Martin's eyes to glaze over and he lost interest in questioning Edwin further.

But now Edwin's own mind turned to the book, and the way he had felt when he was studying it. He knew, in his heart, that he could have spent the rest of his life looking at those pages, caring nothing for anyone or anything else ever again. And that was not a good way to think. If he had to bury any more secrets he wouldn't have room for them all.

A sigh escaped him as he recognised that they were coming into Conisbrough village. It was mid-afternoon so there weren't many people around; most of the able-bodied were out in the fields. Robin the carpenter was there, though – he toiled in a workshop set at the side of his house. He looked up and saw Edwin, then said something to one of his smaller children who was poking around; the boy ran off with his bare little legs pumping. Edwin raised a hand in greeting as he followed Martin along the road.

Edwin supposed they would go straight to the castle, which meant he wouldn't stop at home, but as he neared the cottage he saw his mother come out into the street, the carpenter's boy dragging her by the hand. Beside her was another woman, but it wasn't Cecily, it was …

He pulled so hard on the reins that the horse shied. Martin nosed his own mount back so they were side by side. 'What …?'

Dear Lord, he was seeing things now. He wiped his sleeve across his tired eyes and looked again.

She was still there.

Martin sounded incredulous. 'Is that …?'

Edwin passed the reins to him, his hands shaking so much that he could barely grasp them. He put both legs over one side of the horse and thumped down to the ground. He wasn't sure if his legs would hold him up. They did. He tried walking. It worked.

As he got closer, he was convinced that she was going to disappear. This was a trick, a cruel trick that someone was playing on him. And if she was really here, surely a husband was about to appear?

He didn't care. He reached her and enfolded her in his arms.

She was real. She was here. They were together. Tears streamed down his face. He stood back and held her at arm's length, to look at her. She was crying as well. He touched her face gently, and then embraced her again.

His mother, also weeping, was trying to say something to him, but he didn't hear it. He wanted this moment to last forever. He would never let her go.

'Edwin. Edwin!' It was Martin's voice, but he couldn't listen to Martin just now. Couldn't he see? Didn't he understand?

'Martin. I'm glad to see you safe,' Edwin heard his mother say.

'Mistress,' replied Martin. 'This, I take it, is the girl he's been talking about?'

'Yes.'

'And not married?'

'No. Praise be to God.'

'Well, well. He deserves a reward.'

'Did you … were you successful?'

'Yes. Keep Edwin here for now. When he's ready, tell him I've taken the horses; I'll report to my lord for both of us. He probably won't be all that interested in the details anyway so he may not want to talk to Edwin just now. If he's wanted, I'll send for him.'

'If that happens, I'll make sure he comes, don't worry.'

'Thank you.'

'Martin …'

'Yes?'

'Thank you for keeping him safe. For bringing him back to me.'

'Just doing my duty, mistress.'

And now Edwin's mother was joining in the embrace and shepherding them all into the cottage. He was home.

Some time later, Edwin sat at the table in his home. His *home*, where he had lived all his life, but which was now different, because it had Alys in it. She was still there – she had not vanished. But even now he kept reaching out to touch her hand, just to make sure. She did not seem to mind, brushing her fingers against his and smiling as she looked into his eyes.

Everything had been explained to him, though he thought he'd probably want to hear it again before he understood it properly. For now he kept going back to the two main points.

'You're not married?'

'No.'

'And you want to marry me?'

She laughed and took his face in her hands. 'Yes, Edwin, yes, I want to marry you.'

Mother patted him on the shoulder. 'It's all right, Edwin. Alys is here, we have kept her safe and you will be married in a couple of weeks once Father Ignatius has made it public for all to hear.'

'A couple of weeks?' If she'd said years he couldn't have been more dismayed.

'Yes. And even though you're betrothed I think you'll have to sleep elsewhere until then. William and Cecily will have you, I'm sure.'

'But …' he took Alys's hand once more. 'You'll still be here? You won't go anywhere?'

She looked in his eyes. 'I will be here.'

Mother's comment about lovebirds was drowned out by a knocking at the door. The door was open, as it always was in fine weather, so Edwin turned to see who was there.

It was Martin. And he had a distressed expression on his face. 'Edwin, I'm sorry …'

Edwin jumped to his feet. 'What is it?'

Martin seemed out of breath. Had he run? 'Orders … from my lord …'

'Come in, Martin, and sit down.' It was his mother, taking charge.

Martin obeyed and then looked at each of them in turn. 'My lord has received word this afternoon. Prince Louis has recovered from his defeat at Lincoln and is still in England, in the south. A huge French fleet is being built across the Channel and will sail within a few weeks. There is going to be another invasion. We are marching.'

'When?'

'Tomorrow. All is chaos at the castle – we are preparing. My lord's other retainers will be summoned and will catch him up. But he is riding tomorrow and we are both going with him.' He had an agonised expression as he looked from Alys to Edwin and then back again. 'Your pardon, mistress. I'm Martin, squire to my lord the earl.'

Edwin watched as she stood and curtseyed. 'Pleased to meet you, sir.'

And then everyone looked at Edwin. There was silence.

A massive feeling of relief washed over Edwin. For a moment there he had thought that the lord earl was going to rescind his permission to marry. Thank God, he had not. And what was an invasion compared to that?

He smiled. He reached out and took Alys's hand in both of his, the hand he would hold forever.

'Let's get married now.'

Epilogue

Brother Richard stood in the dawn light and watched in silence as the door to the cell was opened. The anchorite's dwelling where the penitent was to spend the rest of his days had been constructed against the outside of the church, a narrow slit cut in the stone wall of the church itself so that he would be able to see the altar but nothing else. From his position among the brethren Brother Richard could see inside the cell: it contained a mattress and blanket, a wooden stool and a kneeler for prayer. The door had no handle on the inside, but a lock on the outside; it had a small, high barred window through which air and light could pass; it had a trapdoor at the bottom which would open wide enough for a bowl, a jug or a slops bucket to be passed in and out.

That was all.

The man who had once been Brother Octavian was being brought forward by two of the brethren. He was sunk in misery and they were virtually dragging him. As they approached, the monks bowed their heads and the prior began to read out the relevant sections of the Rule. *The abbot must employ the surgeon's knife; he must drive out the wicked from among his flock for fear that one diseased sheep may infect the whole flock.*

The penitent began to struggle as he approached the door. 'Please, Father Abbot, please, don't put me in there. I will atone, I will do anything …' The brothers held him firmly.

None of the brethren may associate with him in companionship or in conversation. He is to be left alone to remain in penitent grief as he reflects on his terrible sentence.

He twisted in their grip and his voice rose. 'Please, Father. At least let me have something to read, to study. That way I …' They pushed him into the cell. The door began to close.

He is to be handed over to bodily death, so that his spirit may be saved …
his food should be taken alone … neither he nor the food that is given him
shall receive a blessing from anyone who passes by.

As the key turned in the lock, Brother Richard heard screaming.
'Please, Father, please – let me have the book! The book!' The voice
became muffled, and thumps sounded on the door, along with
a noise Brother Richard thought to be sobbing. He stared
straight ahead.

The abbot, who would leave that very day for his journey across
the sea, nodded to the two lay brothers who were standing by,
and they began to seal up the gap around the door with mortar.
The noise from within became even more indistinct.

If any brother takes it upon himself to associate with an excommuni-
cated brother in any way, or to talk with him, or to send him a message,
he must likewise undergo the punishment of excommunication.

The prior moved on to the funeral service, his deep voice
intoning the words which indicated that the man inside the cell
was dead to the world, and each of the monks crossed himself
before moving on. Brother Richard could hear the thumping
until he was quite some distance away.

The abbot, allowing that the brethren would be feeling some
emotion and would not immediately be ready for divine service,
had arranged matters so that there was an hour of spare time
before they would assemble in the church. He had given them
permission to walk, to pray, to contemplate, and even to speak if it
were done discreetly and with reverence.

Brother Richard did not feel like talking – although by now he
was well able to, and had even resumed singing during services –
and nor did he wish to go to the library, now his domain after his
appointment as precentor. Instead he let his feet take him around
to the monks' graveyard.

He knelt in the space between the two newest graves, the one
containing his brother, and the other that had been meant for
him, but which now housed the mortal remains of young Brother
Eugenius. He prayed that they would both find peace and that
their paths through Purgatory would be short. He prayed for any

family that Brother Eugenius might have had, who would mourn the loss of their son or brother.

He turned his mind to Alexander. During the time of his illness, his bad dream, he had heard Alexander crying out to him. At the time he hadn't understood why, but now he knew it was because he was in his grave too early. He had not finished his life's work and was leaving this earth with his tasks incomplete. He was also asking for forgiveness: he had broken the Rule and kept a private possession, kept it for years for no reason other than that he did not want to share it. For that he would suffer, but he had not deserved to be murdered for it.

But at least since the truth had been discovered, Alexander's blood cried out to him no more. He was at peace. One day Richard would join him again, but not for some time. He himself owed it to the abbot, to the Order and to the miracle of his cure to live longer, to atone for his own and his brother's sins, and to do God's work on this earth.

Brother Richard thought of the man who, by all accounts, had effected the miracle. He put his hand up to his face as he recalled the terrifying, awful sensation of his face cracking open. But the suffering had been alleviated thereby, and he gave thanks. The abbot had asked the man to stay, but he had returned to his duties in the outside world. And those duties were likely to be onerous, for there was war throughout the land. Father Abbot had received many letters over the past year and asked the brethren to pray for those affected. Thank the Lord the fighting had stayed away from Roche and the lands nearby, but in other places people were being killed, tortured, their money and goods stolen. The Benedictine abbey of St Albans, where Alexander might have ended his days had matters turned out differently, had been raided and robbed on several occasions by men of both sides.

And the young man whose face he couldn't quite recall was heading out into all this. Into danger. Brother Richard asked the soul of his departed brother to intercede for him with the angels and saints, and together they prayed to the Lord to watch over Edwin and to keep him safe during the troubles to come.

historical note

The Cistercian Order of monks arrived in Britain in 1128, and by the time of this book in 1217 they had a large number of houses spread across England and into Scotland. Roche Abbey was one of a group of influential Cistercian monasteries in Yorkshire, having been founded in 1147 on land donated by two local lords on either side of the Maltby Beck. By 1217 all the original wooden buildings had been rebuilt in stone, which was sourced from the local quarry, and the abbey must have been a fine sight.

The Cistercian Order was prosperous, with its wealth based primarily on the wool trade and supported by donations from wealthy patrons concerned with the state of their souls. One of these was Earl William de Warenne, who in the early thirteenth century gave Roche a grant of fish from his manors; the words which Brother William writes down at the beginning of this book are quoted directly from the earl's original letter.

The Order held a General Chapter for all heads of houses at its birthplace of Citeaux (in France) in mid-September each year, and all abbots were required to attend. The abbots from the north of England were slightly unfortunate in this respect: their colleagues in Scotland and Ireland had dispensation to attend only once every four years, due to the distance they had to travel, but this was not extended to even the furthest-flung parts of England. Thus the abbot of Roche – together with the companion he was allowed to bring with him – would have to undertake the month-long journey every year, leaving his flock in the hands of his deputy.

As depicted here, the monastic community both at Roche and in other houses was divided into two unequal parts: the choir monks and the lay brothers. The choir monks were generally from noble or knightly families, and they would make a donation to the Order before they could join. They undertook all three parts of the order's duties: the cycle of canonical hours, theological study known as *lectio divina*, and manual labour. Naturally the number of hours each monk spent in church or in study every day meant that he had less time for manual labour, so the lay brothers did more of this, including not only fieldwork but also everything else which the community needed to be self-sufficient: they were blacksmiths, bakers, masons, shepherds, tanners, millers, and so on. The lay brothers were generally from peasant families but a few among them were nobles who chose to enter the Order at this level in order to demonstrate humility. They attended only morning and evening services and spent the rest of each day at their work, but they still had to take the same vows of poverty, chastity and obedience as the choir monks.

The plan of Roche Abbey which appears at the beginning of this book is based on what the abbey would have looked like in 1217. It differs slightly from those you will see now at the site or in guidebooks, as more buildings were added later in the thirteenth and fourteenth centuries which Edwin would not have encountered. Like all Cistercian monasteries, Roche had a well-stocked library of dozens of volumes; we do not have a full inventory from the early thirteenth century but some of its books survive to this day, including the writings of Augustine of Hippo and Gregory the Great, and we do know that all Cistercian monasteries of this period had copies of the *Carta Caritatis* and the writings of one of the great Cistercians, Aelred of Rievaulx.

Roche Abbey was destroyed in the Dissolution during the sixteenth century, bringing an end to four hundred years of continuous worship and monastic life on the site. The remaining monks were dispersed, the abbey buildings destroyed, the lead from the roof melted, the timbers ripped out, the tombs broken and defaced. The only pieces of the abbey left standing now are the gatehouse and a small part of the church, but careful excavations have revealed the most complete ground plan of any Cistercian monastery in England, and you can walk around it, in and out of the doorways and into each 'room', today. The beautiful abbey grounds were later landscaped by Capability Brown, and the site is now a peaceful spot for quiet reflection or for a visit and picnic.

———◆———

Although the Cistercian Order as a whole was wealthy, individual Cistercian monks were allowed no money or personal possessions. The Order interpreted the Rule of St Benedict more strictly than the Benedictines, and their churches contained no gold, jewels or silks; their abbots, priors and monks wore no costly garments or ornaments. The daily lives of the choir monks were strictly regulated and divided into the three parts detailed above, with all having to undertake all duties including manual labour, although the old and the young were given work more appropriate to their strength and physical capabilities. The day ran from sunrise to sunset, divided at all times of year into twelve 'hours' which were therefore much longer in the summer than they were in the winter. Sext, 'the sixth hour', was at noon, with the morning and afternoon subdivided by terce, 'the third hour', and nones, 'the ninth hour'. The monks also attended the services of prime ('the first hour') in the morning, and vespers and compline in the evening. The twelve hours of darkness were broken for all except the novices by the night services of matins and lauds, so sleep deprivation must have been constant.

For most of the year the monks ate only once per day, in the late morning, but in the summer months they also had an evening meal to help sustain them through the longer days. Meat was strictly forbidden for all but the sick, so the principal foodstuffs were bread, pulses and vegetables, with some dairy produce or fish added on special occasions. Silence was observed throughout the monastery except in the monks' parlour and the lay brothers' parlour, and a form of sign language developed which helped the monks communicate on day-to-day matters.

The daily life of the monks and lay brothers, including their food and clothing, their duties, and the timings of church services, Chapter, meals, reading and labour, was more or less as I have described here.

Abbeys also allowed (male) guests to stay within their outer walls, and had a dedicated guesthouse and guestmaster for that purpose. I have made two specific changes to abbey life in order to suit my plot points. The first is that the Order was even stricter about the presence of women than I have depicted here – not only were they not permitted to enter the abbey proper, they were not even allowed in the main church except on feast days (and even then not if they were breastfeeding) – so Edwin would not have seen Anabilia at a regular vespers service. The second is that, although I needed them to have their hoods up, when undertaking the *lectio divina* the monks actually sat with their hoods down, to make sure they were not making up for their lack of sleep with a quick nap!

Anchorites – or anchoresses, if they were women – did exist at this time. They took rather more extreme vows than other members of religious orders and spent their lives in complete solitude, often in cells adjoining churches or chapels. They underwent a funeral ceremony as they were sealed in, to demonstrate that they were now dead to the world. However, they did this on a voluntary basis, and as far as I am aware enforced vocation was not used as a punishment. However, the casting out of a monk from a house or from an Order was a penalty for those who had committed very grave sins (members of religious orders were not subject to lay justice, meaning they could not be tried in a king's court and could not be sentenced to death). The words which Prior Henry uses in the epilogue here are taken directly from the Rule of St Benedict on that subject.

———

The abbot of Roche Abbey in 1217 was Reginald, who had been in post for four years after the long and successful abbacy of Osmund (*c.*1184–1213) under whose leadership the abbey had expanded and prospered. Henry, Helias, Durand, Richard, Jordan, Walter, Eugenius, Amandus, Thurstan, Waldef and Sinnulph are all names of monks or lay brothers who were associated with the Cistercian Order in Yorkshire during the Middle Ages, though not all at Roche and not all at the same time. Of most of them we know only their names, though we do have small details about some of the Roche men: Prior Henry was later to be abbot of Roche's mother house at Newminster in Northumberland, and Brother Richard became abbot of Roche in 1229. Brother Helias, Roche's cellarer, was 'a man full of energy, fully practised in dealing with outside affairs', who later became abbot of Kirkstall. In the later thirteenth century there was a female hermit named Anabilia who lived in the woods and who had a corrody of five monastery loaves and three gallons of ale per week; she evidently lived longer than expected, as she sued the abbey for withdrawing the corrody which she claimed had been granted for life. Brothers William, Guy, Godfrey and Octavian, Benedict and the other novices, and the abbey guests Aylwin and Sir Philip are entirely fictional, as are Edwin and Martin.

The character of Brother Alexander is based very loosely on Alexander of Neckham, a real person who lived from 1157 to 1217, though there is no indication that his death in that year was due to murder. He was actually an Augustinian monk, but I became so interested in his writings that I gave in to temptation and placed him in the Cistercian abbey of Roche following his travels. He was the author of the *De naturis rerum*, a compendium of the scientific knowledge of the twelfth century, and was the first European author to mention the use of a magnetised needle as a guide to sailors. He had completed volume one of his *Speculum Speculationum* and was working on volume two at the time of his death.

Prior to his return to England Alexander had travelled widely in Europe and may well have encountered the famous intellectual Daniel of Morley (died 1210). A native of Norfolk, Daniel initially travelled to Paris, a great centre of learning, but was unimpressed with the masters there and so went to Toledo to study with Arab masters – something which certainly enlarged his learning but which did not meet with the approval of all Christian churchmen. He returned to England sometime around 1186 with a collection of books, which is what gave me the idea of having my fictional Alexander also bringing back a precious volume.

The book which I have written about here as the cause of all the trouble is fictional, but it does bear some resemblance to the celebrated Maciejowski Bible (also sometimes known as the Morgan Bible as it is now in the Pierpoint Morgan Library in New York; MS M.638). This volume is one of the most astonishing artistic achievements of the thirteenth century, depicting the Old Testament from the Creation to the story of David in ninety-two brilliantly illustrated pages; it would certainly have been an incredible sight for any normal medieval person, never mind for a scholar who could interpret it as well as being moved by the quality of the pictures. Throughout its life this Bible has journeyed through many countries, and the pages contain annotations from different centuries written in Persian and Arabic as well as Latin. The entire work is available to view on the Morgan Library's website; if you think the Middle Ages were dull and mud-coloured, take a look at this manuscript and think again.

To our somewhat jaded modern sensibilities it may be difficult to understand just how strange and frightening some phenomena were to medieval people who had no way to explain them. Think about it: if you had never in your life seen a pair of identical twins, and you had no idea that they existed, how would you react? Twins were not unheard of in the thirteenth century, but they were certainly much more of a rarity than they are now. The rates of conception of twins were probably similar to those of the 1970s (before modern fertility treatments became available), but very few of them survived. A woman pregnant with twins was more likely to suffer complications resulting in miscarriage; and bearing in mind that approximately one in six of *all* newborns died at birth or shortly afterwards, we can extrapolate that mortality rates among twins were even higher given that they were generally smaller than singleton babies and were liable to be born earlier. Even riches and the best medical care available at the time could not save most of them: Prince Louis, heir to the French throne and the man holding much of England in 1217, was both the brother and the father of twins, but all four babies died at birth. Thus it is entirely plausible that a less-travelled man such as Edwin has never seen an adult pair of twins at all – never mind an identical pair – and that he is unfamiliar with the concept.

Other seemingly inexplicable phenomena were also attributed to divine intervention. It was believed, for example, that a corpse would bleed in the presence of its murderer, and that the saints had intercessory powers of healing. The descriptions in this book of Brother Richard and his sufferings are based on a real case reported in 1172 where one Gaufrid had three teeth extracted and then ate too much supper, resulting in a horrendous reaction:

> His whole head swelled so much that he presented the appearance not of a man but of some portentous and horrid monster: his skin was stretched like a bladder so that those who saw him wondered that it did not break. The prominence of his nose was reduced to flatness; the eyes were sunken and dimmed; the mouth closed by the swelling of the lips and the power of breathing obstructed. His friends inserted a reed into his mouth to enable him to breathe.
>
> (From *The Life and Miracles of St William of Norwich by Thomas of Monmouth*)

Gaufrid, a native of Norwich who was at that time in Canterbury, was taken to the tomb of the recently martyred St Thomas Becket; prayers were said to St William of Norwich, and candles put all about the sick man's head, after which: 'on the left side of the throat the skin cracked and burst as if pricked by an awl, and a great discharge came out. The swelling subsided with extraordinary quickness; the pain departed and the sick man recovered.' Modern research has put the swelling down to post-operative infection causing the formation of a massive abscess which subsequently burst, possibly related to the heating of the skin, but Edwin would have had no way of knowing this as he watched events unfold, so it would be natural for him and for others to put it down to divine intervention. There is, incidentally, plenty of further reading available on medieval dentistry, but it is not for the faint-hearted.

Also not for the faint-hearted was the ongoing war in England, although the common people could not escape it and had no choice but to live with the consequences if it came near them. Some lands, particularly those in the south and east of England, were fought over time and time again, the inhabitants pillaged, murdered or tortured for their money and goods. The abbey of St Albans was looted several times by men of both sides. Louis's quest for the English crown had stalled a little after the defeat of his forces at Lincoln, but his wife had been active on his behalf and in the summer of 1217 she was building and equipping a huge fleet of reinforcements on the other side of the Channel. William Marshal, the regent acting on behalf of the boy king Henry III, gathered an armed force to try to prevent the landing of this fleet, and it is towards this muster that Edwin is about to ride …

Further Reading

The Cistercians in Yorkshire online research project,
   http://cistercians.shef.ac.uk/index.php

The Rule of St Benedict, trans. Abbott Parry OSB (Leominster: Gracewing,
   1990)

Birkedal Bruun, Mette (ed.), *The Cambridge Companion to the Cistercian
   Order* (Cambridge: Cambridge University Press, 2013)

Burton, Janet, and Julie Kerr, *The Cistercians in the Middle Ages* (Woodbridge:
   Boydell, 2011)

Lloyd, T.H., *The English Wool Trade in the Middle Ages* (Cambridge:
   Cambridge University Press, 1977)

Moorman, John, *Church Life in England in the Thirteenth Century*
   (Cambridge: Cambridge University Press, 1945)

Acknowledgements

Once again it is a pleasure to thank Matilda Richards and the rest of the team at The Mystery Press for their help, support and encouragement during the writing of what I can now justifiably call a series of books. I've lost count of how many chocolate cakes I owe you now …

The research for this book was made considerably easier thanks to the amazingly in-depth work carried out by the 'Cistercians in Yorkshire' project which was based at the University of Sheffield from 2001 to 2003; further information is available on the project website, listed on the Further Reading page. Many thanks also to Dr Andrew Buck for supplying references on Daniel of Morley, and to Dr Joy Hawkins for pointing out that saying the paternoster was a method of timing used in mediaeval medicine.

Stephanie Tickle, Susan Brock and Maddy McGlynn all read drafts of *Brother's Blood* and offered much valuable insight and constructive criticism. Stephanie and Susan are both old friends of Edwin, while Maddy is a new one: their very differing points of view as readers were of enormous help in the redrafting process.

I am extremely fortunate to have a collection of friends who keep me going with support, pep talks, research references, tea, speaking and review opportunities, and all the other necessities of life: thanks in particular this time round to Sean McGlynn, Julian Humphrys and Sarah Preston.

Astonishingly my family continue to put up with me with good grace: James and our children deserve some kind of medal. And on the subject of family, thanks and love to Helen and Steph, who have been there longer than almost anyone else. It's fitting that this book about brothers should be dedicated to them, my sisters.

About the Author

C.B. HANLEY has a PhD in mediaeval studies from the University of Sheffield and is the author of *War and Combat 1150–1270: The Evidence from Old French Literature* and *Louis: The French Prince Who Invaded England*, as well as her Mediaeval Mystery series, *The Sins of the Father*, *The Bloody City* and *Whited Sepulchres*. She currently writes a number of scholarly articles on the period, as well as teaching on writing for academic publication, and also works as a copy-editor and proofreader.

Also in this series

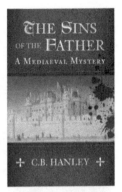

1217: England has been invaded. Much of the country is in the iron grip of Louis of France and his collaborators, and civil war rages as the forces of the boy king try to fight off the French. Most of this means nothing to Edwin Weaver, son of the bailiff at Conisbrough Castle in Yorkshire, until he is suddenly thrust into the noble world of politics and treachery: he is ordered by his lord the earl to solve a murder which might have repercussions not just for him but for the future of the realm.

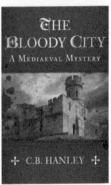

1217: Lincoln is not a safe place to be. A French army has captured the city and the terrified citizens huddle in the rubble of their homes as the castle, the last remaining loyal stronghold in the region, is besieged. Edwin Weaver finds himself riding into grave danger after his lord volunteers him for a perilous mission: he must infiltrate the city and identify the traitors who are helping the enemy. Edwin is pushed to the limit as he has to decide what he is prepared to do to protect others. He might be willing to lay down his own life, but would he, could he, kill?

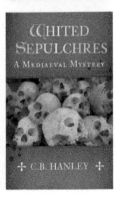

1217: Edwin Weaver has returned to Conisbrough from his blood-soaked adventure in Lincoln, but he has no chance to rest: preparations are underway for a noble wedding at the castle. When the household marshal is murdered and a violent band of outlaws begins terrorizing the area, the earl asks Edwin to resolve the situation but Edwin is convinced that there's more to the situation than meets the eye and, with growing horror, he realises that the real target might be someone much closer to the earl.